BEDEVILED

ELIZABETH ROSE

All rights reserved.

No part of this publication may be sold, copied, distributed, reproduced or transmitted in any form or by any means, mechanical or digital, including photocopying and recording or by any information storage and retrieval system without the prior written permission of both the publisher, Oliver Heber Books and the author, Elizabeth Rose, except in the case of brief quotations embodied in critical articles and reviews.

PUBLISHER'S NOTE: This is a work of fiction. Names, characters, places, and incidents either are the product of the author's imagination or are used fictitiously. Any resemblance to actual persons, living or dead, business establishments, events, or locales is entirely coincidental.

Copyright © by Elizabeth Rose Krejcik

Published by Oliver-Heber Books

0 9 8 7 6 5 4 3 2 1

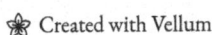 Created with Vellum

Prelude

In a time of great darkness and despair, three powerful kings are obsessed with greed and the quest for power. Battling each other, the land of Mura is in distress. The kings have agreed on one thing only, and that is to ban all magic. Those found to be using magic of any kind are severely punished, or even killed.

Now, hope is naught but the dying flicker of a long-forgotten flame. With the greed and hatred of the nobles at its highest, it has caused imbalance on Mura. A tear in the veil between the land of the living and the dead has occurred, and it will take more than the wealth of these kings to fix it. Only magic can close the portal and hopefully right the wrongs that have darkened the hearts of many.

People in fear cry out for a hero, but is this what they really need? Even with a savior, who, or what, will save them from themselves in the end?

We are what we are.

We do what we do.

Fate brings us here and our destinies are decided before we are even born. We must travel the road that the hand of fate has dealt us.

No one can alter their destiny even if it is naught but a burden to behold.
We can do nothing to change it ... or can we?

One

Sin eating wasn't hard to do, but then again, neither was it a desirable occupation.

The feared profession only demanded one simple task – taking on the sins of the dead. Food and drink were always present at the event, and the pay was twice the amount of a skilled mercenary.

Yes, the job did have its strengths, the only downfall being that the Sin Eater's soul was doomed to The Dark Abyss for all eternity.

Darium Blackseed traveled atop his horse, approaching his destination as the early morning sun broke the horizon, the rays of orange and pink lighting up the vast, cloudless sky. Macada Castle, the home of King Leofric Sethor, rose up majestically before him, a remarkable yet foreboding sight to see. Tall, round turrets reached up into the sky from each corner of the citadel. The stronghold loomed over the cliffs in an attempt to scare away armies as well as those arriving by the Masked Sea to the land of Mura. Flags attached to long poles atop each turret fluttered in the wind. A crossed ax and sword over an azure field boasted the crest of the king. Above this, floated a large golden crown with rays shooting out in all directions.

The intimidating castle was constructed of stone, the thick walls making it an almost impenetrable fortress. The large wooden doors at the entrance made of algeeba wood, from the strongest trees on Mura, were surprisingly open. Even still, a strong iron portcullis blocked Darium's way. He hadn't expected to be received with an open-armed greeting, or to even be welcomed at all. It was also too early in the morning for traveling merchants or traders to be here.

It was no secret that Darium wasn't welcome here. He was a Sin Eater and had not been summoned by the king. No one liked unannounced visitors, especially not one who represented death.

With his raven perched upon his shoulder, Darium rode with his head held high as his horse crossed the moat in a steady cantor. The clip clop of his large black steed's hooves on the wooden drawbridge echoed off the stone walls, reverberating in his ears like distant drumming. The morning fog swirled around him, creating a slight haze in the air. Darium almost found it hard to breathe.

Then the wind picked up, biting against his face with an annoying sting. It was nature's reminder that winter had recently left the land and spring was still trying to find its footing, not quite sure if it was welcome or not. He felt the same way about being here right now. It was a risk to come at all, and a bold move for a Sin Eater to show up to surprise anyone.

Darium's eyes continuously swept from one side to the other and then back again, as he scanned the area, watching for danger. It wouldn't be the first time that assaults happened as brigands emerged through the fog. Attacks by soldiers, bandits, and even simple commoners lately had been happening more and more often. Things were changing on Mura, and it wasn't in a good way.

Being aware of everything around him came as second nature to one of his kind. Darium always watched for trouble, and highly expected it anywhere he went. Something wasn't right here. He felt the unease. There was an uncomfortable tugging in his chest, and an undeniable chill running up his spine. A pungent flavor, like bitter herbs, coated his tongue. This is always how he felt before chaos broke loose. Something bad was about to transpire.

His focus now was upon King Sethor's soldiers stationed atop the battlements. They stood still and stiff, peering down at him through the fog. They watched him with cautious, yet curious interest. The soldiers made no secret of having their weapons at the ready. Darium got the impression that they weren't exactly sure if they should attack or possibly let him pass.

He stopped his steed in front of the closed gate, highly anticipating shouts from the guards, warning him to leave. To Darium's surprise, no one said a word. Then, the sound of the creaking winch and pulley filled the air, before he even had a chance to speak. The gate groaned as it rose slowly, allowing him passage into the castle's bailey. Tension filled the air. His raven flapped its wings from its perch on his shoulder, obviously feeling as anxious as he.

Continuing forward with caution, Darium rode into the courtyard that was paved with round, colored, cobbled stones. Some of the stones sparkled with precious gems, making him wonder if the king possibly stole them from the Whispering Dale, the home of the magical Fae on the other side of the Picajord Mountains.

Statues carved from linden wood or granite lined the entranceway, depicting warriors and fierce beasts.

While Darium had never actually been allowed inside Macada Castle to sin eat, he had visited the courtyard on numerous occasions to carry out his job there. The greedy King Sethor was wealthy, but most everything he owned had been obtained at a steep price. Not at a price to the king, but for those he fought and killed to steal the belongings to claim them as his own.

Darium knew first hand each dead man the goods had been taken from, since he'd had to eat the sins of most of them, because of the king's obvious guilt. While King Sethor didn't think twice about killing others to claim his riches, he also didn't want the guilt of those men's doomed souls weighing heavy on his shoulders. That's why Darium's services had been summoned more times than he could count. He'd been called to the side of not only King Sethor, but also the man's rivals, King Drustan Grinwald of Evandorm, and King Rand Osric of Kasculbough.

Fear thickened the air wherever he went, so it was no surprise he felt the discomfort surrounding him here too. No one ever wanted to be anywhere near a man who was destined for the raging fires of The Dark Abyss. People ran from him, always hiding their faces and crouching in the shadows. They did not want him to see them, even though he always knew exactly where each of them was positioned. It was an inborn ability of his kind, to be able to follow the scent of fear, dread, and grief. It was not unlike a hound of the hunt tracking down a rabbit.

Guards, as well as servants, quickly cleared the way for him, giving him a wide berth. He rode to the center of the courtyard and stopped his horse once more. The whispered conversations he'd heard when he'd first passed under the gate, drifted off as soon as he'd made his presence known.

Darium scanned the area once more, looking over the heads of the soldiers. The scent of a recent death strongly filled his nostrils, smelling to him worse than the garderobes in summer. That told him he was not wrong in his assumption. Someone had died here within the last day, he was sure of it. It was someone who never had the chance to confess their sins. The odor of the damned was intense to him. It stunk worse than one who had confessed their sins before dying. The worst stench of all was on the battlefield, where Darium was often paid to tend to those who died quickly in war. Even still, he was here for another reason besides this. He felt something, or someone inside these walls who didn't belong here. This presence called to him silently, drawing him to the castle like a moth to a flame.

Although he waited for someone to speak to him, it didn't happen. Knowing who and what he was, no one ever wanted to be the first to approach him. Still, that didn't stop them from staring at him behind his back. His skin crawled from the intense searing gazes fixated upon him from all sides now. He didn't need to see the people to know they watched with terrified yet curious eyes, wondering why he was even here.

His raven cackled and fluttered its wings once more, feeling the intensity of the situation.

"Settle down, Murk," Darium commanded in a low voice, looking at his bird from the corners of his eyes. "You're only going to scare them more."

Each second lingered, feeling like an hour as Darium sat without moving atop his black stallion, waiting . . . watching for someone to approach. A muscle twitched in his jaw, and he started to wonder if this had been a good idea to come here after all. He didn't like being the center of attention. He also hated waiting for anyone or anything. Ever. He was not a patient man.

"I want to talk to the king," he finally called out, breaking the silence. He spoke loud enough for everyone to hear him.

"There are three kings of Mura," shouted a guard from the steps of the battlements. "I'd think you'd realize that by now, Sin Eater. Which one did you want to see?"

Knowing they were goading him, Darium blew air from his mouth and shook his head, biting back his frustration. "I'd think you'd know by now which king I speak of since you are the henchman of Macada. Now call him to me," he commanded. Darium lifted his gaze to stare at the guard, just to instill more fear amongst the men so they wouldn't cause him trouble.

There were three kings in Mura, although the land was only big enough for one. Three men had claimed their small kingdoms, always fighting to be the one and only ruler, the way it should be.

"You haven't been summoned, Sin Eater." Another guard called out who was twice as brave as the first, or possibly just two times as foolish. The man actually walked toward him with his sword gripped tightly in his fist.

Being a Sin Eater, Darium could feel others' emotions, on occasion, and sometimes he could even read minds. The strongest emotion he could pick up was fear. That is, the fear of dying from the wounded person just before they perished. That, and also grief from the family members who were left behind.

As strange as it seemed, what he felt right now was neither of these things. No, right now he felt turmoil weaving through the courtyard like an arcine slithering through a field of weeds, hunting its prey. Something was severely wrong here, but he couldn't decipher exactly what it was. It didn't actually feel physical, but rather of the spirit world. Still, he couldn't be sure. It was too soon to tell. All he knew was that he was drawn here, and there was something he needed to do.

Dressed all in black leather from head to toe, Darium's long cloak fell over the sides of his horse. His feet were clad in boots and his hands were covered with fingerless gauntlets. Most warriors protected their fingers in war, but then again, Darium wasn't a warrior of the living, but rather an emissary of the dead.

The hood of his cloak covered his jet-black hair that hung nearly down to his shoulders. The covering hid the streak of white down the middle of his head that continued to grow thicker with each sin he consumed every time he freed a tormented soul. The sight of his two-toned hair was shocking to others and caused alarm as well as gossip. The damned streak made him feel like a skunet, one of the hairy black and white pesky animals of Mura hated by all because of its pungent stench.

Lucifer, Darium's black steed, snorted its discomfort. The tack jangled as his horse danced beneath him anxiously, feeling the emotions as well. Murk let out a shriek and flew up into the sky, making the soldiers jerk backward and raise their weapons. When the raven settled itself atop one of the turrets, the guards once again lowered their bows and swords.

Death called out to Darium, resounding like an eerie whistle in his ears. He'd heard this sound his entire life. However, this time it was more than just a sense of duty that called to him to make this journey to Macada Castle. There was an urgency here that he had never felt before in all the times he'd visited this courtyard. He was sure he felt the presence of magic nearby.

Magic had been outlawed by the kings ever since

Darium could remember. It had been the only thing the three rulers could agree upon. By outlawing magic, none of the three would use it to their advantage, and therefore it put them all on the same playing field. Those found using magic were severely punished or even sentenced to death.

Some said that what Darium did was magic, however he had never been punished for it. Instead, the nobles and even the kings themselves summoned him often, saying he was doing naught but the work of Zoroct, one of the main gods of The Haven. Ironic, thought Darium, since his profession was more the work of Belcoum, the god of the underworld, and they all knew it.

Still, those in high places didn't care what happened to Darium since he eased their conscience, making them feel as if they'd done naught wrong. Nay, the kings of Mura only cared about themselves, worrying for their own souls when their time came to leave this world. Money was no object to them, and they would do whatever they needed to get what they wanted in the end. All three kings of Mura had all already paid Darium double the normal price to sin eat at the time of their deaths, whenever that might be.

Calling sin eating religious, it somehow exonerated the fact that Darium's actions were nothing more than magic . . . but in a twisted, unmentionable sort of way.

Finally, a dozen guards ran down from the battlements with their swords drawn, surrounding him in a full circle.

"You shouldn't be here, Sin Eater," growled a soldier who was three times the size of the others. He was dressed in leathered armor, made from the tough hides of the seyadillos, large rodent-type animals, with such tough skin that not much could penetrate it. This man's beard was red and down to his waist, marking him as one of the giants that came from the clan of seafaring men from the far north, at the Isle of Denwop.

"Mmmph," grunted Darium, his sharp sense of smell picking up the odor of the giant that was worse than the foul stench of slimy arcine eggs. "Stand back, Mercenary. I have no qualms with you. I'm here to see the king only." His hand went to the hilt of his sword – a weapon he very rarely ever had to use.

The ring of a dozen soldiers unsheathing their swords was a new sound to Darium and it took him by surprise. No one ever threatened him with a weapon. He knew how to fight and defend himself, even if he rarely needed to do it. Still, he would do what he had to in times like this. His quick reactions made him twice as good of a warrior with a sword than any of these lame excuses for soldiers.

"Stand down," commanded a low voice from the stairs of the castle. "Sin Eater, I'm surprised to see you here since you haven't been summoned." It was King Sethor. The tall man with gray hair looked down his hooked nose. Darium always thought the man's beak of a nose looked like it belonged on a bird instead. The king descended the stairs slowly with his long ermine-lined cloak billowing out behind him in the breeze as he walked. Six guards were on his heels with their weapons drawn, ready to protect their liege lord.

"Am I wrong in saying someone you care for has died here in the last day, before they had a chance to confess their sins, my lord?" Darium's eyes roamed over the courtyard as he spoke. He saw something odd, something that didn't belong here. His gaze settled on two soldiers who emerged from behind the mews. They held the arms of a beautiful woman who struggled to be free. He immediately smelled the sweet scent of lippenbur lilies, the flowers of the Fae folk. The lilies only grew were the Fae resided in the Whispering Dale. The girl was a Fae, he was sure of it. His only question was, why was she here? Also, why were the guards holding tightly to her as if she were a prisoner? He hoped it wasn't because they knew she had magic. The Fae usually kept hidden from humans, so they stayed safe. But now, with the law of no magic laid down by the kings, this Fae would surely be tortured or killed if discovered, no matter if she was a beautiful woman.

"Nay, you're not wrong, Darium," said the king, calling him by name. "Men, put away your weapons. The Sin Eater is only here looking for work, not to fight us."

"But my king, we have no need for him," growled one of the soldiers who stood near him. "Not now that we have her." The guard's eyes darted over to the Fae and then back again, making Darium wonder exactly what he meant by that.

"True. Bring the body," instructed King Sethor, raising his hand in the air. The many jewels in the rings that covered each of his fingers sparkled in the early morning light. It caught the Fae's attention as well. Darium saw her staring at the man's hand with great interest. A Fae was a lot like Darium's raven at times, attracted to anything shiny or sparkly.

"But my lord," whined the king's right-hand man, starting to protest but being stopped by the king himself.

"Now! And don't forget the ceremonial bread and wine."

"Aye, my lord." The guard backed away, bowing, and whispering instructions to several other soldiers. They ran off in a hurry to carry out their ruler's orders.

"So, who is the girl, and why are your guards

holding on to her so tightly?" asked Darium, dismounting his horse. His eyes remained focused on the beautiful woman. Her lengthy, chestnut-colored tresses were wound in fairy knots, creating a long braid that traveled down her back, reaching all the way to her pear-shaped bottom. She wore a circlet of white and pink lippenbur lilies on her head like the crown of a noblewoman. Now, he only hoped that the king didn't know these were the flowers of the Fae folk. If so, she could be in dire trouble.

The Fae was dressed in a green velvet gown, with a brown bodice that laced up the front. Earth colors, he realized. That meant she was probably a Fae of the land, and not one of the other elements. His knowledge of the Fae was limited, but he planned on finding out more now that he actually saw one close up. This one was careless enough to be caught. He wondered if she was daft to be here at all. Her element was the earth, but her mistake was wandering inside this fortress made of stone.

The girl's head snapped around, almost as if she could read his thoughts about her. With a turned-down mouth, her eyes narrowed to slits momentarily, and then opened wide once again. When they did, he could see her wide, green orbs, the color of emeralds, perusing him from his head to toe.

"See something of interest, my lady?" he asked sarcastically, not liking when anyone looked at him too long. He felt the sting of her stare burning into his skin and it made him uncomfortable.

"She's not a lady," said King Sethor. "Far from it."

The scent of fear was strong on the girl now, and this disturbed Darium immensely. Usually, the Fae folk were happy and loving sprites, not filled with dread and despair like this one seemed to be.

"I heard them call you Sin Eater," she replied. "I've never seen one of your kind before. Remove your hood so I can gaze upon your face clearly."

He didn't appreciate her demands, and neither did he like displaying his hair to anyone. "Well, neither have I ever seen a f-" He stopped in midsentence, seeing her eyes spring open in fear. He was going to say Fae, but if he did, it could bring about her demise. "I've never seen such a fine princess such as you, either."

"Princess? Hah!" spat the king. "She is naught but the king of Evandorm's new healer."

"Really?" he asked in surprise, never having heard of a Fae working for a human before. "You answer to King Grinwald?" he asked her.

"I do not answer to anyone," she retorted. "I am King Grinwald's healer only." She quickly looked the other way.

One of Darium's brothers worked at Evandorm Castle as the king's huntsman. His other brother was a knight at Kasculbough. Darium wanted to ask if the Fae knew either of them, but decided against it. Mentioning this inside the walls of Macada probably wasn't a good idea. After all, both the kings of Evandorm and Kasculbough were enemies of King Sethor.

"She's our prisoner," announced the king's head guard, confirming what Darium already suspected.

"Prisoner?" Darium raised a brow. "What could this delicate girl have done to cause you to imprison her like a murderer or a thief?"

"Not that it's any of your concern, Sin Eater, but she's a spy from Evandorm," answered Sethor. The man's crooked jaw ticked, and the corner of his mouth twitched.

"A spy?" Darium almost cringed in front of the man. Being a spy was almost as bad as being arrested for using magic. It was one of the worst offenses possible. This wasn't looking good for the Fae at all. Spies were usually drawn and quartered and hardly ever spared. Often, they were brought to the gallows. Once dead, the accused spy was left hanging for a fortnight from the front gate, as a warning to others. "I'm sure you're mistaken. She's just an innocent girl, my lord."

"Nay!" bellowed the king. "She's not. Besides, how would you even know? This girl is my rival's healer from Evandorm Castle, I told you. My own spies tell me they've seen her sitting at the side of Drustan Grinwald lately, whispering in his ear. The bastard is plotting to overthrow me and take my castle and land as his own, I just know it."

"That's not true!" shouted the girl. "I would never do such a thing and know nothing about that."

"I hardly think a king would consult a mere healer in his plans for war," Darium pointed out, in the girl's defense.

"You deny being at Evandorm?" the king asked the girl.

"I – well no, of course not. I don't deny it. I was there, I cannot lie. I was hired recently as the castle's new healer," explained the girl.

When Darium heard the wench say she could not lie, it reminded him of something he'd heard from his mother when he was naught but a child. The story was that the Fae folk were honest, and couldn't lie if they wanted to. This, he was sure, was only going to put the girl in more trouble, and would certainly end up getting her killed. If the king asked if she was a Fae, she would not be able to say no.

"I found you sneaking around my dungeon. Why?" asked the king.

"I was only here looking for my father who is one of

Lord Grinwald's guards," she explained. "He has gone missing. I've heard talk that you've taken him prisoner."

"Grinwald is sending wenches now to retrieve his soldiers?" That amused Sethor and made him laugh.

"No one sent me," she spat. "I come of my own accord."

"Is your father a big man with a scar down the right side of his face?" The king's hand went to his chin in thought.

"Yes, that's him," she said, sounding so filled with hope that it almost made Darium sick. If she thought for one moment that the king had spared the man, she was even more addled than he'd originally thought.

The Fae's head snapped around again and she glared at Darium once more. Aye, she must have the ability to read minds, he determined. He curiously wondered what else one of her kind could do.

She turned back to the king. "Is my father here as your prisoner or not?" she demanded to know. The girl's face darkened as she waited for her answer. Darium believed she had just read the king's mind that he'd already killed the man. It was too late to save him.

"He was here, but I disposed of him after he killed two of my men," said the king with a deep, hearty laugh. "Your father squealed like a child, begging me to spare his life. He said he had children to care for, but he never told me one of them was a beautiful full-fledged woman such as yourself." His eyes raked down the girl's body, and lust seemed to drip from his pores.

"Y-you really killed him, then?" The girl's voice came out as a stutter, and her sense of fear grew stronger, as well as her hatred of the man.

"Besides killing two of my men, he was a spy. I couldn't let him live to run back and tell the king of Evandorm all my secrets," said Sethor nonchalantly.

"Why would I spare him when it would only endanger me?"

It was no surprise to hear the man talk this way. Darium already knew Sethor would do anything and everything for his own benefit, not caring a bit about anyone else.

"If my father killed your men, I am sure it was only in self-defense. You killed him, just like you're going to do to me now," said the girl, her emotions now under control as she held her head high. Her bravado was amazing and impressive. Especially after hearing her father was dead and that she was accused of being a spy.

"Oh, on the contrary, I think I'll keep you for my own pleasures." The king chuckled once again.

"So, that's to be my punishment? To warm your bed?" she asked boldly. "Even though I've done nothing wrong?"

"Nay, that is your reward, wench. I have other plans on how to punish you." King Sethor waved over his soldiers who brought out a dead person on a stretcher and placed it at the king's feet. Darium could see it was the body of a young man.

"W-what do you mean?" asked the girl. Her fear grew stronger now as her eyes drank in the corpse.

"Place the bread and wine atop his chest," the king instructed his men before answering her. "My son, Muldor died from a sword in his back. A sword that your father put there."

"Nay!" screamed the girl. "My father would never do such a thing. He was honorable and wouldn't kill someone from behind."

"My son never had a chance to confess his sins before he passed."

"I understand," said Darium stepping forward to do his job. The sins of the dead were absorbed into the food and drink that were placed atop the corpse's body. When Darium ingested it, he would therefore take on the sins himself. Doing this helped the dead one's soul, but his soul was doomed to The Black Abyss for all eternity because of it.

The king's arm shot out to block Darium.

"Nay, not you, Sin Eater," said the king. "Bring the girl forward," he instructed his men, making Darium realize just what he planned to do.

"Lord Sethor, you can't make the girl do this," said Darium, feeling overly concerned. "Her soul will be damned to The Dark Abyss for all eternity. Please, allow me, instead. It's my job, not hers."

"The girl will sin eat for my son, as punishment for her father's deeds. Then, she'll be my plaything to pleasure me whenever I want her." This seemed to amuse all the king's men, making Darium even angrier than before.

"I will never be yours," cried the girl as the guards dragged her forward and threw her to the ground alongside the dead body. "Torture me if you must, but you will never lay a hand on me."

"Shut up!" screamed the king, using the toe of his boot to kick at her. "Now do it, wench. Eat the bread and drink the wine from the body of my dead son, so his soul will be released and he'll go to The Haven in his afterlife where my dead wife already resides."

The girl didn't plead with the man, protesting the act of sin eating, and Darium found that odd. She only objected to being the king's whore, and naught more. He could no longer sense her fear, and he didn't understand it. Slowly, her head turned, and she looked up at Darium from the ground.

Darium's hand went to his hood and he lowered it, showing the girl and everyone else his hair. He heard gasps from the people hiding in the shadows of the courtyard, but the Fae didn't even flinch or look away. She blinked two or three times in succession, then turned back to look down at the dead body.

"Do it!" screamed the king. "Hurry up about it." His guards drew their swords and held them to the girl's back.

Darium's hand covered the hilt of his own sword. He was ready to protect her if need be. She looked back over her shoulder once more and slowly shook her head, telling him silently not to do it. His hand slid off the hilt and lowered to his side.

He watched in horror as the girl reached out and took the bread and cup of wine, preparing to do a job that was his destiny, not hers.

Two

Talia-Glenn was right where she wanted to be. When she'd heard her father was caught and deemed as a spy by King Sethor, she immediately realized he would be killed before he could return with the information he was trying to gather for her. This had nothing to do with the king, and everything to do with saving the Fae race. She needed to know the information her father sacrificed his life trying to get. Since he was already dead, there was only one way to do it now.

She held up the bread and wine, feeling a little nervous. Sin eating, she realized, would doom her soul to The Dark Abyss, or the Land of the Dead, or wherever it was that the unfortunate souls of the dead went who hadn't had a chance to first confess their sins. Then again, that is exactly where she needed to go to find her father and get the information from him that could save her kind. If she was a Sin Eater, she'd be able to cross over to the Land of the Dead and speak to him. She would sacrifice her soul for a higher purpose.

Just as she was about to bite the bread, the Sin Eater's hand shot out from behind her. He grabbed the food from her, shoving it into his own mouth. She gasped, not expecting this at all. Then, before she even had a chance to object, he snatched the cup of wine from her and guzzled it down in two gulps.

"What did you do?" She jumped to her feet, her hands resting on her hips.

"It was nothing," he answered nonchalantly, throwing the cup to the ground and rubbing his hands together to free them from crumbs. "You can thank me later."

"Darium!" shouted the king. "You weren't supposed to do that. It was the girl's punishment."

"Consider her punishment over." Darium flashed a smile. "No charge for this one, Your Majesty," he added, almost beaming with pride. Talia wanted to hit the streak-haired man right now for taking away her only chance to contact her father. Still, she couldn't let on in front of King Sethor that she had actually wanted the punishment he had bestowed upon her.

Darium turned and strutted back to his horse, pulling himself up into the saddle in one fluent movement. The cry of a raven split the air. A huge bird swooped down and landed on his outstretched arm before hopping over to his shoulder.

"I ought to have you killed for that, Sin Eater," Sethor ground out.

"Now, now," said Darium with a tsking sound after his words. "We both know you won't do such a thing, since I'm more valuable to you alive than dead." He turned his horse, preparing to leave.

"You're right," snapped Sethor. "Kill the girl in his stead."

"What?" gasped Talia. This was something she hadn't expected, and also a bump in her plans.

"Nay!" shouted Darium, turning his horse and riding back toward them.

"Call the executioner at once," commanded the king. Two guards grabbed Talia by her arms and they started pulling her with them to the gallows that stood in the far corner of the courtyard.

"You can't kill me. I'm a healer!" she protested.

"Then heal yourself after you're dead," Sethor answered with a sarcastic smile plastered across his face.

"I thought you wanted me to warm your bed." It was the last thing Talia would ever do, but she was stalling for time, trying to figure out how to escape this situation. She was an Elemental of the Earth and could call nature to aid her. However, she wasn't in the forest right now surrounded by plants, animals, and trees. Nay, she was in a stone enclosure, and the rocks weren't going to do a thing to help her out of this mess.

"I no longer want you. You're more trouble than you're worth." The king shrugged his shoulders as if he were doing naught but changing his mind about what to eat for dinner. "Besides, I recognize those flowers in your hair. They're lippenbur lilies, aren't they? The flowers of the Fae folk. You've got magic, and so you need to die."

She swore she heard the Sin Eater groan from atop his horse.

"They're just flowers. I picked them outside the walls of Evandorm Castle." She struggled with the guards. Being a Fae, she didn't have the ability to lie. Therefore, she had to try to twist the truth right now, or she was going to wind up dead. She did pick the lilies outside the walls of Evandorm, but it was in the Whispering Dale, which was the home of the Fae. That was on the far side of the mountains.

"I know who you are, Fae. Your father revealed the

secret to me as I was torturing him. I know all about you and your kind. You've got magic and are dangerous. You must die."

This was worse than Talia could ever imagine. First, her father was killed, and now she would die too. As horrendous a thought that it was, the worst part was that the Fae were going to suffer because of her. It was all her fault for being so careless.

"Let her go," ordered Darium in a low voice, but the king wouldn't hear of it.

"You'd better leave now, Sin Eater, before I change my mind and dispose of you as well," the king warned him.

The world was getting darker, and so were the people around her, Talia realized. She knew the cause of it, and if something wasn't done quickly, it would be too late. They would all be doomed forever.

"There is a rip in the veil," she blurted out, hoping that by telling the king, he would stop her execution and at least want to know more.

"If your gown is torn, I don't really care," answered the man, not understanding what she meant at all. The Sin Eater's head jerked upward when he heard what she had to say. The king might not care, but the Sin Eater seemed extremely interested in this information.

"Nay, I'm not talking about my gown, you fool!" She became angry now, as this was just wasting precious moments. The sky blackened above them and the wind became stronger. A howling or whistling noise could be heard. She was certain it was from the dead souls and it came from the rip in the veil. The thought of it made her shiver. "Something bad has happened, and it must be stopped. Listen to me."

"No one calls me a fool! Hang her," commanded the king with a careless flip of his hand. The guards dragged her up the stairs of the wooden gallows, and tied her wrists behind her back. The executioner held a noose, ready to slip it over her head.

"Nay! You can't do this. You need to listen to me." She continued to try to reason with the king, but he was so dark-hearted that nothing she said could seem to stop him from this heinous act.

"Put the bag over her head to shut her up," instructed the king. "Besides, I don't care to see her eyes bulge out when she chokes to death."

"Nay! Wait a minute," she pleaded, but the executioner covered her head with a burlap bag causing everything to become dark around her. Talia's thoughts were now frantic. She couldn't die this way! In one last desperate attempt, she silently called out in her mind to all nature to come to her aid. A sinking sensation within her made her wonder if it was already too late. She felt the guard starting to put the noose over her head, and knew this was the end now. She had failed in her mission, and there was nothing more she could do. By the time nature heard her call and responded, she'd already be dead.

The shriek of a raven pierced the air, and then she heard the cry of hundreds of birds from up above. Her hopes picked up. Mayhap her luck had not run out just yet.

"What is that?" screamed the executioner.

"We're being attacked by birds!" cried out another of the soldiers.

She heard the snorting of a horse from nearby, and then the thundering of hoofbeats moving closer to her. With her hands tied behind her back and the bag over her head, she had no idea what was going on.

"Hold on, princess," came the deep voice of the Sin Eater. She felt herself being lifted off her feet and thrown over the horse in front of the man. The bag fell off her head, enabling her to see the ground below her now.

"I think I'm going to be sick," she mumbled, feeling very dizzy.

"Not on my horse, you don't." Darium used his dagger to cut the ropes from her wrists, and then pulled her to an upright position in front of him. She sat with her feet over one side of the horse. The animal moved beneath her, causing her to reach out and clasp her arms around the Sin Eater's neck so she wouldn't fall. Pressed up tightly against him, she could feel his chest move in and out with every breath he took. She felt the rumbling against her of a rapidly beating heart, but wasn't sure if it was his or hers.

"Close the gate. Quickly!" yelled the king. "Don't let them leave. Man your weapons."

"Lucifer, get us out of here," Darium commanded his horse. As they turned a full circle, Talia was able to now see the many birds flying at the soldiers and the king. The birds clawed at the men, scratching them, and making them cry out. Her animals drew blood to protect her, and would gouge out the enemy's eyes if need be. She admired the loyalty of her earthly subjects, but didn't like this at all. She'd never meant for anyone to get hurt.

"That's enough," she called out, causing the birds all to lift up into the sky and fly away at hearing her command.

"Murk, let's go!" Darium shouted for his raven as he rode for the gate. They just made it through the exit before the gate came crashing down, almost atop their heads.

They traveled at breakneck speed down the path away from the castle, with a barrage of arrows landing behind them from the archers atop the battlements. The raven shrieked as it flew above them, thankfully not getting hit. They didn't stop riding until they'd reached a hidden stream in the forest. Darium held out his arm and the raven landed atop it like a perch.

"Well, that's one way to start the morning, although I can't say it's my favorite." He ran a finger over the head of his bird. "Thanks for the help, Murk. You too, Lucifer." He reached over Talia and patted the horse's neck. Still clinging to him, Talia's heart raced in her chest. The man's scent of leather and spice filled her senses, making her curious about him. She had always thought Sin Eaters would stink, but it wasn't so. "You're safe now, princess, thanks to me."

"You act as if you want me to be grateful, but mayhap I'm the one you should be thanking instead," remarked Talia, not liking the man's arrogance. "After all, I'm the one who called the birds to our rescue." She removed her arms from around his neck.

"*Our* rescue?" He chuckled deeply. "I wasn't aware I was in any danger. At least, not until I tried helping you."

"I'm not so sure about that."

The raven flew off. She looked up to see the Sin Eater raising one bushy brow in question. "Really? I wasn't the one whose life was in jeopardy. You were, in case you've already forgotten."

"That's not exactly true. I heard the king give the order to close the gate and for his soldiers to man their weapons. He told his men not to let us leave. Your life was in danger as much as mine, Sin Eater. Those arrows weren't being aimed just at me."

"All right, fair enough. Mayhap I was in danger, but it was only after I decided to save your neck . . . Fae."

Her eyes darted over to him. For a moment she was

surprised that he knew she was a Fae, but then realized she'd given her secret away when she told him that she'd called the birds. Besides, the king said aloud that her father had divulged this information. "Did you know before you heard it from the king? That I'm a Fae?" she asked, her curiosity making her want to know.

"Of course, I did. I'm not that easy to fool. I picked up your scent long before I even entered the courtyard. By the way, I'm also not about to thank you for anything, since all you did for me was almost get me killed. Even if thanks were in order, I wouldn't do it. I know a little about your kind. You don't like to be thanked because that makes it seem as if something is then owed in return."

"I owe you nothing! I don't want anything from you, and I never asked you to help me in the first place," she spat. Talia slid off the horse and got to the ground.

"Good, since I wasn't offering anything that I haven't already given you." Darium followed, rubbing his hand over his horse's nose as he led the animal to the stream to drink. "I kept your soul unblemished, princess, by sin eating so you didn't have to do it. I should think that was enough."

"You ruined all my plans!"

"What?" he looked at her as if he thought she was crazy. "You were about to take on the sins of the king's son, and I'm sure they were many. You would have been cursed because of it."

"That's right. And with a doomed soul, I would have been able to talk to the dead like you do. I'd then be able to contact my deceased father in The Dark Abyss."

"You mean, Land of the Dead. He couldn't possibly be in The Dark Abyss this fast. He just died."

"Whatever," she said, feeling flustered just thinking of her father in either position. It was almost as if she could feel the heat of the flames against her face from that horrid place just by thinking about it.

"Who said I can talk to the dead?" he asked.

"Can't you?" she rallied with a question of her own. "After all, you are a Sin Eater."

"It doesn't work that way. Not really."

"Then tell me, how does it work?"

"Never mind. Your father is dead and it is over. Now, forget about it, and just let him be." He stopped at the water's edge and allowed Lucifer to drink.

"My father was on a mission to uncover some very important information when he was killed. I need that information to save my kind."

Darium felt another chill run up his spine. He turned to face the girl. "A mission? Information? Does this have something to do with the odd feelings I've been getting that something is severely wrong? And what did you say about a tear in the veil?"

"In case you haven't noticed, there is a tear in the veil between the land of the living and the dead."

When she said the words, Darium closed his eyes and he let out a deep sigh. He had known something was wrong, but had no idea it was of this extreme. How could something like this have escaped his notice? His mind had been preoccupied lately, and this wasn't like him at all. "Nay, this can't be. Tell me it isn't so."

"It's true. It's been brought about by the extreme greed and deceit and hatred that is overtaking mankind," she told him. "This is a bad omen. Things are only going to get worse and many will die. The veil needs to be closed because we don't know what is going to come through. My father was meeting in secret with an elven sage inside Macada Castle, to find out how to do that."

"A sage? An elven sage?" Darium shook his head, never thinking of elves as extremely wise before. "I didn't think a fae like your father would need the help of one of them. Besides, you know you can't trust bloody elves."

The lands of Mura contained mountain ranges, thick forests, lush vegetation, lakes, streams, and several glens and vales. While the three kings of Mura ruled over the south side of the island, the north side, over the mountains, were the lands where the magical creatures resided. Humans never went there, and the creatures of magic usually stayed put as well. It was a long, treacherous journey to get there, and not worth the risk.

The Whispering Dale was filled with the fae folk, down in the valley where the lippenbur lilies grew. Glint was the home of the elven kingdom, right next to it. The gnomes lived in the caves of Quamm, while the Isle of Denwop was where the giants made their home.

Across the water from Mura was the land of Lornoon. Further still, across the Masked Sea could be found Tamiras, the land of sand and sheiks, where it was dry and barely ever rained. Not much was really known of these places since no one from Mura ever went there. All that Darium knew about them was from the stories his parents used to tell him when he was a child.

"My father was not a fae," she explained. "Only my mother is. He was naught but a mere human."

"Mere human," Darium repeated, not at all amused at her choice of words. "I see." His horse finished drinking and he led it back toward the road. "So, you're really only a half-fae then and not a princess at all?"

"I never said I was a princess. That was all your idea.

Besides, it doesn't matter. We're all in danger as long as that portal stays open. I'm sure there is extreme darkness and evil on the other side, just waiting to come through."

"Yes, I can vouch for that," said Darium with a nod of his head.

"So, you've been there, then," she told him, not asking. "In the Land of the Dead." Her eyes were wide with interest as she waited for him to say more.

"I have." It was only once and when he was a child, but she didn't need to know that. It was also the most terrifying thing that had ever happened to him in his life, and he'd tried to block the memories from his mind. What little he did remember, he'd rather forget. "I'm sure since I'm able to cross over into the Land of the Dead and return, you're now counting on me to close the damned portal, aren't you?"

"Nay."

"Nay?" That truly surprised him. It wasn't at all what he expected her to say.

"I want to go through the portal myself into the other realm to find my father. Then I can still gather the information he died collecting for me."

"What information? This isn't about closing the portal, is it? This has something to do with the information the so-called sage was going to give him."

"It is about closing the portal, and . . . more."

"More?" He perused her, feeling as if she didn't trust him. She had a secret, and was keeping things from him. Even though it bothered him, did he really care? He was about to try to read her mind, but then decided not to. "Never mind, I don't want to know." Darium waved his hand through the air in a dismissing manner. "It doesn't matter. You can't go through that portal, and that's all there is to it. You need to be dead in order to enter that world, and if that's the case, you are never coming back."

"But you did it and survived! I've heard Sin Eaters can do it. You told me yourself just now that it is possible. That's why I wanted to sin eat, but you ruined my chances."

"Listen, princess, I've seen things in the Land of the Dead that you couldn't even imagine. It's not a place for a frail wench like you."

She fixed the crown of flowers on her head. "Wench? I'm half-fae, I told you. And stop calling me princess. I'm an Elemental of the Earth."

"Whatever." He didn't really care.

"I think I might be able to cross the threshold and still return after all." The addled girl's eyes lit up as if she really believed it.

"You are only half-fae, and you think you can do anything." He groaned. "That diminishes your chances by half, you realize. Nay, you can't do it, so don't even mention it again."

"Then you do it for me," she said, raising her chin in the air, almost in a manner that challenged him not to deny her request. "You're a Sin Eater. You can cross the threshold and even talk to the dead. That can come in handy for us."

"Us? What do you mean, us? There is no us. This has nothing to do with me, and everything to do with you." Darium turned away, busying himself with checking the straps of the horse's saddle.

"But you have the ability to do what I cannot."

"So, what if I can? What does it matter?" He spoke without looking at her. It was hard to deny a beautiful girl what she asked. He figured if he wasn't staring at her, mayhap it would be easier. There was no way he was going to purposely enter the Land of the Dead for anyone.

"Forget it," she snapped, sitting down on a rock and hiding her face in her hands. "I don't know why I ever thought I could count on someone like you. Any man who would purposely sin eat, obviously cares about nothing but money."

"Now, wait a minute," he said, crossing over to stand in front of her. "No matter how much you don't like me, I assure you, that statement is not true. Sure, I like money as much as the next man, but this is totally irrelevant."

"How so?" She peeked up at him when she spoke.

"It's my destiny to be a Sin Eater, precious. Do you think I'd really choose this profession because I wanted to do it? No one is that stupid!"

Talia removed her hands from her face and looked up to see that she'd really angered the man. His hood was down, and the white streak in his black hair was stark and a bit frightening. She swore she saw fire in his eyes.

"How can it be anyone's destiny to do such an awful job?" she asked softly. Mayhap she should have just let it go, but being a fae and curious in nature, she couldn't.

The Sin Eater's jaw was clenched tightly. He looked off in a different direction rather than to meet her eyes. She didn't think he was going to answer. Then, he sat down on a stone opposite her, and looked as if he were ready to speak.

"It is the hand that fate has dealt me," he said softly. "For the gods' sake, it's the last thing I ever wanted to do, but I didn't have a choice. Don't you see? I inherited the position from my father."

"We all have choices," she told him, honestly believing it, even though it seemed as if he didn't agree.

"My father was a Sin Eater," he explained. "I am his eldest son. As his first-born son, it is my destiny to be a Sin Eater as well."

"Nay," she said, shaking her head. "It might be fate that you are the first-born son of a Sin Eater, but it is not your destiny to follow in your father's footsteps."

"Yes, it is. You don't know what you're saying."

"Of course, I do. Fate is something that can't be changed, but destinies can. It's all up to you and the choices you make."

"Nay, I have no choice in his matter." He was too convinced and wouldn't listen to a word of what she was saying.

"Do you have siblings?" she asked.

"Yes. Two brothers."

"Then, why can't one of them sin eat instead of you?"

"Nay. It doesn't work that way," he said, giving her an appalled look that she should even suggest it. "We all have our destinies – our reasons for being here. Sin eating just happens to be mine. My brothers are plagued with . . . other things."

"Plagued?" she asked, questioning his odd choice of words.

"That's what it is, really. I'm doomed to do this until the day I die. If I have a son, he'll inherit the sin eating destiny from me as well. That's why I'm never going to marry or have children. I wouldn't wish this profession on my worst enemy, let alone my own child."

"Never marry?" she asked in shock, since that is all she'd been thinking about since she came of age. "You don't want children? Really? How can you say that?"

"Nay, I don't want children of my own since they're only going to end up like my father, and me. Or like my brothers, which is almost as bad. There is no reason to have sons of my own."

"Well, what if your children were girls?" she asked curiously. "Then would they be free of this curse you speak of?"

"Yes, I suppose so. But it doesn't matter. If I ever did have children, they would all be boys."

"You don't know that."

"I do. You see, for generations, there have been nothing but boys born in my family."

She giggled and he gave her an odd look.

"That's funny to you?" he asked.

"Nay. I was just thinking how I'm the opposite. My family is all girls."

"Is that common amongst the fae folk?"

She wasn't sure she could trust him, but decided she needed help so she had to divulge the whole story to him. "Darium, I don't know you well, but I am trusting that if I tell you this, you won't use it against me or my kind."

"What are you talking about?"

"The fae," she told him. "We're . . . a dying breed."

"How do you mean?"

"Never mind." She started to change her mind about it, and got up, heading to the horse. He jumped up and followed her, touching her on the arm.

"Princess, tell me the rest. Please."

She stopped, looking down to his hand on her arm. Why did she feel so warm? She slowly looked over her shoulder, up at his face once again. He was a handsome man, besides the streak in his hair. She was sure someday he'd have beautiful babies. He had a strong nose, and high cheekbones. Stubble formed on his jaw, just kissing his face lightly, making him look rugged in an exciting sort of way. He was very masculine and she liked that. His eyes were probably the most mesmerizing thing about him. This close up, she realized they weren't brown or blue or even green. Nay, they were a shiny, bright gray that to her looked to be silver.

"Can you stop calling me, princess?" she asked.

"I can. But only if you tell me your name."

It was at that moment that she realized he truly didn't know her name. She supposed that is why he called her by that silly title.

"The fae don't like to tell our names to humans." She was hesitant to do it. "It gives a person power over us."

He chuckled. "You really believe that, yet you scoff at my belief of not being able to change my destiny?"

"I – I don't know," she said, staring at his mouth now. It was a good, strong mouth, and his lips looked inviting. It made her wonder how it would feel to kiss him. For a moment, she almost thought they would kiss, but then he stepped away.

"Never mind," he said, clearing his throat. "Let's keep riding before the king's men catch up to us. We're not safe yet." He mounted his horse and then reached down for her hand. She didn't think twice about giving it to him. Once she was seated in front of him again, his arm closed around her waist and he held her tightly up against his body as they started to ride.

"Talia. Talia-Glenn," she said after a few minutes of silence.

"What?"

"My name. You asked me my name and now I've told you."

"Oh. Talia-Glenn. I like that name. It's different."

His breath blew against her hair as he spoke. She felt his essence encompassing her, making her feel warm and alive.

"I'll tell you the rest," she said. "I mean . . . about the other information that my father died trying to get."

"You don't need to."

"Don't you want to know?" She looked at him quizzically over her shoulder. One moment he seemed interested, and the next he acted as if he didn't care at all.

"I admit, I'm curious, but I also get the feeling that the more I know, the more I'll somehow be involved in the crazy plan that is rolling around in your head."

"Mayhap your true destiny is to help me. Have you ever thought of that?"

"I doubt it," he said, his low voice rumbling in his chest. She felt it against her back. "Besides, I've just met you, so that can't be true. My only purpose is to take on the sins of others so their souls are free to get to The Haven – not that I believe they'll really end up there anyway."

"So, you think anyone with sins is going to end up in The Dark Abyss instead?" She glanced over her shoulder, waiting for his answer.

"I don't know. I'm not even sure I believe in either place anymore."

"What?" she gasped. "That's blasphemy. How can you, of all people, say such a thing?"

"It's because of who I am that I *can* say that."

"I don't understand."

"Enough of this conversation." He sounded really irritated now. "Tell me the rest of your story before you burst."

"What does that mean?" She turned back around

and looked out at the forest, since nature always calmed her.

"It means, I have the ability to pick up on others' feelings and emotions."

"You do not."

"Yes, I do. It's natural for someone of my kind. I suppose it's because I've taken in so much from others, that I'm able to feel things from the living as well as the dead."

"Really. Well, then, what am I feeling right now?" she challenged him. "Tell me, so I know you're not lying."

"You're attracted to me," he said without hesitation. "You're also wondering what it would feel like to kiss me."

Talia's eyes sprang open wide, and she jerked around so quickly to look at him that she almost fell off the horse.

"Whoa, careful there, my little fae," he said, holding her with two arms now, stopping his horse.

She looked up into his beautiful silver eyes. "That's not what . . . that's not . . ."

"Not what?" he asked. "Are you trying to deny you want to kiss me?"

"Nay," she said, feeling the heat rise to her cheeks. Her tongue shot out to lick her dry lips. Her gaze lowered. She couldn't look directly at him now that he knew the truth. She had started to lie, but it didn't work. The fae folk were happy, giddy people who could only tell the truth. They might be curious by nature and troublemakers just for fun, but they were good people and would never hurt anyone purposely. "I am incapable of lying, even though I wanted to do it to keep from being embarrassed," she admitted.

He gently lifted her chin with one hand and she

looked up into his eyes getting lost within their depths.

"I have to admit something as well, Talia. Even though I can read minds on occasion, I didn't really know you wanted to kiss me."

"You didn't?" Now, she felt even worse for telling him the truth. "Then – then why did you say that?"

His eyes dropped to her mouth, making her very nervous. Their faces were so close together, and it would be so easy to share a kiss right now. She'd never been kissed by a man before, and had longed for this for quite some time now.

"I suppose, it was only because it was what I was thinking." With that, he leaned in to her, pressing his lips gently against her mouth. Her eyes closed. The connection immediately made her tingle. A wave of emotion surged through her. He tasted like mead and smelled like wood smoke mingling with pine and fresh air. Their lips parted, and she boldly lifted her chin, kissing him once more. The sound of leather creaked as he shifted in the saddle, drawing her closer to him with both his arms around her waist. Now, she knew what it felt like to kiss a handsome man . . . even if he was naught but a Sin Eater.

"Someone's coming," she said, hearing nature calling to her, warning her of an approach. She had been so caught up in the kiss that she had nearly missed it.

"What? Really?" He abruptly released her, reaching for his sword. When he did, she lost her balance and tumbled off the horse, letting out a scream as she hit the ground.

When she landed, she came face to face with a big white wolf that she had never seen before. All the wolves of Mura were brown or black or sometimes even gray. This one was white. She tried to talk to the wolf with her mind, but the animal snarled and showed its teeth. It didn't make any sense. She was an Elemental of the Earth. She could talk with all the animals and plants and had a connection with each of them. That is, all but this one. Fear entered her. She wasn't sure what to do, nor what was going on. Nothing like this had ever happened to her before.

Help me! She cried out in her mind. Instantly, the vines of the ground snaked over the top of the wolf. The wolf fell, snarling and growling, trying to bite off its restraints. Then a stricat bolted out of the shadows, ready to fight the wolf. The large wildcat was a species of the land that was hardly ever seen, and nearly extinct. It was orange with black and brown stripes, and a shaggy mane that could be lifted up at will to make the wildcat look even larger. On its back were folded two black wings that it used to fly when the animal needed to escape quickly. The stricat had razor-like claws and was a ferocious fighter.

"Nay, stop it!" shouted Darium, jumping off the horse with his sword outstretched. The wolf thrashed about on the ground, ripping at the vines with its teeth. "Talia, call off the cat," he commanded. "I know you can."

"Nay, it's here to protect us," she explained from the ground. "Darium, I can't talk to this wolf and I've never seen it before. It is dangerous. Perhaps, it is some dark entity that came through the portal."

"I assure you, it's not. Now call off the damned cat as well as the vines. You can't hurt this wolf. It's not evil and not from the Land of the Dead."

"How do you know that?" she asked, wondering why Darium seemed so sure of this, when she knew all about nature and had no idea where this wolf even came from or why she couldn't speak to it at all.

"Talia, please. Call off your attack on the wolf, and I

promise to explain everything."

"I don't know," she answered, still not convinced it was the right thing to do. "Why do you even care about this animal?"

"I ask you once again to do it, because I do care. I don't want anything to happen to the wolf, because it is my brother."

Three

Darium was used to his brothers showing up at random times, but this had to be the most inopportune moment ever. He'd been enjoying kissing the fae, and now he was standing with his sword at the ready while the fae was sprawled out on the ground. She held the power in her hands to decide if the wolf would live or die.

"Your brother?" asked the girl in confusion, as the stricat crept closer to the wolf, ready to lunge at it or take a bite.

"Please, I'll explain. Just let him go." Darium, did not want his brother to get hurt, and at the same time he didn't want to hurt the wildcat either. "The wolf won't hurt anyone, I swear."

"Release him," commanded Talia. The vines around the wolf loosened, enabling the animal to spring up, snarling at the stricat now.

"Are you sure we're safe?" asked Talia once more, peering at, not looking as if she believed him.

"Zann, stop the growling. You're making matters worse," said Darium, causing the wolf to pull back. "Now, get rid of the cat," he commanded the fae, still holding his sword aimed at the stricat to take down the animal if need be to protect his brother.

"Go on, Seka," said Talia softly, sending the cat bounding away into the thicket as a rider approached. "It's the king's men," she cried, jumping to her feet.

"Nay, it's just my youngest brother, Rhys," said Darium, seeing his other sibling heading toward them at full speed atop his horse. When Rhys saw Darium, he came to an abrupt halt.

"Rhys, what is going on?" grunted Darium. "It's not the best time for a visit."

"There's trouble," announced Rhys, jumping off the horse and hurrying over to him. "That's why I sent Zann ahead to track you down."

"Who are these people and what is going on?" Talia made her presence known.

Rhys wasn't expecting to see anyone there and jerked back, startled, ripping his sword from the scabbard at his waist. Then, he realized what he was looking at, and slowly lowered the tip of his blade. "A girl? With you, brother?" asked Rhys. A smile turned up the sides of his mouth. "You're such a demon, Darium. She's a pretty one, too, but highly unexpected, I must say. Are you going to introduce us?"

"Aye, but not yet. Zann, please shift so we can speak like humans." Darium spoke to the wolf.

"Shift?" Talia looked confused.

The wolf let out a long howl, and put its head down on the ground. Then, he started to shapeshift back into his manly form.

"Oh!" cried Talia, grabbing on to Darium's arm, and half-hiding behind him.

When Zann shifted back into a man, he was naked. He always was whenever he shifted.

Talia gasped. Darium pulled her against him, to hide her view of his naked brother.

"For Haven's sake, give him some clothes," Darium told Rhys.

Rhys replaced his sword and then pulled clothes out of the travel bag that was tied to his horse. He tossed some garments to the ground for his brother.

"Sorry about that," said Rhys. "Zann doesn't usually shift around people, and especially not in front of pretty girls."

"Arrrgh," groaned Zann, hurriedly pulling on his clothing, shaking his head since it took a few minutes to focus after he shifted.

"All right, you can look now," Darium told Talia, gently turning her to face his brothers. "Talia, these are my brothers, Rhys and Zann. Guys, this is Talia-Glenn. She is a fae."

"Elemental. Of the earth," Talia corrected him, nodding to his brothers. "Nice to meet you."

"A fae?" asked Zann, flashing her a smile. "I've heard about your kind but never met one before."

"I've heard about your kind too, but for the life of me have never seen anything quite like that!" She stared at him with wide eyes, still seeming shaken.

"I often get that response from women who see me naked." Zann grinned and walked over, taking a hold of Talia's hand, kissing it.

Then Rhys stepped in front of him, kissing her hand as well.

Talia wasn't sure what to think of this. She'd been kissed by three men in one day, and she rather liked it.

"Darium, you didn't tell me your brothers were just as handsome as you, and twice as charming," she said, smiling at them just to be pleasant. "They seem to like to kiss girls just like you do."

"You kissed her?" asked Rhys, looking up at Darium in surprise.

"On the mouth?" asked Zann, looking like he wanted more details.

It was the nature of the fae to play tricks and games, and sometimes purposely cause trouble. After the kiss from Darium, Talia was convinced that he liked her. Mayhap it wasn't the right thing to do, but she purposely said these things to see if Darium would become jealous.

"What is it that is so important that you had to hunt me down to tell me?" Darium didn't sound jealous at all. He actually just dismissed the whole kissing question, acting like it didn't even exist. Mayhap it didn't matter to him like it had her. That made her feel a little disappointed.

"Brother, there is a rip in the veil between the worlds." Zann relayed the information, sounding out of breath. Talia figured it was probably from all that running in his wolf form.

"Aye, I know about it. Talia already informed me," answered Darium.

"Um, excuse me," Talia interrupted. "Before we talk about the portal, can we talk about . . . that?" She looked at Zann and then at the ground where he'd shifted.

"Oh, she doesn't know?" Zann glanced over to Darium. Zann was a little shorter than his brother, and had blond hair that stopped at his shoulders. It was so light, that it almost seemed white. His eyes were wolf-like, bearing a glowing orange tone.

"What have you told her?" asked Rhys, sounding cautious. He was the youngest of the three and had the shortest hair out of the brothers. It was oaken in color. His eyes were a striking green. He was dressed in chain mail and wore the crest of the King of Kasculbough on his chest.

"You're a knight," said Talia, eyeing up his attire. "At Kasculbough?"

"Aye," Rhys proudly answered.

"Can you shapeshift like your brother?" she asked eagerly, wondering what else these men could do. They intrigued her, and she wondered why she had never come across them before. She supposed it was because her whole life had been spent in the Whispering Dale. It was only recently that her family moved to the Goeften Forest so they could be close to the castle where her father worked and lived.

The smile on Rhys' face turned into a frown. "Can I shift? Damn, of course not. I'm the youngest son. I'm the one with the super strength, and who's unbeatable with a sword." He drew his sword again, and flipped it around, then slipped it back into his scabbard with a snap.

"All right, then," she said, her eyes glancing up at Darium. She really didn't understand any of this, but decided not to pursue it further at this time.

"Only Zann can shapeshift into a wolf," Darium explained. "It's a trait, or ability, passed down from our grandfather."

"Oh, I see. So your grandfather wasn't a Sin Eater."

"Nay, he was the second-born son," said Darium.

"So, then he could shapeshift into a wolf, too?" she asked, thinking she was starting to understand this.

"Nay, of course not," said Zann, making a face. "He was a bear-shifter."

"Oh," she answered, feeling very confused now.

"Our great-grandfather's strength was passed down

to me since I'm the third son," eagerly explained Rhys. "Thank the stars I wasn't first or second born," he mumbled under his breath.

"I see," said Talia. "Each son inherits the traits or skills or powers of the male from a previous generation."

"That's partially correct," said Darium with a nod. "It just depends on how many sons are born, of course, but each has a different . . . skill, shall I say?"

"What if there are four or five boys in the family?" she asked. "Can they do other things? Mayhap turn invisible or fly?"

Darium and his brothers glanced at each other and shook their heads. "Never mind," said Darium. "This isn't important right now."

"Well, then what about your mother?" she asked. "What was her skill, and would her daughters have inherited it if you three had been female instead of male?"

"What?" Zann looked at her as if he'd smelled something bad. "Mother didn't have any skills. She was just . . . human."

"That's right. And please don't even suggest that we might have been girls," said Rhys, making a face as well. "That is an insult, and highly unthinkable."

"I don't see why," said Talia. "What's wrong with girls? My family has many."

"Don't take offense for the rudeness of my brothers," Darium told her. "All they mean is that the Blackseed line has only birthed sons for as long as anyone can remember."

"Right," said Rhys. "We don't have anything against girls, or kissing them." He smiled at her, making Talia feel uncomfortable now.

"Can we get back to the matter of the rip in the veil?" asked Zann impatiently. He shifted from foot to foot and his eyes continuously scanned the area, the way an animal would. He seemed to be the nervous type.

"Yes. What do you know about it, and where is it?" asked Darium.

"It's near the Lake of Souls somewhere, but it keeps moving and disappearing," explained Rhys. "We heard it open earlier today, but we can't find it now."

"We've got to find a way to close it." Zann heard a twig snap in the forest, and he spun around and cocked his head to listen. Then, he sniffed the air.

"There is nothing to worry about," said Talia calmly. "If there is trouble, I'll be alerted by nature."

Zann and Rhys exchanged glances.

"She's an Elemental of the Earth, like she said," Darium told his brothers. "She has powers like the rest of us, just different. Now, does anyone know if anything has come through the portal yet?"

"No one can be sure, since the portal keeps moving," Zann answered. "But I can feel it. Something's either already happened, or is about to." His flipped his hair, his whole body moving like a dog shaking water off its back.

"I've felt the disturbances too," agreed Darium. "It's important we move quickly. What we've got to do is to figure out how to close the portal before anyone else knows it is even there."

"Only the sage knows the answer to that," said Talia. "He is who my father was supposed to meet at Macada Castle."

"Sage?" asked Rhys.

"Elven sage," grunted Darium. "I hate elves. They are so irritating. Why couldn't the sage just be an old man? A human?"

"Where is the sage?" asked Zann.

"Inside Macada Castle," Darium relayed the information, shaking his head.

"We need to get to Macada Castle as quickly as possible, and find this sage," suggested Talia, even though she knew Darium didn't want to do it.

Darium let out a sigh. "Nay, not we. Me. You're not going anywhere, Talia. "It's not safe." He put his fingers to his chin in thought, and looked up at Rhys.

"I'm happy to help, of course, but right now I need to get back to Kasculbough before I'm missed," said Rhys. "If I don't report for my next duty, King Osric will send out a squad to look for me."

"We don't want that," said Darium in thought. "It's better if we try to keep everyone away from the lake until we find the portal."

"I need to rest after shifting," said Zann. "I won't be any good for at least an hour."

"Mayhap King Kasculbough or King Evandorm can help us," suggested Talia.

"Nay!" Darium and his brothers all said together.

"The kings are the reason this rip in the veil happened to begin with, I'm sure," said Darium. "I don't want them involved."

"That's right," agreed Rhys. "Besides, the less people who know about this, the better. If any of the three kings realize the portal is open, they might decide to use it to gain power over the others. It could be disastrous and very dangerous. We don't know what kind of darkness will be coming through."

"Oh, I see. I already said something about it to King Sethor." Talia looked up at Darium, feeling worried.

"I'm sure it's fine. He didn't seem to believe you or even understand it," Darium pointed out. "Either way, I'll go back to the castle and try to contact the bloody elf and find out what we need to know."

"You've got to also find out from the sage the rest of the information that he's given my father," said Talia.

"About what?" asked Zann. "I don't understand."

"The fae are near extinction," Talia explained. "Or at least a pure line, I should say. You see, a male fae hasn't been born in so long, that the females have had to mate with humans. Because of it, most of us are only half-fae. Eventually, the human side will overpower us, and our abilities that make us who we are, will fade away until we are naught but mere humans too. There is a way to ensure male fae are born, and that is the answer we are searching for."

"And only the elf knows?" asked Darium.

"He's a sage. And yes, he is the only one who knows the answer," said Talia.

"What does it even matter?" asked Darium. "If the fae birth males, they'll still be half-fae only."

"Not so," said Talia. "You see, the male fae power is even stronger than the females. So, in a generation or two, there is a chance that babies will be born as full-fledged fae once again."

"Well, I'll do what I can, but I can't make any promises," said Darium, feeling agitated by all this. "Remember, I'm not welcome inside the castle walls, so I'll have to wait until I'm summoned. Hopefully, I'll sense there's been another quick death and that my services are needed."

"Nay. We can't wait that long," cried Talia. "This is important. We need to act now, right away."

"She's right," agreed Zann. "The longer we wait, the more chance for trouble to happen."

"All right, I'll go," grumbled Darium, not really wanting to do this. Talia didn't need to read his mind this time. His words and body actions made his feelings transparent. "In the meantime, we all need to keep our eyes and ears open. To keep you safe, Talia, I'm taking you back to your kind."

"Isn't that on the other side of the mountain?" asked Zann.

"Aye. It'll take a good day to get to the Whispering Dale and then another to get back," protested Rhys. "We need to do something about the rip in the veil now. It can't wait, brother."

"He's right," said Talia, looking up at Darium. He was very tall, and she had to stretch her neck to see his face since she was so short. "I'll just go back to my home here, in the Goeften Forest instead. I'll be safe."

"I don't know," said Darium with a shake of his head. "Talia, it's better if you stay with me for now so I can keep an eye on you."

"Nay, I'm safe in the forest. The animals and all nature will protect me, as you've already seen. Besides, I haven't been living in the Whispering Dale lately. My home is here now."

"Fine. Then, I'll stay with you," said Darium, scaring her yet exciting her at the same time with his comment. After the kisses they'd shared, and the intense attraction and warmth she'd felt, she wasn't sure what to expect.

"If you insist. I suppose you can stay with me in my earth hut," she told him.

"Good. Then its settled," he answered.

"However," she added, "I must warn you that my place is small and pretty crowded."

"I don't mind."

"I don't suppose you do." She turned to lead the way through the woods. "I just hope my six sisters will feel the same way about it."

Four

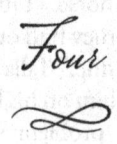

"Six sisters?" asked Darium, not liking the sound of this at all. He was used to being a loner, and living by himself, with only Zann as company on occasion. He didn't have sisters, and wasn't even sure if being around all these women was going to drive him crazy.

"Six sisters?" Zann and Rhys said together, sounding as if they liked the idea a lot.

"Yes," answered Talia. "I am the eldest. Then comes Shaylyn, Poppy, the twins Tia and Zia, Aubrette, and the youngest of my sisters, Joy."

"Great," answered Darium, wondering just what he was getting himself into.

"Darium, how old are you and your brothers?" she asked. The curious nature of the fae kept her asking so many questions. Darium wasn't sure if she'd ever stop talking.

"Darium is twenty-five, I'm twenty-four, and Rhys is twenty-three," said Zann, not waiting for Darium to answer.

"My, you are close in age." Talia giggled. Giggling

must be something that the fae did a lot, Darium realized.

"Well, let's go and meet all these faeries," said Darium. He mounted his horse. "I just hope they won't be frightened of me once they find out I'm a Sin Eater."

"Oh no, they'll be fine." Talia took his hand and settled herself in front of him on his horse.

"It won't cause a problem with them, then?" he asked, just to be sure.

"Not at all," she answered with a smile. "However, I'm not sure how my mother is going to react."

Darium let out a loud groan, glancing over to his brothers to see them both holding back their laughter.

"Well, go on," Darium told his brothers. "Do what you have to do. Then head to the lake and look for the portal. I'll take Talia home to get settled, and I'll meet you there later."

"Oh, I don't want to get settled," Talia told him, being the defiant little fae that she was. "I want to be a part of the plan as well."

"Impossible. You'll only get in the way," remarked Darium.

"Or hurt," added Zann.

"I agree," said Rhys. "It's best if you leave the tear in the veil to us. We'll make sure to close it somehow."

"Not before you contact my father, you won't," Talia reminded him.

"I said I'd contact the sage at Macada Castle," Darium answered. "I never agreed to try to talk to your father."

"Where is your father?" asked Zann. "Perhaps I can contact him for you."

"He's dead," Talia answered.

"Oh." Zann shook his head. "Can't do it, then. Sorry."

"He died before confessing his sins, so that means he's in the Land of the Dead, and most likely headed for The Dark Abyss," added Darium. "Talia wants me to go find him."

"In the Land of the Dead? On purpose?" Rhys' mouth fell open. "You can't be serious."

"Isn't that a little risky?" asked Zann.

"I'm not really sure, since it's been so long," said Darium, not even remembering anymore how he visited there with his father in the first place. He also didn't remember much about how they returned.

"But you are a Sin Eater. You can do it. Right?" asked Talia.

"Is it possible? Can you visit the Land of the Dead and return afterwards without father to assist you?" Rhys wanted to know.

Things seemed to be going from bad to worse in Darium's opinion. He had no intention of visiting the Land of the Dead. All he wanted was to close the damned portal to keep anything or anyone from coming through. If he didn't, he wasn't sure what would happen. The last thing he wanted was to purposely be going through it.

"We'll meet at the lake later," Darium told his brothers as they headed away. "I'll take Talia home and then sneak back into the castle and try to find the sage. What is his name?" he asked Talia.

"His name is Elric," Talia informed him. "However, don't call him a sage, and certainly not an elf."

"Why not?" Darium was starting to think these magical beings were very odd.

"Because no one there knows who he really is. You see, he's also the court jester."

"It figures," mumbled Darium, knowing it was a fool's journey going back to the castle where he'd almost been killed this morning. Now, he would be risking his life, and only to contact a bigger fool than himself.

"Stop here," Talia told Darium when they got to the thickest part of the forest.

"Here?" He looked around, feeling confused. "Why? I don't see a house."

"Of course not, silly." She giggled and slid off the horse. "Elementals blend in with the environment. Our abodes remain hidden to others unless they know where to look. Since a human tends not to see the nose on his own face, they never see what is right in front of them."

Darium found himself looking cross-eyed, trying to see his own nose, wondering exactly what that meant.

"It's all right. You can come out. He won't hurt you," she called out to her sisters. Then, one by one her sisters poked their heads out from behind trees and rocks, and slowly made their way over to them.

"So, these are your siblings," he commented, dismounting and tying the reins of his horse to a tree.

"Let me introduce you," she said, waving the girls forward. Darium wasn't sure how to tell the age of a faerie, but Talia said she was the eldest and she seemed to be about twenty years of age. The youngest of the sisters looked to be about eight. "This is my sister, Shaylyn," she said, nodding to the tallest girl. Each of the girls had brown hair, and honestly looked so similar that Darium didn't know how he was ever going to tell them apart, let alone remember their names.

"Hello, Shaylyn," he said. "I'm Darium."

"You're that Sin Eater, aren't you?" asked Shaylyn, saying it like it was a bad word. She stared at his head, reminding him that he hadn't covered his hair.

"He is," said one of the other girls. "Look at that streak of white in his black hair. He looks like a skunet!"

"Tia! That wasn't nice," scolded Talia.

"He doesn't smell like a skunet," said one of the girls sniffing the air.

"Why, thank you, Tia," Darium said sarcastically.

"I'm Zia!" the girl responded, scowling at him.

"I think he's handsome. For a Sin Eater, that is," said one of the other girls.

"This is Aubrette," said Talia, motioning to the one with red flowers in her hair. "And Sister, that wasn't proper of you to say that, either."

"I like it better than being called a skunet," Darium said with a shrug.

Next, Darium felt a tugging on his tunic, and looked down to see the smallest girl looking up at him with wide, brown eyes. "Are you going to marry our sister?" asked the little one.

"Well . . . I . . ." He looked over to Talia to see a flush cover her face.

"This is Joy, and she's a pest. I'm sorry about that," said Talia, pulling her youngest sister to her, and holding her against her skirt.

"Well, nice to meet you all, but I really need to go now." Darium turned to mount his horse, and felt the slap of a branch hit him hard across the face, knocking him to the ground. Then, the vines covered him, winding around him, tying up his arms and legs.

"What in damnation was that?" he ground out, struggling to get free. "Talia, what are you doing? Call it off, anon."

"It's not me doing it," she said, but he didn't believe her.

"You're the one who controls nature, so tell it to stop and release me."

"Honest, Darium, I did not do it." Since the fae couldn't lie, he realized she was telling the truth.

"Then tell your sisters to stop it. I don't think it's

funny." He struggled, trying to get a hold of his dagger, almost able to reach it, but not quite.

"My sisters are still learning but are not yet skilled in the elemental art of controlling nature," Talia explained.

"Then who is doing this to me?" He reached his blade and used it to sever the vines, hearing a screech of some sort as he pulled the vines off of him and jumped to his feet.

"How dare you treat nature with such disrespect!"

He looked up to see an older woman appear right behind Talia. She was a short, busty woman, who looked a lot like all of the sisters. She wore a crown of flowers in her hair as well.

"Mother, it was you!" cried Talia. "How could you?"

"How could you bring a Sin Eater to our hidden, sacred spot in the forest?" snapped her mother. "You led him right to our door. Talia, you have no idea what you've done. You've put us all in grave danger."

"Darium is here to help us," explained Talia.

"We don't need his help." The woman looked down her nose at him as if he were naught but trash. "I sent you to find your father, not bring back one of *his* kind." Her eyes narrowed to slits. Darium wouldn't have been surprised if a forked tongue shot out of her mouth next since she hissed at him like an arcine protecting her eggs.

"Father is dead," said Talia, getting gasps and cries from the sisters.

"Dead?" Her mother's stone-like face softened just a little. "Are you sure, Talia? How can this be? He was supposed to be meeting with the sage."

"Elf," said Darium, wiping his blade on his breeches and securing the dagger back to his weapon belt.

"He did go to Macada Castle, Mother," said Talia. "Lord Sethor killed him, saying he was a spy."

"He wasn't a spy!" shouted her mother. "He was our only hope of closing the portal, and saving the fae from extinction."

"Nay, Mother. Darium is our last hope. That is why he is here. He, and his brothers have agreed to help us."

"Really." Her mother eyed him up and down.

"Look, Talia's mother," said Darium.

"Her name is Maeve," Talia whispered.

"All right, Maeve. I'm sorry about your husband, and I'm sorry your kind is headed for extinction. But honestly, my only concern is closing that portal. You have no idea what kind of darkness and evil is on the other side."

"Hrmph," sniffed the woman. "I suppose someone like you feels at home in a place like that."

"Mother," gasped Talia, but Darium held up a halting hand.

"It's all right, princess. I'm used to it," he told her.

"Princess?" repeated her mother, glaring at Talia. "Daughter, did you tell him that's who you are?"

"Nay, Mother. He just calls me that, and doesn't mean anything by it." Talia looked over to him with begging eyes.

"That's right," agreed Darium. "I know she's just an Elemental."

"Just?" Her mother seemed insulted by that. Darium figured he was only making things worse and needed to stay quiet. Nay, what he really needed was to get out of here quickly.

"I'll go to the castle and try to find the elf, since I promised you I would." Darium quickly mounted his steed. "However, I have no intention of crossing into the Land of the Dead to try to speak with your father, Talia, I'm sorry."

"But we need you to, Darium," cried the girl.

"I'm going to figure out how to close the portal, and that is the end of this nonsense." He turned the horse and rode off quickly not wanting to accidentally insult the fae again. He also wanted to leave before they tricked him into doing another thing that he had no intention of doing.

"Talia, what were you thinking bringing that man here to our private glen? He's a Sin Eater!" Talia's mother looked as if she'd smelled a foul stench. It pained Talia's heart to know that Darium was always treated in this manner.

Talia watched Darium riding away, with his long cloak billowing out behind him in the breeze. His raven flew down from the treetops, leading the way. Her mother and sisters hadn't given Darium the welcome she had hoped for. Then again, they didn't know a thing about him, so they judged him like everyone else . . . by his profession.

"Darium saved my life as well as my soul today, Mother," Talia said in a soft voice. She couldn't stop thinking about the man's kisses and how her whole body tingled when his lips touched hers.

"You kissed him?" snapped her mother, having read her mind.

"Yes, Mother," Talia admitted. "Now, please stop reading my mind."

"What do you mean he saved you?" asked her sister, Tia.

"I mean, I was a prisoner of Lord Sethor," Talia explained. "The king accused me of being a spy, just like he thought our father was."

"Did the king hurt you, Daughter?" Her mother walked over and put her hand on Talia's shoulder.

"No, but he did try. To punish me, he first ordered me to sin eat."

"Nay!" gasped Shaylyn, holding her hand to her mouth in horror. "Tell me this isn't so."

"Sister, please tell us you didn't do it," said Zia.

"I was going to do it." Talia glanced out at the woods where Darium had already disappeared from sight. "I planned on doing it, so I could enter the Land of the Dead and speak to father. King Sethor said father killed two of his guards, but I'm sure it was only in self-defense. Father also died before he could tell us what he learned."

"Why didn't you just seek out the sage yourself?" asked Poppy.

"Aye," agreed her mother. "That was all you had to do."

"I was captured before I could locate the sage. Right as I was about to sin eat, Darium pulled the bread and wine away from me and took it into his own body instead."

"How romantic." Aubrette smiled and held her hands to her heart.

"Aubrette, you're smitten with any man," snapped Shaylyn.

"That's right," agreed Poppy. "This one is doomed to spend his afterlife in The Dark Abyss, or are you forgetting?"

"Darium did it to save my soul," Talia continued. "Then, when Lord Sethor tried to hang me from the gallows, Darium saved my life as well."

"The gallows?" cried Poppy.

"Nay!" shouted little Joy.

"Why didn't you just use your powers to call nature to your aid?" asked her mother.

"I did, but it wasn't enough, Mother." Talia turned

to face them now. "If Darium hadn't been there, I'd be dead right now, just like Father."

"Why was Darium there?" asked Shaylyn.

"I'm not sure, but what does it matter? Darium has agreed to help us, and I want all of you to be nice to him when I return. I have decided that I need to be with him. I will take our horse and follow." Talia started to walk away, knowing this was the right decision.

"Wait!" Her mother grabbed her arm and spun her around. "Where do you think you're going?"

"To help Darium, of course," she answered. "I don't expect him to do this by himself."

"You said his brothers were going to help him," Poppy reminded her.

"I did. However, I think they're going to need my Elemental powers to help in this case. We don't know yet exactly what we're dealing with."

"Talia, I don't want you near that Sin Eater," spat her mother.

"I like him," said little Joy.

"I think he's handsome," agreed Aubrette.

"Stop it!" shouted their mother. "Girls, it is time to get back to your studies. And Talia . . ."

"Yes?" asked Talia, looking up at the concern on her mother's face. She was sure that her mother was going to demand she stay there and not go after Darium. Instead, her answer surprised her.

"Be careful, dear," said her mother gently, releasing her arm.

"I know there is darkness and evil beyond the portal," Talia replied. "I will be careful, Mother, I promise."

"Not just that. I mean be careful of the Sin Eater, too."

Talia smiled. "Darium's not going to hurt me. He saved my life. That should be proof enough."

"That's not what I mean, Talia. What I mean is, protect your heart. The last thing I want is for any daughter of mine to fall in love with a man whose soul is blackened by the sins of others. A man who is destined to spend his afterlife in The Dark Abyss."

Five

Darium left his horse a little ways from Macada Castle so he wouldn't be spotted by the guards atop the battlements. Then, he hid under the hay in the back of a passing merchant's cart, managing to enter the castle undetected. Slipping out of the back of the wagon into the courtyard, he hid hunkered down in the shadows, waiting and watching, wondering where to find this so-called sage.

"Has anyone seen my fool?" yelled the king, storming across the courtyard. "I'm in a sour mood and need amusement."

"I believe he's gone to the stables to prepare for the show he'll present during the meal, my lord," answered one of his guards.

"Good. Steward, see to the meal. I'm hungry," snapped the king, heading to the great hall. "Guards, keep your eyes open for the girl and that Sin Eater. If you find them, bring them to me anon."

"Aye, my lord," answered a few guards, dispersing to their posts.

Darium was about to make his way to the stables, when he felt a shiver run up his spine. Then, a stabbing sensation to his chest made him double over. A strong wind picked up, whipping his cloak and hair around him. Something made him look up to the sky. Dark clouds overhead parted slightly, and a black wispy form swept down, coming right for him! He closed his eyes and braced himself, feeling the air go right through him. His body became so cold that his joints could barely bend. When he opened his eyes, the clouds had smoothed over, and nothing seemed amiss.

"What in the name of Belcoum was that?" he asked out loud, almost falling over when he tried to stand upright. He smelled the strong scent of death, but this time it was different. This time he realized it wasn't from someone recently departed. Nay, this was the scent of an entity that had come through the portal from the other side, he was sure of it. His biggest fear had come true. The dead were coming through the portal, and it wasn't going to end well.

There was no telling what could or would happen now. All he knew was that the longer he waited to get that portal closed, the bigger chance of more spirits coming through into the realm of the living where they didn't belong.

He hurried to the stable, entering it and thankfully seeing a small man sitting atop a bale of hay, dressed in the clothes of a jester. He was cross-legged and his eyes were closed. His palms were turned upward and he was humming a low chant. It surprised Darium that the man was so young. He thought at first it was just a boy since he was so small and short, but when he got closer he saw it wasn't a child but a mature man. Blond, curly hair stuck out in all directions from under a three-pronged hat made of red and blue with little bells attached to the ends. A stick wrapped in colorful ribbons lay across his lap.

Darium stood up, looking around, thankful not to see any soldiers or even a stablemaster nearby. Then, with a limp, since his joints were still stiff, he made his way over to the fool.

"Sage?" he asked in a low whisper.

The man's eyes opened slowly and his head turned slightly. "I was wondering when you'd show."

"Huh?" Darium had no idea what the elf meant, and neither did he have the patience or time to question it. "I need to know what you told the fae's father."

"Oh, you mean, Necos?" The elf's voice was wiry and grating on Darium's nerves just listening to it.

"I – I guess so. I don't know the man's name. He's the one accused of being a spy and killed by the king."

"Yes, that is unfortunate," said the sage, showing no emotion at all. "I suppose you're here because of the tear in the veil between the worlds."

"Aye. I need to know how to close the portal. The fae said you knew how to do it."

"Mayhap, I know something. But tell me, what do you have to trade me for this information?" The elf giggled, either from nerves or because he somehow thought playing this game was fun. Darium didn't agree.

"What do you mean?" Darium asked, starting to lose his patience with the fool. "I'm here for the sake of all of us. I'm about to risk my life to save many, and you so selfishly ask me to trade for the information? I can see now that you really are a fool! Forget it, I'll figure it out on my own." He turned to leave but the man's words stopped him.

"Why don't you ask Necos yourself? Mayhap he will tell you what you want to know."

Darium turned back to face him. "I am not going through the portal to talk to the dead, so just forget it."

"Your father took you there when you were a boy,

don't you remember? You can go through the portal, get your information from the dead, and come back without being harmed." He chuckled. "You don't need my help, and you know it."

"How do you even know about that? I don't know who you are, and you certainly don't know me." Darium looked at him suspiciously, wondering what the story was behind this fool elf.

Darium did remember the one time as a child when his father took him to the Land of the Dead. His father told him he'd been preparing Darium for his destiny. Darium, on the other hand, was just a child and frightened out of his mind. What he saw inside the portal was something he would never be able to forget. It was an horrific, and frightening place. Evil and darkness resided there and he had been very scared. Even though he was born a Sin Eater, Darium honestly had no intention of ever going back there again if he didn't have to.

"I'm a sage. I know a lot of things." The elf played with the stick, tossing it in the air and catching it again. His beady little eyes glanced over quickly and his mouth scrunched up on one side.

"I'm sure King Sethor would like to know a few things as well." Darium reached out and yanked off the elf's hat, exposing the tips of his pointy ears.

"Nay! Stop that." Elric's face turned dark. He grabbed the jester hat back, pulling it over his head and quickly covering the tops of his ears.

"You play a dangerous game, and I want to know why," said Darium. "What is it that is so important that you're willing to risk being exposed and possibly killed just to be here?"

"I'm done with you, Sin Eater. Leave here now, before I expose you to the king," answered Elric with a sniff.

"You wouldn't. Not if you want me to keep your secret."

"Are you so sure about that?" It was that last giggle that pushed Darium over the edge. He no longer cared what information the sage had, he didn't want it.

"I'm leaving," he said, gritting his teeth. "If all of Mura is covered by darkness because you refused to tell me answers of how to close the portal, then this is on your head, not mine."

"You play games with the fae as well," said the elf. "She's in much danger."

Darium's body stiffened. "She?" he asked.

"Talia-Glenn."

"She's in no danger. I saw to that. She is safe and back with her family."

"Is she?"

"What are you saying?"

"Are you sure she hasn't followed you back here to Macada Castle?"

"By the gods, she better not have." Darium didn't waste any more time with the fool. Was Talia really here? If so, what was she thinking?" He ran from the stables, leaving the sage sitting there chuckling to himself like some kind of madman.

Darium dodged a few guards, and once again managed to hide in the back of a cart as a merchant left the courtyard. As soon as he was through the gate and over the drawbridge, Darium rolled out of the wagon, seeing a man and a girl standing under a tree nearby talking. It had to be Talia, but who was with her? He collected his horse and rode toward them, stopping when he saw Talia look up at him and smile.

"Darium! My father lives," she cried, hugging the man standing in front of her.

"How can this be?" he asked from atop his horse. "I thought the king killed him."

"He managed to escape," said Talia. "Darium, this is my father, Necos," she introduced him as Darium dismounted. "Father, Darium is a Sin Eater and he saved my life."

"Sin Eater?" the man's head snapped around, and for a brief second, Darium felt odd. He swore he picked up the scent of death on the breeze and didn't want to go back to the castle for sin eating again. It made his head ache just thinking about it. Darium blinked, not sure if he was becoming ill since he didn't think his kind ever got sick. He figured it was only the energies from the rip in the veil that were affecting him so. "Oh, thank you for saving my daughter," said the man, sounding sincere. Necos smiled, but it still didn't do a thing to make Darium feel better. He didn't understand any of this. Right now, neither did he care.

"How do we close the portal?" Darium ground out, getting right to the point.

"The only way to do it, is for you to go through the portal first, Sin Eater," said Necos.

"Go through it? Why?" asked Darium. "That doesn't seem necessary."

"I – I'm not sure," said the girl's father, rubbing his head. "I seem to have forgotten a few things. It probably is from the king's beating."

"What did the sage tell you, Darium?" asked Talia.

"He was worthless and didn't tell me a thing. However, we don't need him anymore since we now have your father."

"That's right," agreed Talia. "Father, what did the sage tell you? You've got to remember."

"Sage?" He sounded confused again.

"The fool who gave you the information," Darium prompted him.

"What did he tell you about how to save the Fae from being a dying race?" asked Talia anxiously.

"I–I can't seem to remember." The man rubbed his head. "I guess when the king tried to kill me, he must have hit me over the head hard. I seem to have lost part of my memory."

"Oh, Father, that is horrible." Talia took him by the hand. "Do you remember Mother and your other daughters?"

"I–I'm not sure."

Darium rolled his eyes, not believing this at all. He didn't know why the man was acting stupid, but Darium sensed that he knew more than he was letting on. Perhaps he was working for the king in secret, being a spy but for the other side. Darium decided he needed to be careful.

"I have a horse in the woods, Father. I'll take you back home," offered Talia.

"I'd like that," said the man, looking back up at Darium. "Will the Sin Eater be coming with us?"

"Please don't call him that, Father. His name is Darium. Yes, he will be coming with us," Talia told him.

"Nay, I won't be," said Darium, watching as Talia's eyes opened wide in surprise. "I promised to meet my brothers at the lake so we can look for the tear in the veil. I'll catch up with you later."

"We'll come with you," suggested Talia. "The more eyes the better."

"Nay!" he said, not wanting the two of them along. He wasn't exactly sure why he felt this way, but he didn't want Talia or Necos to go anywhere near that rip in the veil.

"Well, be careful," called out Talia, as Darium

turned to go. "Hurry back. We'll all share a meal together later. It'll be a feast to celebrate the return of my father from the dead."

Talia's words jolted Darium. He looked over his shoulder at the man once again. It seemed as if King Sethor lied about killing the man, and that concerned him. Necos could be working for the king in secret. He'd have to keep a close eye on him.

Darium kicked his heels into the sides of his horse, riding fast with the wind in his hair. Breathing in the fresh air, he immediately felt better. No longer did his head ache. Mayhap spending some time with his brothers was just what he needed right now to clear his befuddled mind.

Six

"Brother, we were starting to think you weren't going to show." Rhys sat impatiently atop his majestic steed at the lake, with Zann atop the horse as well, sitting right behind him. Rhys was a knight of King Rand Osric from Kasculbough, and one of the king's favored soldiers. Therefore, he'd been rewarded with a Silver Snowflake steed. These horses had a silvery tone to their hides, with small white spots that looked like snowflakes. Their manes were long and white and snowy as well. It took a strong man to control such a large, powerful beast. Rhys, with inherited extreme strength was just the man to do it.

"I'm sorry. I was a little detained." Darium stopped in front of them.

"Did you get the information from the sage that we need in order to close the portal?" Zann hopped off the back of the horse, almost falling when he hit the ground since it was such a long way down.

"Nay. The fool wouldn't tell me a thing." Darium dismounted as well.

"Then, we'll just have to figure this out by ourselves,

since the only other person who knows the answer is dead." Rhys dismounted next.

"Speaking of that," said Darium. "It seems the fae's father is alive and well after all."

"What?" asked Zann.

"How can this be?" Rhys wanted to know.

"I don't understand it, but I saw him in the flesh," Darium told his brothers. "Talia is taking him home."

"Well, that's great. Right?" asked Zann. "He can give us the answers."

"Wrong," said Darium, shaking his head. "It seems that when the king left him for dead, the man lost part of his memory."

"So, he's hurt badly then?" asked Rhys. "Mayhap the fae can heal him."

"Nay, that's the odd part," said Darium, scratching his head. "He didn't look hurt at all."

"So, he's lying then, about the king killing him." Zann tried to come up with an explanation.

"Either that, or he's working for King Sethor as a spy now," said Rhys. "The traitor."

"I thought of both of those things, but I'm not so sure either is true." Darium shivered.

"What's the matter, brother?" asked Rhys. "You look like someone walked over your grave."

"I don't know, it's just a feeling I have," said Darium. "Something tells me that mayhap evil has already escaped through the rip in the veil and come to Mura. If so, this is only the beginning of our troubles. We need to find the portal quickly, and figure out how to close it before anything happens that we can't reverse."

Darium looked out over the waters of the Lake of Souls. It was one of the largest lakes on Mura, and also had the deepest water of any of the lakes or streams. The water always looked black it was so dark. Tall weeds and grasses surrounded the lake, making it hard to even get close to the water. Not many animals even seemed to want to drink from this reservoir. It was usually foggy around the lake and rather dreary. When he was a child, Darium was told by his father that the lake was so named because too many men had lost their lives in it.

It was here that Darium's father, Ambrose, took him through the portal into the Land of the Dead when he was six years old. Darium remembered his mother and father arguing about something, and his mother crying when they left. It was even more disturbing to Darium, because once they returned, things changed. The next day, he was told his mother had died in the night. He never even got the chance to say goodbye. He missed her dearly, and barely could even remember her face anymore. Bad memories filled his mind of this area, and it was the last place he ever wanted to be.

"Have either of you seen anything out of the ordinary lately?" Rhys asked, looking around the area.

"Not really," said Zann.

"I did," Darium told them. "I am sure I saw an opening in the sky, and something come through it when I was at the castle right before this."

"Was it the portal?" asked Zann.

"I think so," said Darium. "I could feel something odd."

"Like what?" Zann cocked his head in concern.

"You wouldn't understand."

"I feel something odd every time I shift into a damned wolf, Brother. Try me."

"Sorry. I wasn't thinking." Darium rubbed his chest, starting to feel the pain again. "It's like a sword stabbing me in the heart. I was almost overcome by the stench of death as well."

"Do you feel it now?" asked Rhys.

"I–I do," said Darium, taking a deep breath, not wanting to feel the pain.

"That must mean the portal is close by. Or about to open again." Zann looked up into the sky.

"Look!" Rhys pointed to a place at the edge of the lake that was between two tall standing stones. "I think I see it."

The horses started to go wild, confirming that something was amiss. Rhys held on to his horse's reins, since the horse was powerful and tried to pull away. It reared up on its back legs, neighing loudly.

"Down, Sampson," Rhys commanded, having a hard time keeping the steed from bolting away.

"I've got Lucifer," called out Zann, grabbing the reins of Darium's horse. "Go, Brother. Check it out before the portal moves again."

"Aye," answered Darium, not looking forward to this task, but knowing that he was the one who had to do it. Damn, being a Sin Eater only seemed to get less and less desirable all the time. He ran over to the tall standing stones, stopping in his tracks when he saw the tear in the veil. A swirling portal of black hovered just above the water with a jagged stream of dim light in it. The tear wasn't large yet, but the whole portal looked unstable. Black swirling masses of fog circled around now, and when it cleared, he could see right through the opening, and into the Land of the Dead.

Skeletons, and dark entities swarmed around just inside, making Darium's chest start to ache so badly that he felt as if he'd been stabbed with a sword for real. He reached out and held on to a standing stone to steady himself, wanting to run back to his brothers. He was unable to move. Not sure if it had anything to do with his own will, deep down Darium knew he couldn't just ignore this. It was up to him to save Mura. He needed to be their savior. He was the only Sin Eater in the land left since his father died. He was also the only one who could go through the portal to the Land of the Dead and come back out again.

The winds picked up, blowing his hair in all directions. It whipped into his eyes, causing them to sting with pain. He pulled back his long hair, using a leather band from around his wrist to hold his hair in place.

His raven cried from atop the rock, and he looked up at it.

"Go on, Murk. Go back to my brothers. You're in danger here."

When the bird did nothing to leave, he picked up a stone and threw it at his pet. He hated doing this, but if his bird followed him through the portal, it would die. The raven squawked, and flew back toward his brothers and the horses.

"What is it?" asked Rhys, still struggling to hold back his horse as he yelled into the strong wind.

"Do you see it?" Zann called out, pushing his long hair out of his eyes.

"Aye. I see the portal, but I'm not sure what to do," Darium called back to them, squinting from the dirt being kicked up from the swirling mass. He held on to the rock and stepped closer to the opening. That's when he saw his father inside the portal, and it caused him to stop in his tracks.

"Father?" His voice came out as a mere whisper. He felt sickened by what he saw. His father was naught more than a gaunt man with sunken eyes. He had sores all over his body, and his limbs were twisted. "By the gods, what has happened to you?"

Darium supposed he shouldn't have been surprised to see his father looking this way. After all, he'd been dead for quite some time now. He'd also been a Sin

Eater his entire life. All the sins of others that he'd consumed seemed to eat away at him now. His father's past profession made him not more than a pathetic shell of the man he once was.

"Darium. You've got to . . . close the . . . portal." His father held out a hand, trying to make his way toward him.

"I don't know how," Darium shouted into the wind.

"Come, Son. Come to me and I'll tell you." He held out that bony arm again, and Darium felt a distinct pull to go to him. He stepped forward, now at the edge of the portal of the damned. "Step through, Son. Just like I've taught you to do. Do it . . . now. Hurry."

Darium's foot was up in the air, and he was about to take a step through the portal, when something grabbed him from behind and threw him down. He hit the ground hard, shaking his head to clear his vision. When he looked up, he saw the stricat brooding over him, looking like it was about to eat him.

"Get out of my way, damn it!" He pushed the stricat and lunged for the portal, but he was too late. The portal closed quickly. Instead of going through it, Darium ended up in the lake. He came up sputtering, and spitting water from his mouth.

"Darium? What are you doing?"

He looked up to see both Zann and Rhys standing at the edge of the lake peering out at him. The stricat bounded away, being chased by his raven. Then, the stricat spread its long, black wings and took off up into the sky.

"Dammit, I was almost through it!" Darium ground out, sloshing his way out of the water. When he emerged from the lake, he saw a horse. Talia and her father sat atop it.

"Darium? Are you all right?" Talia slipped off the horse and ran to him, throwing herself into his wet arms. It surprised him that she seemed to care what happened to him. "Thank goodness we were in time to stop you."

"Stop me?" He pushed away and looked down at her. "I don't understand. Wasn't it you who begged me to go through the portal in the first place? Plus, your father told me that I needed to do it. Now, you're trying to keep me from doing so?"

"You don't need to go through it anymore," she told him. "My father is here now. As soon as his memory returns, he'll tell us everything we need to know."

"Really." Darium squeezed the water from his hair, looking up at the man on the horse.

"I was wrong to say what I did, Darium, forgive me. I was confused. I do remember something now," said Necos. "That sage told me no one should ever go through the portal of the dead."

"Funny, you should first mention this now."

"Like I said, I was mistaken. Sorry about that. I get confused since my little endeavor with the king has scarred my mind. I told my daughter she had to stop you, and that's why we came."

"I'll bet you did." For some reason, Darium found it hard to trust Necos. His headache had returned and he felt like he needed a drink of whisky since he was feeling agitated.

"Come, let's go back home for now," said Talia. "Mother has made a meal and has invited your brothers to join us as well."

"A meal? With meat?" asked Zann, his animal cravings coming out.

"Nay, we only eat fruit, seeds, nuts, and vegetables from the earth," Talia told him.

"I'll take a pass." Zann looked sorely disappointed. "I'm going to go to town and see if I can find anyone else who knows anything about the portal."

"I've got to get back to Kasculbough," said Rhys. "I'll meet you back here tomorrow, Darium."

Darium looked back to where he'd almost gone through the portal, but now, nothing was there at all.

"Are you coming?" Talia called out from atop her horse, her father riding with her.

"Fine," Darium grumbled, wringing out his wet cloak. He didn't like being around a lot of people, and certainly not so many giggling faeries. However, he didn't trust Necos. Until he believed Talia was not in any danger from him, he decided to keep a close eye on things. "Let's go, Murk," he called out to his raven, pulling himself up atop his horse. "And next time you see that pesky stricat, you have my permission to peck out the damned thing's eyes."

―――

Later that night, Talia sat around the fire in the forest with her family, having enjoyed one of her mother's delicious meals. Darium was there as well, and it seemed to make her sisters all giggle more than usual.

"How did you enjoy the food?" Talia asked Darium, pouring him another cup of spiced mead.

"It was . . . interesting," he answered, not sounding as if he were excited about eating such an earthy meal.

"I am still wondering where the meat is," complained her father. "Mayhap a little rabbit or even some ground squirrel would have been nice."

"Necos, you've never complained about eating from the earth before," said Talia's mother.

"I suppose my brush with death has made me crave meat." He fidgeted atop the stump where he sat.

"Father, you always liked mother's cooking and never complained," Talia told him.

"Aye, you're right, I suppose. I am having a hard time remembering the simplest things since the king tortured me. I'm sorry." Necos threw the leftover food from his plate into the fire.

The girls gasped.

"Necos, what did you do?" asked the man's wife. "We never waste food."

"It's an offering. To the gods, and nature." The man smiled, and this seemed to calm down the others.

"So, tell us how you managed to escape the clutches of King Sethor." Darium looked up at the man, waiting for an answer.

"I don't remember," answered Necos, taking a stick and stabbing at the fire.

"Aye. It seems to me, you conveniently only remember things when it is beneficial to you."

"Darium! That's not polite," Talia retorted, not wanting any trouble.

"I'm only asking the questions that we all want to know the answers to, Talia. We can't sit around and wait forever until your father's memory returns. We have bigger problems to tend to."

"Girls, clean up the dishes and then get to bed," said Maeve, glaring at Darium. Talia could tell that her mother still didn't like him. She didn't need to read her mother's mind to realize it, because it showed in the woman's actions, words, and expression.

"Necos, I'll be in the hut waiting for you," said Maeve.

"I'm going to stay out here and talk with the Sin

Eater for a while," said the man, chugging down mead and pouring himself another cupful.

"Husband, I was hoping to spend time with you." Her mother tried to convince him. Talia knew she missed him, and wanted their intimate time together.

"I'll not be rushed!" snapped the man, not sounding at all like her father. This made Talia curious as to why he was acting this way. She always knew him to be a very patient man, never raising his voice to her mother or her sisters. He always put the needs of his family before his own. Until now. She wondered what he was going through, or what King Sethor did to him to make him lose part of his memory and act so unusual. His time with King Sethor seemed to have really changed him.

"Talia, leave the men and come inside." Her mother motioned with her head.

"I'll be there soon, Mother. I promise." Talia sat down on a stump by the fire, next to Darium. She cradled a wooden cup of mead in her hands. She heard her mother sigh, and head inside with Talia's sisters.

"So, Sin Eater, do you ever regret your profession?" asked Necos.

"Father, please," said Talia. "That is not a proper thing to ask. And I told you, his name is Darium."

"Nay, it's fine, Talia," answered Darium. "It's my destiny to be a Sin Eater, Necos. I couldn't change it even if I wanted to."

"I'm sorry, Darium, but I still don't believe that." Talia sipped mead from her cup. "We always have choices."

"Not me."

"What if you didn't continue sin eating?" she asked. "What would happen, then?"

"Yes, that's a good question," said Necos. "I'm sure

Mura would be no worse off if you didn't continue in this profession."

"How can you say that?" Darium asked. "Especially, since you almost died without the chance for a confession," he told Talia's father. "It seems to me, you'd think Sin Eaters were very important about right now."

"That's true, father," Talia said, coming to Darium's defense since she knew he'd had a hard day. "It's because of Darium that everyone doesn't end up in The Dark Abyss."

"Is it really such a bad place?" asked her father, taking a gulp of mead, then looking up at both Talia and Darium staring at him. "I mean . . . The Land of the Dead, not The Dark Abyss of course."

"I've seen things in the underworld that I will never be able to forget. They are things that I assure you, no one would ever welcome," Darium informed them. "I also saw my father today through the portal."

"You did?" This almost seemed to startle Necos.

"Darium, why haven't you mentioned this before now?" asked Talia.

"I don't know." He looked down and ran his finger over the rim of his cup. "I suppose I didn't think anyone would be interested in hearing it. After all, my father is probably the darkest soul there, after years of being a Sin Eater."

"What did he say?" asked Necos. "Tell me everything." Talia's father leaned in, cocking an ear.

"He wanted me to enter the portal," Darium explained. "He called me to him, and I found myself wanting to go."

"Nay. Really?" asked Talia, swallowing hard. She had been ready to do just this, and she also had asked Darium to go there to find her father. Now, she regretted it all. Now that her father was back and alive and well, she realized just how foolish she'd been. There was too much danger involved to ask this of anyone.

"Nay, you mustn't go into the portal. Ever. Don't go there! Don't even go near it." Talia's father got up and started pacing.

"Why not?" asked Darium. "A minute ago, you asked me if it was such a bad place."

"You do it, and you'll never return. You'll be trapped there forever," continued her father.

"How do you know this?" asked Talia.

"I know it because I died, Daughter. I didn't want to tell you, because I didn't want to upset you. I died and went to the Land of the Dead briefly, but then somehow I was alive again."

"Father, this is horrible," gasped Talia. "So, you were really down there? In the Land of the Dead?"

"I believe so." He nodded, and then sat back down. "It was horrible, Talia. Just like the Sin Eater said. I was hoping he could confirm that it wasn't so bad. If so, I would have thought I dreamt the whole thing. But now . . . now I am sure it was real."

"Why didn't you mention this to Mother?"

"Nay. I didn't want her or the girls to hear it. It would only frighten them."

"I've never heard of anyone dying, going to the Land of the Dead, and then returning alive again," said Darium, sounding as if he didn't believe her father.

"Darium, if my father said it happened, then it did. I have never known him to lie. Ever since he married and had a family of fae who can't lie, he has chosen to be honest with us as well."

"Prove it," said Darium, making Talia upset. "If you were in the Land of the Dead, then tell me about it, Necos."

Why was Darium doing this? Talia wondered. Her

father almost died, and had to experience the Land of the Dead. It must have been horrifying. Now, Darium was making him relive it all again.

"Nay, Father. You don't have to even think about it." Talia glared at Darium, not understanding why he was acting this way.

"If he says he was there, then he should tell us about it," said Darium. "I've been there too, so I'll know if his story is right or not."

This shocked Talia to hear Darium speak this way. "Are you saying my father is a liar?"

"He's not a fae, sweetheart." Darium narrowed his eyes, finishing off his mead, and then throwing the cup to the ground. "Even though you believe he always tells the truth, you must remember that he is only human."

"My father doesn't lie!" She stood up and put her hands on her hips. She loved her father and would do anything to protect him. "He also doesn't have to prove a thing to you. He has been through a terrible ordeal, so please just leave him alone."

"Nay, Talia, I'll tell him," said Necos. "If it'll make him stop glaring at me the way he's been doing since he met me, I'd be happy to."

"Go ahead," Darium challenged him.

Her father looked over at her before continuing. "Talia, you might want to go inside. This isn't going to be something you'll want to hear."

"Nay, I won't leave. I'm old enough to listen. Tell me what it was like in the Land of the Dead."

"It was dark, and murky, Daughter."

"Anyone could guess that," Darium replied with a sniff.

"Souls wail in misery continuously, and the dead one's sins eat away at them until they look worse than a leper." His words seemed to make Darium stir.

"Go on," said Darium.

"You know as well as I, Sin Eater, about the wall of skulls and the feeling of being trapped, as well as the weight of the world on one's shoulders."

"Oh, that sounds so horrible." Talia held a hand to her mouth and sat back down.

"It feels like a blade to the heart," continued her father. "You can barely move since it freezes your joints and makes your head spin."

Talia saw Darium's head snap up when her father said this.

"I've seen your father there, Sin Eater. He is so bony with festering sores and sunken eyes that I–"

"Enough!" shouted Talia, jumping from the stool, not wanting to listen to any more. She also didn't want Darium to hear such horrible things about his father. Especially, since someday Darium was going to end up there as well. Nay, he was going to end up in a worse place. No one even knew what lie in wait in The Dark Abyss.

"Well, I hope I've convinced you that I'm not a liar." Necos shrugged and got up and stretched. Then he looked over to the house. "Where did your mother go, Daughter? I'd like to join her for the night."

"She's in the cottage, Father. Go on in. She is waiting for you."

"Aye. Of course." He took a few steps forward, looking one direction and then the other. She could tell he was lost. For some reason, he couldn't seem to see their dwelling, although he could before. She supposed it was because of his memory lapse. "I'll take you there, Father. Darium, will you be spending the night here as well?"

"Nay," Darium answered, seeming suddenly quiet. "I need to get home." He headed for his horse. Talia's heart sank. She didn't want to see him leave. Not now, after the horrible things he'd heard about his father. This night had started out as a celebration, and it couldn't end on such a sad note.

"I'll be right back," she told her father, running to catch up to Darium. By the time she got there, he was already atop his horse, preparing to leave. His raven flew down and landed on the pommel of the saddle.

"Are you all right?" she asked him, reaching up and gently placing her hand on his leg. She liked the feeling of their bodies touching.

His eyes lowered, and he reached out and covered her hand with his. He gave it a slight squeeze, then gently pushed her hand off his leg.

"Of course, I am. Why wouldn't I be?" he asked.

"Well, I thought after hearing all those things about your father that mayhap it upset you."

"I'm not upset."

"I'm sure my father remembered things wrong. After all, he has seemed to lose part of his memory."

"He's not wrong," said Darium, closing his eyes slightly and then opening them once again. In his silver orbs, she saw sadness and despair. "I saw my father through the portal, and it is exactly as your father relayed. He's not lying, Talia. Everything he described about the Land of the Dead is exactly the way I remember it from when I visited there as a child. I don't know how he was able to go there and return alive, but somehow he did it."

"Oh, Darium, this doesn't mean you'll end up the same as your father," she said, trying to comfort him.

"Doesn't it?" He looked tired and as if the events of the day had drawn out most of his energy. She didn't like this at all. She read his thoughts. All he wanted to do was to get away from everyone and be alone. As always.

"It could be different. For each person, I mean." She tried to comfort him once again, but it did naught to ease his mind. She could feel his inner turmoil.

"I'll end up just like my father, Talia, and we both know it. I'm going to the Land of the Dead when I die, and I will afterwards end up in The Dark Abyss. There is nothing anyone can do about it. That is where I belong."

"Please don't say that."

"Why not? It's the truth."

"Mayhap things can change."

"Nay, sweetheart, things will not change. Not for me, not for anyone. We all have to live out the life that fate has handed us. There is nothing we can do to alter it. I'm supposed to end up in the same place as my father. It's my destiny, taking on the sins of others, and bearing the punishment of all. Not you or me, nor anyone can change that. Good night, Talia," he said, riding away and leaving her there, not looking back.

Talia almost cried thinking what would happen to Darium someday. He didn't deserve it. No one did. He gave up everything to help others. Surely, that should be rewarded instead of punished.

After the kisses they'd shared, she found herself wanting to know him better. He was her savior. Now, she needed to somehow save him as well.

Today, when Darium saved her life as well as her soul, something happened between them. She started to see him–a Sin Eater–as something more than just a doomed soul. She'd looked into his eyes and read his thoughts, realizing he was no different than anyone else. He was human and had wants and needs and desires just like any man. She somehow saw right into his heart, and could feel the hurt lodged there. He didn't deserve to feel such loneliness and such pain.

Darium said he lived his life as a loner, but she didn't believe it was what he really wanted. She saw the way that others treated him because of the profession he inherited that was once his father's. Was it really his destiny to do this, and end up no better than the man who sired him? She refused to believe it. His brothers were sired by the same man, and yet it didn't seem as if either of them would be doomed for all eternity. Nay, they didn't have to worry for their souls the way Darium did.

She couldn't . . . she wouldn't accept it, she decided. Tomorrow, she would go to Darium and tell him how she felt about him. She would do whatever it took to help him change his destiny. Her only hope was that he would have a strong enough will to try. Darium was a good man and deserved to be happy. What he really needed was to be loved. By her.

Tomorrow, she would take the first step to make Darium feel loved. She would find a way to help him believe that his life was not determined for him. He needed to believe in himself.

"Good night, Darium," she said softly, feeling her bottom lip quiver as she watched him ride away into the night.

"Is something the matter, Daughter?" asked her father, coming up behind her.

Be strong, Talia told herself, holding back her tears. It might not be easy, but perhaps this was her destiny – to help Darium change his future. To change that which he believed could never be anything but what it was now.

She turned around and smiled at her father. "What could be wrong? After all, I thought I lost you today, but now you are back. Everything is fine now that you are home with Mother and me and my sisters again. Yes, everything is good now that I have you back in my life."

She took her father's hand in hers, leading him to the cottage. His hand felt cold. The feeling of love between them that she had sensed her entire life seemed off somehow. Talia dismissed the thought, knowing that she was too upset about Darium to think clearly. Tomorrow, she was sure, was going to be a much better day.

Seven

Darium drifted awake the next morning, lying in his bed with his eyes still closed, not even wanting to move. He'd been dreaming about the fae girl. He had picked up a lippenbur lily that had fallen from Talia's hair yesterday, not telling her that he kept it. He'd placed it on his pillow before he went to sleep. He enjoyed smelling the sweet scent of the flower all night long. It somehow made him happy. It even got into his dreams. He was holding Talia and kissing her in his dreams all night long.

He'd oddly also dreamed of his mother. This was something he hadn't done in many years now. She was at the side of his bed, holding his hand and humming a tune that used to always calm him when he got upset. It was so real, that he had almost believed she was really there.

His thoughts drifted back to Talia, and he found himself wanting to be with her again. She was a beautiful woman, and a feisty fae. Ever since he'd kissed her, he'd been having thoughts that he'd never had before. She spoke of children and marriage. These were things he'd dismissed in his mind, since someone like him should never be married. He also didn't want his fate passed on to a first-born son either. The art of sin eating in the Blackseed family would end with his death someday.

"Darium, wake up! Your services are needed." It sounded like his brother, Zann.

"What?" He opened his eyes, sitting up in his bed, not even having removed his clothes last night before he went to sleep. His gaze fell to the lippenbur lily. He picked it up from the pillow and sniffed it, feeling the presence of the fae girl, even though she wasn't there. He wanted her so badly, that it was driving him mad. Nay, it could never happen. He wouldn't let it. Throwing the lily to the floor, he called out. "Zann, is that you?"

He looked up to see not only Zann, but also Rhys standing in the open doorway of his home. They both looked extremely upset. Murk cawed wildly from outside. Something was wrong. Really wrong.

"What it is? What's happening?" he asked, jumping to his feet, pushing his hair from his eyes. He had to wake up. He needed to get focused.

"Grab your weapons, brother, you're going to need them," came Rhys' warning.

"All right," he said, strapping on his weapon belt and then throwing his cloak over his shoulders. It was odd, since he'd never been told before to don his weapons. There had never really been a need. His brothers were the ones who went to battle. Darium's job was to approach the battlefield after the fighting was over. He dealt with the dead. Sin eating had everything to do with saving souls, but nothing to do with saving lives. "What's got you both so excited?" he asked, slipping into his boots and heading to the door.

"There is something you've got to see." Rhys moved

aside and so did Zann. Darium didn't understand any of this, but stepped outside and closed the door behind him.

He immediately doubled over in pain, feeling the sensation of something sharp driving into his heart again. "Argh," he ground out, holding his chest, looking up to the sky, already knowing what it was. The sky was dark with black clouds. And where the sky met the ground down by the lake, he saw what looked like the portal to the Land of the Dead. It was open. His eyes grew wide as he saw black wisps of spirits entering into their realm.

"The portal's open, and some nasty things are coming through," said Zann with urgency in his voice.

"King Kasculbough has called for you, Darium," said his brother, Rhys. "This morning, several of his best warriors died instantly and no one knows why. He wants you to sin eat for them."

"Nay," said Darium with a shake of his head. "That will have to wait. We need to get to the portal quickly and try to close it before anything else comes through."

"I'll shift, and get there first. It might prove beneficial to be in my animal form. Tell me what to do," said Zann.

"I had a thought," Darium relayed his idea to his brothers. "Mayhap all we need to do is to send something through, and then it will close by itself."

"Like what?" asked Rhys.

"Should a throw a rock through the portal?" asked Zann. "Or mayhap a branch?"

"Nay," said Darium, heading for his horse.

"By the gods, don't tell me we'll need a live sacrifice like an animal," said Rhys, sounding disgusted by the idea.

"Nay, I should hope not." Zann looked horrified, since he'd just offered to shift into his wolf form.

"Of course not," Darium answered. His head spun and he felt as if he were going to retch. "I saw father in the portal and he called to me. I'm the one who needs to go through."

"Oh, no! You can't do it, Darium. We won't let you," cried Rhys, following him and mounting his steed, Sampson, ready to ride.

"Do you really think you can stop me?" asked Darium.

"Seriously," Rhys continued. "We don't even know if that will stop anything. Don't risk your life."

"Aye," agreed Zann. "We don't know that you'll be safe or even able to return." Zann removed his clothing as he spoke, getting ready to shift.

Darium's head swarmed with all the wailing voices resounding in his ears, driving him mad. Damn, this was one of the worst parts about being a Sin Eater. It brought back memories of his time that he'd spent in the Land of the Dead when he was just a child. The wails never seemed to subside, only get louder.

"We've got to try. There is no other way," Darium told his brothers, hoping he could really stop this. "The spirits of the dead are in our realm now, and killing people. This isn't good. Somehow, they need to return."

"I'm on my way," said Zann, hunkering down on the ground and shifting into his wolf form. Then he jumped up on all fours, and took off at a sprint toward the lake.

"I'm supposed to bring you back to Kasculbough," said Rhys. "I have my orders from King Osric himself. What am I going to tell him when you're not with me?"

"Tell the King of Kasculbough whatever you want, I don't care. He's not the only one with troubles. Nay, tell him I'm busy and will be there soon," Darium changed his mind. "I want to take a look at those who died. It might give us a clue as to how to stop all this."

"All right, but please, Darium. Do not enter the portal. I mean it. Not yet, at least. Wait until I return."

"Why?" asked Darium. "There is nothing you or Zann can do to help me. This is something I need to do alone."

"Be careful, brother," said Rhys. "I'll be back as soon as I relay the message to the king."

"Rhys," Darium called out, feeling another stab to his heart.

"Aye? What is it?" Rhys asked, turning his horse to face him.

"Even your strength, and all the weapons in the world won't be able to kill something that's already dead."

"So, what are you saying? That I shouldn't even try?" Confusion painted his brother's face.

"I don't know," said Darium, holding his aching head. He kept hearing the sound of loud wailing coming from the area of the lake. It was so strong in his mind that he could no longer think straight. He could also no longer ignore it. It called to him, and he had to go. "I don't know the answer, but mayhap Father can tell us what to do."

"You're really going to do this, aren't you?" asked Rhys with a shake of his head.

"I don't have a choice, brother. It's my destiny. I have to do it." With that, Darium headed his horse to the lake. His raven flew above him in the sky, shrieking like he'd never heard before. Egads, this noise was getting so loud in his head, that all Darium wanted was for it to stop. He longed for nothing more than to go back to sleep where he could hold and kiss Talia in the silence of his dreams.

~

Talia made her way through the woods atop her horse, heading for Darium's cottage the next morning. She'd never been to his home before, having only lived in the Goeften Forest for a short time, having lived most of her life in the Whispering Dale. Even not knowing the way, it didn't matter. The trees whispered the directions to her. She was almost there when she heard the sound of wailing coming from the lake. The sky was black and it looked as if it were about to rain.

Hurrying, she made her way to Darium's home, dismounting and running to it.

"Darium, wake up," she called out to him, pounding on his door. When he didn't answer, she opened the door and peeked inside. It was dark in there, and the furnishings were scarce. Leaving the door open, she entered the house, looking around. "Darium?" she asked, softly, hearing the words of the plants and flowers, telling her that he had already left.

She looked around at his dwellings. It was a small house with several rooms, and not at all tidy. Clothes were spewed all over the place. There were dirty dishes piled on the counter and on the table with dried scraps of food on them. The blankets on the bed were in a heap, and the entire place was filthy. The windows had no coverings and were so dirty she could barely see out. This was a sad place. How could anyone live here? She felt the loneliness all around her, and it about broke her heart.

"Where is he?" she asked, hearing the answer in her mind as soon as she asked the question aloud. He was headed for the lake. She turned to go, but stopped when she spied something on the floor by her foot. She bent down and picked up a lippenbur lily, knowing immediately it was one she had worn in her hair yesterday. The flower could speak to her in her mind. It was clear to Talia that Darium had taken this with him in secret.

"Why?" she asked aloud, sniffing the flower and twirling it around in her fingers. The next answer came to her as more of a feeling than anything else. It was a feeling that she knew in her heart was true. She looked over at Darium's pillow, seeing the essence of pollen from the flower atop the place where Darium had laid his head. "He took it to bed with him," she said softly, wondering if he had feelings for her after all, that he was not willing to share.

Gently placing the flower back atop his pillow, she turned and ran out the door.

"Darium, don't do it," she cried, mounting her horse, hearing from the fauna around his home that he had told his brothers he was going to enter the portal. "I've got to get to the lake. Hurry," she said to the horse, speeding off to stop Darium from doing something that she was sure they would all regret in the end.

By the time she got to the lake, Darium was already attempting to go through the portal. She saw Zann in his wolf form, biting at Darium's cloak, trying to stop him. It didn't seem to be working at all.

"Leave me alone, Zann," griped Darium, swatting at his brother. The wolf growled and continued to pull at his cloak, trying to stop him from doing this unthinkable thing.

"Darium, wait!" cried Talia, hopping off the horse before it even stopped. "Please, don't do this."

"Talia?" Darium looked up in surprise. "Go home," he commanded. "You shouldn't be here."

"Don't go through the portal," she begged, running toward him.

"I told you, this is my destiny. I have to do this, so don't try to stop me."

"Let's talk about it first. Please." Being a fae, she never really used the word please, because the faes believed that word would make them weak. However, in this case she would say anything to get Darium to change his mind. He was about to do something dangerous, and she couldn't be sure it wouldn't kill him. Part of her felt as if this was all her fault. She had asked him to go through the portal but now she'd had a change of heart.

"Nay, there is no time to talk." Darium looked back at the portal. "It's closing. I have to move quickly before I lose it again. Zann, let go of me or I swear I'll knock you over the head with my sword." He ripped off his cloak and threw it down. The wolf sprang backward with just the cloak in its mouth now, releasing a small whimper.

Talia raced for the portal, approaching it just as Darium started to step through.

"Nay!" she cried, lunging for him, falling to the ground, grabbing on to his leg that was still in this realm. The portal continued to become smaller and smaller. She could see horrible creatures inside, as well as black swirling wisps of smoke. The wailing was louder up close to the portal, and she smelled the stench of something very rancid like rotten meat coming from inside.

"Let go, dammit," yelled Darium, half in and half out of the portal now. "You can't stop me, Talia. I have to do this."

"Then, if I can't stop you, I'm coming with you."

She released his leg and stood up, meaning to go through the portal after him if that is what it took.

"Zann, keep her here," she heard Darium call out as he disappeared inside the portal now. Zann, in his wolf form, latched on to her clothes with his teeth, holding her back.

"Stop it, Zann," she cried, pulling against him, looking back to the portal for Darium. "The portal is closing. I have to go through quickly."

She fought against the wolf but was unable to get out of its grip. Then she heard Darium call her name from the Land of the Dead. She looked back to see him inside staring out at her as the portal started to close completely. He looked so sad and defeated that it about broke her heart. He was alone in the Land of the Dead now, and she didn't like that. All she wanted to do was to help him, but now, she didn't even know if anyone could change this situation. He was all alone, once again.

"Nay! Darium, don't go," she cried out. "I love you!" She felt panicked that she'd never see him again, and the words flew from her mouth without even pondering what that really meant. It didn't matter, she supposed since he didn't seem to hear her anyway. It was too late. The portal had closed and he was gone. If only she had been a few minutes sooner, she might have been able to stop him from leaving.

The sky cleared, and all evidence of Darium and the portal disappeared.

"Oh, no!" she cried, pulling away from Zann and running to the lake, falling to her knees right where the portal had been but was no longer. She lowered her head to the ground and wept. It was too late. She had tried to stop him, but Darium left, thinking it was really his destiny to go to such a horrible place. She had no idea if he would return or if she would ever see him again. Her heart ached and the tears ran in streams down her cheeks. Why hadn't she been faster? Why hadn't she stopped him or at least gone with him? Now, he was all alone once again. This time it was in a place that was so horrible that no man, woman, or even Sin Eater, should ever be there at all.

Eight

Darium watched as Talia faded from sight. He thought he heard her say something to him just before the portal closed, but he wasn't sure what it was. She was most likely warning him to be careful, or still protesting and saying she wanted to come with him. Well, it no longer mattered. He had to focus on the job at hand. He'd finally made it through the portal and now needed to figure out his next move.

Thank goodness, Zann was there to stop her, or the fae would have entered the portal with him. He couldn't protect her here, and never wanted to see anything happen to her. As much as he regretted leaving Talia behind, he realized it was for the best. She was a gentle fae, and could never withstand a trip to the underworld and back. Even if she did survive, there was no telling how it would affect her afterwards. The last time he was here was long ago, but yet it still affected him. He'd had nightmares of this place for years after his father decided to bring him here. Even to this day, he couldn't forget it.

Talia was a happy fae, filled with light and life. Being amongst the dead would only harm her, he was sure. He knew she meant well, but this wasn't a place she should ever visit.

Slowly turning around, Darium took in his surroundings. Black fog swirled around him and there was very little light at all. It felt hot and muggy here and he found it hard to breathe. Then again, the stench was so foul, the last thing he wanted was to breathe it in at all.

A black wisp of something shot past him and he jumped out of the way, drawing his sword. Holding his blade with two hands, he turned a full circle, looking up in the thickened air. Fog hung heavy all around him. It was getting harder and harder to see.

"Put away the blade, Darium," came a voice from the depths. "That won't do you any good down here."

"Father?" Darium recognized the voice. "Is that you? Where are you?" He tried to see through the fog, straining his ears to hear past all the wailing voices in his head. He found himself feeling pity for the dead who ended up here, no matter what it was they did that kept them from moving on to either The Haven, or gods forbid, The Dark Abyss.

"I'm here, son," came a voice from directly behind him. He spun around, still holding out his sword. Sure enough, his father walked through the fog, looking at Darium as if he felt disappointed with him. His appearance was grotesque, and it made it hard for Darium to look directly at him. Rotting flesh hung from his bones, and oozing wounds festered. The stench of his body was worse than the depths of a castle moat where remains of enemies became food for the fish and creatures of the deep. "That sword does you no good here, I told you. You can't kill someone who is already dead."

"It's not to kill anyone, but rather to protect myself from the evil spirits," he told his father, realizing after he said it just how stupid he sounded.

Just then, a loud shriek made him jump. He saw a body flying through the air right at him. An evil face with an open mouth looked like it would devour him. Darium swiped at it with his sword, but the entity was spirit and he didn't even hurt it. Instead, the black wisp went right through his body, knocking him to the ground. It took his breath from him. As if in slow motion, Darium saw his sword flying through the air, and heard the clanging sound as it hit the stones beneath his feet. He fell to his back, seeing swirling masses of creatures above him that he'd never seen before. And then he heard loud laughing, and saw the son of King Sethor hovering over him before the young man swooped away and disappeared.

"What is this? What's happening?" Darium jumped to his feet, trying to make sense of any of this, but couldn't. He was starting to regret coming here at all. It was obvious now that he wasn't going to accomplish a thing.

"Yes, some call this place the home of Belcoum, god of the underworld," said his father. "Then again, some see it only as a holding area as they wait out their time to have a chance to move on. It truly is the Land of the Dead."

"Father, that was King Sethor's son, I just saw," said Darium, pointing to where he'd seen the spirit. "I'm sure of it. What is he doing here?"

"He's dead," answered Darium's father, Ambrose. "This is where the dead go, son. You know that."

"Aye, but I sin ate for him. He shouldn't be here," protested Darium, running a hand through his long hair. "His soul should be free. He should have moved on to The Haven."

"Son, I am finding out I was wrong about a lot of

things I told you. Everything is not always what it seems."

"I don't understand," said Darium, shaking his head. "Why is he here? My action should have kept him from being here at all."

"Well, as you can see, it isn't so."

"Then, what about all the years you've spent as a Sin Eater?" asked Darium. "What good did it do? And what about me? What about my destiny?"

"Darium . . . please come back," he heard a muffled voice, realizing it was Talia calling for him from outside the portal.

"You shouldn't tarry here any longer, son," said his father. "The more time that passes with you here, the harder it will be for you to leave. Go now, while you still can."

"Father, there is a rip in the veil and I need to know how to close it before it is too late. Tell me how to do it."

"Nay. I can't tell you that."

"Why not?"

"Because, I can't."

"You don't know how to close it?" gasped Darium. "This can't be. Father, you've got to know something. Tell me! Tell me before all of Mura is doomed."

"Darium? Darium?" called out Talia, her voice becoming louder. He turned around to see the portal starting to open again. "I'm coming with you," he heard her say.

Instantly, a pack of evil entities swarmed overhead and started toward the portal, drawn directly to her.

"Innocence such as hers attracts these beings. They feed off of it," explained his father. "She shouldn't be here."

"Stay away from her," Darium shouted to the creatures, and bent down and picked up his sword. When he stood back up, he saw a glimpse of someone who looked a lot like Talia's father, Necos. It was so quick and then the man disappeared into the shadows. Darium figured he had to be mistaken. How could it possibly be him? Necos was still alive. "Was that Talia's father?" asked Darium, hoping his own father would give him the answer.

"Go to your fae, son. You need to protect her," was all Ambrose said.

"What I need to do is to close the tear in the veil, but you won't tell me how to do it."

"You know how."

"Nay, I don't," shouted Darium as the wailing voices became even louder.

"Look inside yourself to find the answer."

"Darium? I can see you. I'm coming with you." Darium spun around to see Talia peeking into the open portal. The dark entities hovered around the entrance just waiting to attack her. She put one foot through the portal, and several of the entities latched on to her leg.

"Nay!" she screamed, trying to shake them off, but the evil forces inside the Land of the Dead were strong. The entities started to pull her through the portal, and there was nothing she could do to stop them.

"Go, now!" shouted Ambrose. "Protect the fae. I'll try to close the portal from this side right after you leave."

"But, I need answers before I go," protested Darium. "Why are you even here instead of in The Dark Abyss by now? Father, there is so much I have to ask you."

"It's your destiny to help her, son," said his father in a calm voice.

Suddenly, nothing made sense, because all his life his

father had told Darium his destiny was to be a Sin Eater and nothing more. Darium had no time to question his father about it now. If he didn't move fast, Talia could get hurt. Why couldn't she have listened to him and stayed behind? He needed more time to find the answers, and now he never would.

"Leave her alone!" he yelled, charging at the black wisps with his sword waving in the air, even though it did naught to harm or stop these creatures of the night.

"Darium!" screamed Talia, looking so scared. He picked up her feelings easily, and her fear and confusion was out of control.

"Hold on, Talia. I'm coming." Darium jumped at the portal that was starting to close again, his body smashing against the fae's. He wrapped one arm around her and pulled her with him as he exited the portal, falling to the ground on the other side. His sword fell from his grasp. He looked up to see several black entities come through the portal, just as it closed. The last thing he saw from within was his father's face, grimacing and twisting and contorting as he tried to help Darium from the other side.

"Darium! You're back."

Darium looked up to see Zann standing there in human form, wearing his cloak. The cloak blew open to reveal he was naked underneath.

"Damn it, brother, don't you ever think of bringing clothes with you?" he asked, pulling Talia against his chest in a hug as he sat up. He could feel the rapid beating of her heart against his chest. "I told you to keep Talia here. What in damnation were you doing?"

"She said she wanted to talk with me, so I shifted back into my human form," explained Zann. "Once I finished the shift, I saw her trying to go through the portal. But since shifting takes so much energy, I didn't have enough to go after her. She tricked me."

"Talia, did you purposely trick my brother?" Darium stood up, bringing Talia with him.

"I'm sorry, I did," she admitted with a sniff, wiping a tear from her eye. "I couldn't stop myself from wanting to be with you. I wanted to help you and therefore used this as a distraction to give me time to reach you. I'm sorry. I really did want to talk to Zann, but not until after I helped you to return."

"Help me? All you nearly did was get both of us killed." He shook his head, not believing any of this.

"I'm sorry," she said once again.

The sound of hoofbeats upon the ground made Darium look up to see his brother, Rhys atop his horse. This time, several of Kasculbough's guards rode along with him.

"Darium! What happened?" called out Rhys, hurriedly dismounting. "We heard wails and thought we saw the portal opening."

"Aye," answered Darium, releasing a deep breath. "It's closed now, but a few entities got through. We need to be on alert. They'll probably try to kill again."

"The king needs you, Sin Eater," said one of the guards. "He has summoned you to Kasculbough. You need to come right away."

"Darium, don't go," whispered Talia.

Darium couldn't stop thinking about what his father told him in the portal about his destiny. He wanted time to think about what he saw . . . or whom he thought he saw from within. The last thing he wanted right now was to rush off to do more sin eating.

"Nay, King Sethor summons the Sin Eater," called out a guard from Macada Castle, as a small entourage of soldiers moved forward to meet them.

"Sin Eater!" called out another soldier, leading a group of men to the lake who wore the crest of King Grinwald of Evandorm. "You are needed at Evandorm. You must come right away. We have just had three deaths."

"This is getting serious," mumbled Zann.

"Nay, I'm not going anywhere," Darium told them, but that only triggered the reaction of all three sets of soldiers to draw their weapons.

"You've received your orders from three different kings," Rhys told him. "Brother, you have no choice but to heed the call, or be killed. It is your duty to go to them when you've been summoned."

Darium ran a hand through his tangled hair, wanting nothing more than to have a few moments to himself to ponder what just happened. After hearing what his father said, he was starting to question his profession as well as what his true destiny really was after all. Even still, Rhys was right. If he denied the summons, it would only bring about trouble. He no longer cared for his own life, but now that they'd seen the fae, he feared they might do something to her if he refused to help them.

"All right, I'll go," Darium agreed. "Zann, take Talia home," he told his brother, wanting her to be protected.

"Nay, I am coming with you," protested Talia. "Darium, I will not leave you again. Besides, I feel safer with you than with anyone else."

"Then you'll stay at my side and keep quiet," Darium ordered. "Understand?"

"Wait a minute," said a guard from Kasculbough, riding closer with his sword pointed directly at Talia. "I saw this one in the portal. I think our king will want to question her."

"She knows nothing," snapped Darium. "Leave her be."

"That's our king's healer," said one of Evandorm's men.

"I recognize her. She's that fae that King Sethor tried to kill," said a guard from Macada Castle.

"A fae?" asked the soldier from Evandorm, causing him and his men to become upset. "If she's got magic, she needs to die. It's the law!"

"Stop it!" yelled Darium, raising his sword in the air to get their attention. "I'll go to each of the castles to sin eat, but only if it is promised that the girl won't be harmed."

"We can't promise you that," snarled a guard from Kasculbough.

"Only the kings can decide what happens to the fae," said a soldier from Evandorm.

"Then, you'll just have to speak for your kings right now, if you want my services." Darium laid out his terms, hoping they wouldn't object. Having soldiers from all three of the kingdoms of Mura in one place wasn't going to stay peaceful for very long. "Do you agree to the girl's safety?"

"I'll promise her safety at Kasculbough since I'm head knight," said Rhys, coming forward.

"Good," said Darium. "Then, I'll go to Kasculbough as summoned, but only there and nowhere else."

"What about Macada Castle?" asked a guard.

"Or Evandorm?" asked another.

The guards from the other two kingdoms didn't like the fact that they hadn't been included in this decision.

"Give me your promises, and I'll come," said Darium. "Otherwise, leave now, because I won't be helping you or your kings."

"Speaking for our king can get us killed," protested the Evandorm guard.

"Really," said Darium. "Well, what do you think your kings will do to you when you return and tell them that you let me service Kasculbough, but that I won't be there to do the same for Evandorm or Sethor?"

It didn't take long before all the guards agreed that they would promise Talia's safety. However, it was decided she would stay hidden under a cloak so no one but they knew who she was or that she was even there at all.

"Good," said Darium with a satisfied nod. "Let it be known, that if your kings order any harm to Talia, I'll expect you all to protect her."

"Protect a fae?" snorted one of the guards.

"Deny our king?" asked another. "Never."

"I see," said Darium with a slow nod. "Then, you'd better hope there will be no trouble. Because, if so, I'll personally kill each and every one of you myself. Afterwards, I will refuse to sin eat for you. Believe me, you don't want that to happen. I've just returned from the Land of the Dead, and I guarantee it is not a place where any of you want to go."

Nine

"Everyone, go back to your castles," Darium called out. "I'll start at Kasculbough and I will be there soon."

The guards from both Evandorm and Macada Castle left. Rhys mounted his horse, ready to lead his men back to King Osric's domain.

"Are you sure about bringing the girl along?" Rhys asked Darium, looking down from atop his steed. Darium walked over to talk to him, not wanting Talia to hear their conversation. Zann stood next to Rhys, wrapped in Darium's cloak.

"I'm going to bring her with me, only because I want to keep an eye on her," Darium told his brothers in a low voice as the soldiers from Kasculbough headed away. "I think her life might be in danger."

"I can watch her," offered Zann. "King Grinwald won't need me to hunt until the morrow. I'll keep her protected for you."

"Right." Darium shook his head. "We see how well that worked already."

"That doesn't count. She tricked me," Zann pointed out. "She purposely waited to enter the portal until I was in the middle of my shift. It won't happen again, I assure you."

"Damn right it won't, because she's coming with me. I've got another job for you, Zann."

"And what might that be?" Zann glared at him.

Darium looked back over his shoulder to make sure Talia wasn't listening. She was fixing her braid, sitting on a rock. Satisfied, he turned back to talk to his brothers.

"When I was in the portal, I saw some things I didn't understand."

"Like what?" asked Zann.

"Lots of things, but I don't have time to tell you about it now. All I'm going to say is that I saw some people in the Land of the Dead who shouldn't have been there."

"I'm sure they're supposed to be there, brother," said Rhys. "They're dead."

"I'm not sure of anything anymore," Darium answered. "I saw King Sethor's son there, but I sin ate for him. He shouldn't be in the Land of the Dead at all. He should have moved on to The Haven by now."

"Are you sure?" asked Rhys. "How can that be?"

"Mayhap you just thought you saw him," said Zann. "I'm sure it's foggy down there."

"And loud," added Rhys. "We heard the wailing all the way to the castle."

"Perhaps," said Darium. "But I don't think so. Plus, Father was there and told me that things are not always what they seem."

"Father? He said that?" asked Rhys.

"I still don't understand what any of this has to do with Talia being in danger," said Zann.

"We're all in danger from what came through that

portal," Rhys remarked. "We have dead men at each castle to vouch for it."

"Aye, that's true, but not what I mean," said Darium, once again gazing back at Talia. She looked up at him and smiled, and went back to fixing her hair. Now, she was picking wildflowers and sticking them in her braid. She was such a sweet thing. So good, that Darium felt as if he didn't deserve her.

"Well, tell us, brother. I need to catch up to my men," stated Rhys impatiently.

"I–I thought I saw Talia's father in the Land of the Dead," Darium told the others, knowing how addled this must sound.

"Talia's father?" asked Zann. "But he's not even dead."

"Not anymore," added Rhys. "We all saw him."

"Exactly," said Darium. "Although I don't know the man, it seems he's been forgetting things, and acting odd. Or at least that is the impression I get from the rest of Talia's family."

"What does any of this mean?" asked Zann.

"I'm not sure." Darium scratched the stubble on his chin in thought. "That's why I need you to go spy on him back in the Goeften Forest, Zann. He's most likely still with Maeve and Talia's sisters."

"Me? Why me?" asked Zann. "I don't like being around all those giggling faeries. Besides, I hate their food. I need meat!"

"Then hunt down a hare or something on the way over to their cottage," Darium told him. "Stay in your wolf form. You'll be less noticed that way. Watch Necos' every move and report back to me if he does or says anything that seems to confuse or upset Talia's family."

"What's in this for me?" complained Zann.

"A big, fat, juicy steak when it is all over," Darium promised.

"Fine," answered Zann with a sigh, starting to walk away.

"Hang on there, brother." Darium held out his hand. "I'll need my cloak back to keep Talia undercover."

"Doesn't she have a cloak of her own?" asked Zann.

"Don't you?" Darium matched his words.

"I don't know how you think I can carry clothes with me in my wolf form." Zann begrudgingly removed the cloak, handing it over to Darium. He now stood there naked.

"Oh!" gasped Talia, walking over to join them. "You certainly aren't shy, are you?" she asked Zann with a giggle.

"Go on. Get out of here, Zann." Darium pulled Talia against his chest, trying to block her view once again.

"What were you all talking about?" she asked with a smile once Zann had left.

"Nothing," Rhys and Darium said together, much too quickly.

Darium glared at his brother. This, he was sure, was only going to make Talia suspicious. After all, she was a fae and curious in nature.

"You'll ride with me, and stay covered with this." Darium handed Talia the cloak. "Don't say a word to anyone while we're at each castle. Also, ignore eye contact of any kind."

"Darium, you're being too cautious," said Talia. "Stop worrying. I'm a fae, don't forget. I have all of nature at my beck and call to help me if I need it."

"Just the same, do as I say. Got it?" He headed for his horse.

"Got it," she repeated from behind him.

After Talia wrapped herself in Darium's cloak, she crawled up and settled herself in front of Darium atop his steed. It felt comforting to have his arms around her. She'd been afraid that she would never feel this again.

"What was it like? In the Land of the Dead?" asked Talia as they rode toward Kasculbough, following Rhys on his huge silver warhorse.

"Don't even ask."

"I saw some things through the portal that didn't look inviting."

"They're not."

"Did you hear what I said to you before the portal closed the first time?" She held her breath, waiting for his answer. She had spoken from her heart, blurting out the words 'I love you' when she thought she was about to lose Darium forever. He hadn't mentioned anything about it since he'd returned.

"I heard you calling out some nonsense to me, but I was a little busy."

"Nonsense?" That about broke her heart. "I told you what I honestly felt. At the moment, at least." She was suddenly starting to feel foolish and wondered if she should have said those words at all. After all, they seemed to mean nothing to a man like Darium. Perhaps all those years of being a Sin Eater made him unemotional and hardened to the idea of love.

"I told you how I felt too, yet you kept insisting on coming with me," said Darium. "Don't you see that you almost got us both killed?"

"I'm so sorry to have inconvenienced you. Stop the horse and let me off. I think I'll go home after all."

"Nay," he answered and kept on riding.

"Nay?" She twisted around to see him. "You do know that I could call to nature and have you unseated from this horse in seconds."

"I'm keeping you with me to protect you."

"From what?" she asked. "Those things that came through the portal? I'm not frightened of them, if that's what you think."

"That's not what I mean. And by the way, you should be frightened. After all, nothing is as it seems anymore. Until I figure things out, you're not leaving my side."

Talia figured it would do no good to fight with Darium. Plus, she didn't really want to have to use nature to do her bidding against him. She had feelings for Darium and she honestly didn't want to see him hurt.

"What were you talking about with your brothers that you didn't want me to hear?" she blurted out.

He jerked, his body stiffening. "Don't worry about it."

"You just told me to be cautious and that I should be scared. Now, you're telling me not to worry?"

"If I had wanted you to hear what I said, I would have called you over."

"I see." She didn't like being treated this way, and she also didn't like people keeping secrets from her. Talia needed to know about their conversation. Even though she probably shouldn't use nature to her advantage, she decided to talk to his horse and find out what the big secret was. "Lucifer, you are such a good horse," she said, running her hand over the horse's neck. In her mind she asked the animal to tell her about Darium's conversation with his brothers. She needed to find out. If this was the only way to do it, then she would use her connection with the animal to discover what Darium didn't want her to know.

"My horse wasn't close enough to hear my conversation with my brothers, so don't bother trying to find out from him," Darium growled in her ear.

"I wasn't–"

"Don't even try to lie, either, princess, because I know that you can't," he added.

He was right. She couldn't lie. If she could, things might be different. "Oh, all right," she said with a sigh. "But how did you know what I was doing when I tried to talk to Lucifer?"

"I know you are too mischievous to let it go. Before you try to read my mind next, know that I've purposely blocked the thoughts of me and both of my brothers as well as my horse."

"You can't do that!"

"Can't I? Go ahead and try reading our thoughts if you want. I assure you, that you'll get nothing."

She supposed since Darium and his brothers had special powers that he could block her from reading his thoughts if he so wanted. Right now, she had no idea what he was thinking. Then again, it might be her own unsettled thoughts about Darium that was keeping her from doing so. She would try to read his mind again later, when he least suspected she was doing it.

They approached Kasculbough Castle, the mere presence of the place scaring Talia a little. Unlike Macada Castle or even Evandorm, this fortress was big and black and held a sinister feeling about it. It wasn't on the cliffs like King Sethor's fortress. Instead, it was on a small hill, surrounded by a large moat of water. As they crossed the moat, she looked down into the black murky water, wondering just what kinds of nasty things were hidden at the bottom.

Banners hung from the battlements, wavering in the breeze. They depicted the crest of the resident king, which was a boar with an open mouth and spikes on its back. It was truly ugly.

Rhys led the way into the courtyard where they found King Rand Osric waiting for them, surrounded by his men. There were three dead bodies lying on the ground at his feet.

"Sin Eater," called out the king. "Your services are needed. Please hurry. I hope it's not too late to save their souls."

King Osric was a short man with a round belly. He had ebony black hair that was oily, and smashed down under his crown. His double chin rested on his chest, and his squinty eyes slanted downward.

"My lord," said Darium, getting off his horse. Talia stared to dismount, but he shook his head. "Stay there," he whispered. "I'll make this fast and then we'll be on our way."

"Who is that, you're talking to?" asked the king, looking up and cocking his head.

Talia's heart jumped. At first, no one answered.

"My King, my brother has also been summoned by King Sethor and King Grinwald," said Rhys, dismounting and heading over to his ruler. "I was lucky enough to convince him to come here first."

Hearing the name of the king's rivals made Osric thankfully forget all about Talia. She breathed a sigh of relief.

"If I could stop you from helping my rivals, I would," said the king. "But at least you know which of us is most important and came here first. That's good, Sin Eater."

"Are you ready?" asked Darium, making his way over to the dead bodies.

The king looked over at his men and nodded. They laid bread and cups of ale atop the dead warriors' chests.

In doing this, it was believed that the sins of the dead would be absorbed into the food and ale. Once absorbed, it could be transferred to another by the means of eating the bread and drinking the ale. Darium reached down, and one by one, did his job. He was fast about it, throwing down the last cup and wiping his mouth on his sleeve.

"It's done," said Darium, no emotion coming from him at all.

"Ah, so it is," said the king. He finally smiled. "I suppose you'll expect your normal fee, then." The king nodded and another of his men handed a small pouch of coins to Darium.

When Darium looked down to the pouch in his hand, Talia could feel his disgust.

"What's the matter, Sin Eater? Aren't you going to open the pouch and count your coins like you usually do to make sure I didn't cheat you?" asked the king.

Instead of even looking inside the pouch, Darium threw it to the ground. This surprised Talia. A few coins spilled out atop the cobbled stones of the courtyard, and rolled in all directions.

"Nay," Darium answered in a low voice. "I'm not."

"What are you saying?" asked the king. "Are you asking for more money, because I won't give it."

"It doesn't matter." Darium slowly shook his head. "No amount of coins can buy a soul's way to The Haven."

"What does that mean?" snapped the king. "In order for this to work, I have to pay you. There needs to be an exchange."

"Then give my share of money to the families who lost these men." Darium looked down and shook his head, then turned and walked back to the horse.

"Where are you going, Sin Eater?" called out the king.

"I have other work to do," answered Darium, mounting his horse.

"Ah, yes. I suppose it is your destiny to sin eat, no matter who asks you to do it."

Darium's head snapped up, and once again, Talia felt his body tense.

"Tell my rivals to watch their backs. I'm coming for them, their land and their castles, to make it all mine," finished the king.

"Darium? Are you all right?" Talia whispered. She wasn't sure if he looked so upset because the king said he was basically going to start a war, or if it had something to do with him calling Darium a Sin Eater and speaking of his destiny. It couldn't be the latter, since all Darium had been talking about since she met him was his destiny and what he was meant to do.

"Mmph," Darium mumbled, turning his horse and leaving the castle at full speed.

They didn't say anything to each other on the trip over to Evandorm. Every time Talia started to talk, she stopped, feeling as if she would only be upsetting Darium even more if she said the wrong thing. Something happened when he crossed over into the Land of the Dead, and it bothered him so much that although she tried, she could no longer read his thoughts. After coming back through that portal, he seemed distant and filled with confusion. He also put up a wall around him that seemed as if he wanted to keep everyone out and she didn't know why.

"I'll be welcome at Evandorm since I worked there, so it's not a threat to me," said Talia as they rode across the drawbridge a while later. This was the smallest of the three castles, and in her opinion also the one that was the least frightening. It was made of orange stone, and had beautiful gardens with lush vegetation within the castle's walls. Bountiful orchards were filled with lush apples, pears and even the sweet green limsta fruit that was always her favorite and tasted like the nectar of flowers.

She adored the maze of shrubs that led to a little pavilion and bench that was private, and meant only for the king. There were also many types of birds in the mews and wonderful hounds in the kennels. She loved all the animals there. Since she was an Elemental of Nature, this is what made her happy and relaxed. She even liked the king's crest that was a stricat with its paws up in the air. If only King Drustan Grinwald wasn't so mean, she might consider this a good place to live. That is, for a human.

This time, when Darium stopped the horse and dismounted, Talia got down before he could tell her to stay there again.

"Nay," said Darium. "What are you doing? Get back up on the horse."

"It's all right. Remember, I was, or should I say I am, a healer for the king of Evandorm. My father was one of his guards as well. I am welcome here."

"Correction. Your father is still one of his guards." She turned to see Darium's brother Zann standing there.

"Zann?" asked Darium. "What are you doing here? And what are you wearing?" he asked as they surmised his clothes that looked like he got them from a peddler or perhaps a serf. "You were supposed to be . . ." He looked at Talia, then turned back and finished his sentence to his brother. "Be somewhere else," he said, not wanting Talia to know he'd sent his brother to spy on her father.

"I was," answered Zann. "I followed him and he ended up here."

"Who did? Who were you following?" asked Talia, overhearing them even though they had been speaking softly.

"Talia," said Darium, figuring it was time he told her. "I suspect that your father isn't who he seems to be."

"Of course not. He's lost part of his memories, Darium."

Before Darium could explain that he thought he saw the man in the Land of the Dead, they were interrupted.

"Talia, Daughter, so good to see you came back to work for the king as well."

"What?" Talia spun around to see her father walking out of the great hall with the king.

"Where did you disappear to, Healer?" growled the king. "I have four dead men who might have lived if you had been here to heal them. I should have you whipped for this type of conduct."

"Whipped?" Talia's heart jumped. She looked over to her father, thinking he would come to her aid, but he didn't say a word. "I–I went looking for my father," she answered. Her father stood there with his hands behind his back.

"Zoroct's eyes, I knew this was going to be a problem." Darium left her standing there with Zann and hurried over to greet the king. "Your Majesty," he said with a nod of his head. Talia had never seen him bow and was sure he never would. "How did these men die?"

"It was those dark spirits that came through the portal," explained the king. "My men were attacked. The soldiers' blades went right through them. They couldn't stop them."

"Then I'm sure your healer could have done naught

to help these men either," answered Darium. "The spirits who attacked them are life-sucking creatures who seem to thrive on killing quickly."

"Come, now, Death Eater, you are exaggerating," said Talia's father, Necos with a chuckle.

"It's Sin Eater. Not Death Eater," Darium ground out through clenched teeth.

"Father, what are you doing here?" Talia ran to them with Zann on her heels.

Darium got a bad feeling from Necos. He didn't like the fact that the man was here instead of back with his family where he should be resting and trying to regain his memory. Things just weren't adding up where Necos was concerned. He also wondered about the being in the Land of the Dead that looked a lot like Necos.

"Aye," agreed Darium. "After your near-death experience, I'd think you'd want time at home to recover."

"Near-death?" The king looked over at Necos. "You didn't tell me about this."

"Didn't I?" asked the man nonchalantly. "Ah, yes, perhaps I forgot to mention that King Sethor ordered his men to kill me. I was beaten and tortured and left for dead. I actually visited the Land of the Dead, but was lucky enough to return and live once again."

"How is that possible?" asked one of the soldiers.

"Aye, that's what I'd like to know," said Darium, needing answers that he wasn't seeming to get.

"King Sethor did what?" King Grinwald's face turned red just hearing the name of his archenemy mentioned.

"That's right. King Sethor said I was a spy and ordered my death," explained Necos.

"He also said you killed several of his men, stabbing them from behind," Darium added to the conversation.

"Nay. I don't remember that." Necos looked in the opposite direction. "Sethor is lying."

"I'll not let Sethor get away with this." King Grinwald raised his fist in the air. "I will storm his castle and take it as my own, right after I kill them all off." That seemed to rile the rest of his soldiers and they all started shouting and waving their fists in the air.

"Father, you *were* a spy, weren't you?" asked Talia, causing the noise to settle. "King Grinwald sent you there, knowing you'd be caught and killed and he didn't have a care about it." She raised her chin higher, more or less challenging the king. Darium knew this wasn't good and was only going to cause trouble. Why couldn't the girl stay quiet and on the horse like he'd instructed?

"What did you say, wench?" snarled the king.

"Talia, keep quiet," Darium mumbled. "Get back on the horse. Now." Then he stepped forward to talk to the king. "If you'll show me the dead bodies, I'll get right to the sin eating. I have much to do today."

"Aye." The king glared at Talia, but then led Darium over to a wagon with several dead men thrown in the back. Darium looked down to see the scorch marks on them, just the same as the dead over at Kasculbough. He moved the tunic aside on one of the dead, seeing his neck and chest were nearly black.

"Set them up," said Darium, eager to be finished with this so he could talk with his brothers.

"Calm down, Sin Eater. Where have you got to go that is so important?" asked Grinwald.

"He's going to our enemies to sin eat for them as well," said Talia's father, making Darium wonder if the man was purposely trying to start trouble.

"That'll be fine," said Darium, seeing the soldiers

laying the bread and wine atop the bodies. He stepped in before they were finished, gobbling down the food and gulping down the wine. All this sin eating was making his stomach bloated. He felt as if he had swallowed a rock. Once again, his head began to ache. "All right, my work is done here." He turned to go and stopped in his tracks. The king was holding a knife to Talia's throat. "What are you doing?" shouted Darium. "Let her go."

"Nay. She has upset me with the way she spoke to me," said King Grinwald. "No one gets away with that!"

"Father, please, tell him I didn't mean it," Talia begged, but Necos didn't seem to be rushing to her rescue.

"You did speak disrespectfully to the king, Talia," said her father, making Darium want to belt the man in the mouth. "Still, Sire, she is my daughter and I ask you to spare her."

"Necos, why don't you tell us all how you managed to escape death?" asked Darium, trying to turn the attention to him instead of Talia.

"Me?" That seemed to shake up the man.

"Yes, you," said Darium. "No one dies, goes to the Land of the Dead, and returns without a scratch on them. Or mayhap you were never killed, but for some reason King Sethor wanted King Grinwald to think you were. As a matter of fact, let me see your chest."

"Don't even think of touching me," snarled Necos, gripping the top of his tunic.

"What is going on here?" The king released Talia and lowered his blade. Darium reached out and pulled the girl to him. "Necos, are you a spy for Sethor? If so, I'll have your head."

"Nay, my father isn't," said Talia. Darium turned and hauled her quickly to his horse. He lifted her up into the saddle and followed suit. "Wait. We can't leave now. My father's in trouble," said Talia.

"He started it, so let him end it as well. Besides, he didn't seem to be trying too hard to save your life, so don't worry about his." Darium turned the horse and headed to the gate.

"Wait, Sin Eater. I haven't paid you yet," called out the king.

"Give it to someone else. I don't want it," said Darium, no longer interested in anything these kings would pay him for a service he no longer wanted to do.

"Darium, we can't leave him." Talia tried to get off the horse, but he held her tightly to keep her from moving.

"Princess, things aren't what they seem."

"What does that mean?"

"It means, honestly, I'm not even sure anymore if that really is your father."

"Of course he's my father. I should know. Who else would he be?" She squirmed in his arms. "Now, let me down. I have to go back and try to help him."

"I don't believe he's in any danger that he can't handle." As Darium started down the road, he heard hoofbeats from behind him and turned to see Zann following atop a horse. While Zann usually traveled in his wolf form, there were times when he couldn't do that. To get around quickly in his human form, he also used a horse to assist him. Since he worked for Evandorm, he was able to use a horse from the stables.

"Wait up, brother," said Zann, riding to his side. "What was that all about back there?" He raised a bushy blond eyebrow in question.

"I've got one more stop to make at Macada Castle," said Darium. "Fetch Rhys and meet me back at my place later. I will explain everything then."

"Are you going to tell us exactly what happened when you went through the portal?" asked Zann.

"Aye, and you're not going to like it."

"I'll fetch Rhys," said Zann, turning his horse and heading away.

"What happened when you went through the portal?" asked Talia. "I want to know."

"We've got one more stop to make, and then I'm taking you home. I need to talk with my brothers alone first."

"I don't want to go home. I want to know what is going on."

Darium wanted to tell her, but he honestly wasn't sure yet what exactly was happening. He figured it would be better not to say anything, until he knew more. "Talia, I will tell you one thing right now, and you must heed my warning."

"What warning? What are you talking about? And why did you leave my father when he needed our help?"

"You are in danger. Your whole family is not safe. Until I figure out a few things, I want you to go with your mother and sisters and make your way back to the other side of the mountain to the Whispering Dale where you'll be safe. Stay with the rest of the fae until I come to get you."

"Leave? Now? Nay, Darium, I can't do that. Father needs me."

"Your father is the one who you are all in danger from."

"My father?" She looked back at him innocently and batted her long, curled lashes. "My father would never hurt us. He loves us . . . even if he is a bit confused."

"I'm sure he did love you at one time and wouldn't hurt you, princess. Then again, if I'm right, that man back at Evandorm is no longer really your father."

Ten

"I don't understand. What do you mean he isn't my father?" Talia felt uncomfortable and wanted nothing more than to get off the horse and have a heart-to-heart talk with Darium. Unfortunately, all his sin eating had them too busy to even discuss the serious issue of the tear in the veil, or what he meant by what he said about her father.

"I'll explain everything once we're done here," he said, making his way over the drawbridge of Macada Castle. "I can't say I feel good about coming back here after the last visit we had that ended up with us fleeing for our lives."

"I don't feel good about it either," she admitted, not wanting to think about her close call with death.

"Mayhap you should wait outside the gate," he told her. He was probably right but she didn't want to leave Darium there by himself since he was no longer on good terms with King Sethor.

"Nay," she answered. "I am not leaving your side. We are in this together. Besides, I still need to find my answers."

"Have it your way," he said, not sounding as if he

agreed with the idea at all, but still he didn't stop her. Once in the courtyard, they came face to face with King Sethor. Two dead men lay at his feet.

"If I didn't need your services, Sin Eater, I'd kill you and the girl right now," the king told him. In Talia's opinion, it wasn't a good way to go about getting someone to do what he wanted. Still, they were there and doing his bidding anyway.

"I am surprised you summoned me," Darium told the king.

"Well, I can see that you have a special power that no one else possesses."

Talia felt confused by that. "Darium, what does he mean?" she whispered.

"I don't know, and we're not going to hang around long enough to find out. Now, this time, stay on the horse. If there is any trouble, turn and ride for home. Don't worry about me."

"I won't leave you."

"Well, hopefully we will both be leaving in a few minutes," he said, but she had the feeling it wasn't going to be that easy.

Darium walked slowly over to the king, feeling very unsettled. Something was wrong, more so than usual. The food and drink was already set up atop the dead bodies, so he wasted no time in doing his job, finishing quickly. All this sin eating was making him feel full and uncomfortable. He also felt tired and just wanted to leave and rest.

"It's done," he said, turning to go, eager to get away from this place as fast as possible. "Give my pay to the families of the dead."

"Hello, Sin Eater," he heard, turning around to see

who spoke to him. His mouth fell open when he saw the king's son. It was the same son who had died and for whom Darium had done sin eating the last time he was here. It also happened to be the same young man he saw in the Land of the Dead. None of this made any sense at all.

"You?" Darium looked over at the king and back again to the young man, waiting for answers.

"Aye, my son, Muldor, has returned from the dead," the king told him.

"You saved my life with your sin eating," said Muldor.

"But . . . how?" Darium wasn't sure what to say to that. "It doesn't work that way."

"Who cares how it happened, I'm just glad it did." King Sethor smiled, which was something that Darium had never seen before. "You saved my son's life with your sin eating, Darium. Can you save the lives of these other men as well?" Sethor nodded to the dead bodies at his feet.

"Well, I-I'm not sure," Darium answered, not knowing what was going on. "If you'll excuse me, I need to leave now."

"Not yet," said Muldor, holding a finger in the air. When he spoke, Darium felt a sharp pain shoot through his heart. He doubled over, clutching his chest. "Father, I think we no longer need the Sin Eater's services."

When Darium looked up, he saw the man's eyes. They were black, like death. No life shone in them in the least. He knew now exactly what had happened. This was more dangerous than he had thought. He needed to get Talia to safety fast.

"I'm leaving," said Darium, turning and taking two steps before he felt a nasty blow from behind. His hand went to the back of his head to find it covered in blood.

"Arrrgh," shouted Darium, pulling his sword from his side and raising it in just enough time to block the blade of Muldor.

"What are you doing, son?" asked the king.

"This one needs to die. As well as the wench." Muldor came at Darium mercilessly. It was all Darium could do to block his blows with his sword. The man was possessed by evil. The spirit of one of the dead souls from the other side had taken over his body, and it was quite strong.

"Get out of here, Talia!" Darium shouted over his shoulder, still fighting with Muldor. "Leave!"

Now, not only Muldor attacked him, but the dead bodies on the ground rose up, their black eyes staring at him, weapons in their hands as well. The stench of the underworld filled Darium's nostrils, and the pain in his heart now felt like a burning fire within him.

"Belcoum's breath, nay," he said, barely able to stand because of the intense pain. He wasn't sure if his sin eating had done something to let the evil spirits in, but now he had three men coming after him and he could barely hold his sword because of all the pain.

"My king, we're under attack by King Osric of Kasculbough and his men," called out one of the guards from atop the battlements. To Darium's dismay, this was the moment when Osric decided to try to conquer Macada Castle. The kings never stopped fighting for control. Now, he had to defend himself and Talia against not only the evil spirits, but the evil humans too.

"Lower the gate and man your weapons," cried Sethor. "Whatever you do, don't let them in."

"Nay!" shouted Darium, realizing if the gate lowered, he and Talia would be trapped inside. He turned to see Talia dismounting his horse, once again disobeying his orders and purposely putting her life at risk.

They were about to be trapped inside the courtyard and there was nothing he could do to stop it. He had all he could do to fight off the possessed men, but he couldn't protect Talia from an entire army too, at the same time. Not when they'd be trapped inside these walls. It was looking as if this was where they would both die.

The low growl of an animal caught Darium's attention. He looked up to see Zann in his wolf form, lunging at Darium's attackers. Thank goodness, his brother didn't listen to him, and instead decided to follow. However, now Zann's life was in danger as well.

The damned giant of King Sethor's walked over next, lifting Darium up over his head. Could things possibly get any worse?

"Leave my brother alone!" shouted Rhys, riding his war horse into the courtyard, thankfully before the gate closed. Rhys struck out at the giant, right from atop his horse. One punch to the stomach, and the giant dropped Darium. One more hit from Rhys, and Darium's attacker went crashing to the ground. "Get Talia out of here," shouted Rhys, jumping off his horse. Rhys reached down and used his astounding strength to pick up the giant man and hold him over his head.

Darium, bleeding, bruised, and barely able to walk because of the pain in his chest, headed over to Lucifer as fast as he could.

"Darium, you're hurt," cried Talia, putting her arm around him.

"Forget about me. We've got to get you to safety. Get atop Lucifer. Now!"

He heard the growls of Zann from behind him. When he turned to look over his shoulder, he saw Rhys spinning the giant in circles over his head. Then, Rhys threw him, and the giant landed in a cart of hay, smashing the cart to pieces with his bulky form and weight.

The sound of the creaking winches and pulleys was like a death sentence being announced. "Talia, they're lowering the gate," said Darium. "We've got to get out of here before we're trapped for good."

With her help, he was able to mount his horse. Talia pulled herself up into the saddle with him. "I'll call on nature to help us," she said.

"Nay. Don't risk the lives of any poor animals. We'll do this by ourselves."

"How?" she asked, as the gate came crashing down, now trapping them inside the castle's courtyard.

"Rhys, you're needed," called out Darium, doubled over in pain. It was hard for him just to sit atop his horse. His head began to spin, and his vision became fuzzy. The spirits of the underworld seemed to affect him in ways that were not felt by anyone else. He supposed it was because he'd consumed so many sins from the dead over the years that he was feeling the pain of each and every one of them now. This tear in the veil was really causing problems. Sadly, he was sure it was only going to get worse before it became better.

"I'm on it," shouted Rhys, mounting his horse and riding fast for the gate.

Darium's raven shrieked from the sky, diving down to claw at the heads of their enemies.

"It's about time you showed up, Murk," Darium grumbled, looking up to the sky. "Where have you been?"

"He's doing it," said Talia excitedly. "Your brother is lifting up the gate so we can get through."

"Come on, Zann. It's time to get out of here," Darium called out to his other brother. Kicking his heels into the sides of his horse, he directed Lucifer toward the gate. "Murk, make it quick," he shouted to his raven.

"Hurry!" yelled Rhys. He was off his horse again and holding the gate open over his head. His muscles bulged under the weight. The gate was constructed of heavy iron, and it took much strength to hold it open for very long. Chaos reigned all around them now. The spirits of the underworld were not supposed to be here, and Darium wasn't sure if anything could stop them.

"Talia, reach down and grab Sampson's reins so the horse will follow us out the gate," ordered Darium, doing all he could just to hold on now and not pass out from his wounds and the pain.

"No need. I can talk to animals in my mind, remember?" Talia must have said something to Rhys' horse, because it ducked under the gate just as they passed through. Zann ran out after them, and Murk flew overhead. Then Rhys stepped through the opening and dropped the heavy gate. It came crashing to the ground with a loud clanging noise.

"Let's get out of here," said Rhys, climbing atop his horse. "Oh damn, no. Kasculbough is attacking as well as Evandorm now," he said, noticing the knights approaching. "I'm a knight of Kasculbough. I can't just ride away."

"Dammit, brother. This isn't good," spat Darium.

"I can help," said Talia, chanting something aloud that Darium couldn't begin to understand. To his surprise, he saw all the horses of both the Kasculbough knights as well as Evandorm, rise up and paw the air. Then they turned and ran, each horse heading to its own castle.

"Nice work," he heard Rhys comment from his side.

"Brother, I'm not feeling . . . well," said Darium, as pain from the evil spirits from the other side of the portal seemed to fill him now completely. He looked up to see Talia's father standing nearby, watching him. He was dressed in chain mail, ready to fight. His eyes flashed black, and a shiver ran through Darium's body. This gave him the answer he needed, although it was the last thing he wanted to see. Necos truly was possessed by an evil spirit from the other side. Now, it all made sense. His soul was in the Land of the Dead, but his physical body was still here, under the possession of evil. Talia would be crushed to know this. Her whole family would suffer realizing the truth of the situation. Necos wasn't alive as they had thought. Nay, the man was truly dead.

"Talia, we need to take Darium home. Zann, let's go," cried out Rhys as they rode like the wind, heading for Darium's house with the wolf and raven leading the way. That's the last thing Darium remembered before the pain overtook him, his vision blurred, and his world became black all around him.

Eleven

"Why doesn't he wake up?" Talia wrung out a rag soaked in herbed water, gently placing it against Darium's forehead. "It's been hours now and he's yet to open his eyes." She had been treating Darium with herbs from the earth ever since they brought him back to his home. Talia knew how to heal, using the gifts of nature. However, she was doing all she could, but nothing seemed to be helping Darium. With no idea what he was even ailing from, she felt at a loss as to how to cure him.

"You're the healer and an Elemental. Why haven't you been able to help him by now?" Zann paced the floor anxiously in his human form. She wasn't sure if it was a trait of the wolf always making him seem so agitated, but the man really needed to learn to relax.

"Brother, that's not fair." Rhys leaned back on a chair, cradling a tankard of ale in his hands. "The fae is doing all she can. None of us knows what's even happened to Darium."

"You're right. I'm sorry," said Zann, stopping for a moment and then continuing to pace once again. "This day just isn't getting any better."

"It'll be night soon," said Talia, placing a kiss on Darium's cheek. She stood up and released a deep sigh. "I really should get back to my mother and sisters. They will be worrying about me."

"Zann, take her home," said Rhys, getting out of his chair. It creaked under his weight.

"Me?" Zann looked at his brother and scowled. "Why don't you do it?"

"I've got to get back to Kasculbough before King Osric starts to think I'm working for the other side."

"So, drop off the fae on your way there. I've got things to do," snapped Zann.

"And what might that be?" asked Rhys snidely. "It's not like you have a real profession."

Zann's head snapped up at that comment, and he clenched his jaw. "I'm huntsman for King Grinwald, and you know it. That is a profession." Zann glared at his brother. "The king will want food on the table and is expecting me to bring it. I'll have to hunt in my wolf form now since I've lost so much time."

"You're going to kill the poor animals of the forest?" This thought sickened Talia. She knew the humans needed to eat, and liked their meat. However, it was always sad to see any of her forest creatures die senselessly when there was so much other food to consume instead. She would never understand humans.

"I like meat, and so does the king and his soldiers of Evandorm," Zann told her. "I'm sure you know this from your short time as healer at the castle."

"She's a fae, brother, so stop it," said Rhys. "She'll never understand you. Actually, I'm not sure I understand you, Zann. You truly can be quite insensitive at times."

"You try living the life as a shifter, feeling the carnal

needs of a wolf. Then mayhap you'll think differently, brother," Zann told him.

"Never mind," said Talia, not wanting the brothers to fight. "I don't need an escort. I am at one with nature. I'll be fine." She was sure everyone was upset by the happenings of the day, especially since now their brother was not responding. Still, she got the distinct feeling that Darium's brothers didn't really like her.

She heard the men conversing softly. Finally, Rhys spoke to her.

"Darium wouldn't like it if we didn't watch over you."

"I'll take you home," said Zann, sounding like he was doing it out of duty to his unconscious brother and not because he really wanted to, or even cared.

"I don't think we should leave Darium alone right now," said Talia, looking back at the bed, changing her mind about leaving. "Someone needs to stay with him. I have an idea."

"What's that?" asked Zann.

"I'd like to be here for Darium to care for him. I also want to be the first one he sees when he opens his eyes," Talia explained. "Rhys, I know you have duties as a knight, so you should return to the castle. Zann, if you wouldn't mind, can you go to my mother and sisters and tell them I am here, before you go on your hunt?"

"I suppose so," said Zann. "But will I be able to find the fae hovel? After all, isn't it only noticeable by your kind?"

"I'll have the animals and plants guide you," she told him. "I'll make sure that you'll be able to see the cottage, don't worry."

"I don't know," said Rhys, shaking his head. "It might not be a good idea to leave the fae here with our unconscious brother. They won't be safe. Darium's not going to be able to protect her," he said to Zann as if she wasn't standing right there, listening.

"Go," said Talia. "Really. I'm sure we will be fine. I'll stay with him until the morning."

After a minute, the brothers agreed. "All right then," said Rhys. "We'll check back at sunrise."

"We'll also try to find out more about what is going on with the tear in the veil," said Zann.

"That is kind of both of you. I'm sure Darium will be fine and just needs some rest." Talia sat down at the side of the bed and held Darium's hand. She wasn't totally sure about anything, but she thought by saying it aloud, perhaps it would make it so.

"Are you certain you'll be all right, here without us?" asked Zann as he and Rhys headed for the door.

"I'll ask the plants and animals to watch over the house and to warn me if anyone arrives," said Talia. "I will be well protected by the forest."

"Let's go, then," said Rhys, sounding impatient. "I have a feeling this is all far from over."

∾

Darium found himself surrounded by fog, and the sound of distant wailing filled his ears. He seemed to float instead of walk, and wasn't at all sure where he was.

"Hello?" he called out, hearing a sound and spinning around on his heel. He grabbed for his sword, but it wasn't there. "Who goes there?" he demanded to know.

"Darium, you need to return," came the voice of his father just before his father's image walked out of the fog. The man no longer looked dead. His body seemed normal, and his eyes were no longer sunken on his face.

This is the way Darium had always remembered him when he walked upon the earth.

"Father?" he asked, moving closer. "Where are we? Am I in the Land of the Dead again?"

"Nay. Not really. You are in between two worlds, Son," was his father's answer. The man smiled but that smile did not reach his eyes.

"I don't understand. I thought the Land of the Dead was the place between two worlds."

"It is. But that is not where you are right now. Not yet, anyway. You are naught but in the dream state, Son. Don't end up dying with regrets, Darium. Don't be like me."

"What regrets do you have, Father?" asked Darium.

"I have many. Too many to tell you about now. I took my own life, Son, and that was a big mistake, because now I have no choice but to end up in The Dark Abyss."

"Nay, that's not so, Father. You died at the hands of bandits."

"You and your brothers were young when I passed, and only know what it was I wanted you to think. I shoved the knife through my heart because I didn't deserve to live after what I did to my family."

"What are you saying, Father? I don't know what you mean."

"It no longer matters. All that you need to concern yourself with, is not ending up in The Dark Abyss someday."

"Of course, I'll end up there. I don't have a choice," said Darium. "I'm a Sin Eater, just like you, Father. It is my destiny to carry on with your work. When I die, I will end up in The Dark Abyss for all eternity as well. This is what you always told me."

"Well, I was wrong. They're all wrong." His father's face began to slowly change.

"What does that mean?" he asked. "Explain."

"You make your own destiny, Darium, just like the fae said. No one, no profession, nothing, can choose that for you. Life is all about making your own choices." His father's face started to contort, and it looked as if he were in much pain.

"How can you say this? I was born into this, Father," Darium reminded him. "It is in our blood. This is what the Blackseed line does. I am first-born and must follow the ways of the Sin Eater. I never had a choice."

"Mayhap you didn't, before. But like I said, I was wrong. Now you do have choices, Darium. Make the right ones for all concerned."

"Nay. It's too late for me, Father," said Darium, shaking his head. "I am a Sin Eater, and have taken on the sins of many. In the end I will pay for all those deeds. I can't do anything about it, and neither can I end up anywhere but in the Land of the Dead and eventually The Dark Abyss. My path has been chosen for me. That is where it leads, whether I like it or not."

"Anything . . . is . . . possible. If you just . . . believe," said his father, screaming in pain now. Then he looked up at Darium and his eyes glazed over with black, just like those evil spirits that had escaped through the portal.

"Nay! Father," shouted Darium, reaching out for the man. His father shook his head, holding up his palm and backing away. "Change, Darium. Do it quickly . . . while you still can. Save yourself. Save others. Close the portal before darkness wins."

"How?" asked Darium. "How can I do that? Tell me."

His father screamed out again, a shrill, bone-chilling sound that Darium would never forget. Then his image dissipated into a wisp of black smoke that swirled around Darium's feet and shot off up over his head. When Darium looked down to his arms, he saw them starting to change as well. Just like his father, he would soon be filled with oozing sores.

Darium's hands cramped up and his fingers curled. The pain felt intense and he couldn't help but scream loudly. Then, through all the chaos, he thought he heard soft humming. It was a familiar tune. It was the song that his mother used to hum to calm him as a child. The humming became louder, starting to cover up the screams of agony that filled his ears. The scent of sweet lippenbur lilies masked the awful stench of death, filling his senses with light and life. Something had changed.

He swore he heard someone saying I love you, but none of this made any sense to him. A struggle within himself made him feel as if he were being pulled in two directions at once. Part of him longed to leave here, yet another part of him felt as if he should stay. A hissing voice in his ear told him that being a Sin Eater is all he would ever be and that The Dark Abyss is really where he belonged.

"Darium, it's all right." The soft voice of an angel floated in the air, growing louder now. He shook his head, trying to clear his thoughts, but they were as muddled as the darkness surrounding him. "Open your eyes. Come back to me. I'm right here." The calming voice he heard became even stronger.

He screamed again from the intense pain, and bolted to an upright position. His eyes popped open. His breathing was labored and his gaze flashed back and forth as he searched for whatever entity it was that had started to invade his body. "Nay! Leave me alone," he yelled, flaying his arms in the air, expecting to see evil black wisps of spirits flying around his head, but there wasn't any.

"Darium, stop it. It's me, Talia. You're home. You're safe now."

He finally realized he was no longer in that horrible place, or mayhap it was only a dream. Either way, he was home and in his own bed now. The fae girl sat at his side, holding his hand as she tried to comfort him.

"Talia?" His eyes settled on the radiant image of the most beautiful woman he'd ever seen. Her bright green eyes twinkled like gemstones and her face looked so smooth. Her smile warmed his heart and fed his soul. Releasing a deep breath, Darium finally brought his breathing back to normal. His heart continued to beat rapidly in his chest.

"Thank the gods, you're all right," said Talia, her words so sweet, that he started feeling foolish about the dream he'd just had. "I've been here with you the whole time," she explained. "I never left you. I've been holding your hand all night, humming songs to comfort you."

"Then, it was you I heard?" he asked, realizing now that it hadn't been the humming of his mother. It was Talia who pulled him back from that horrible place. Whether it was real or just a dream, it no longer mattered to him. All he cared about was being here with the woman who healed his spirit with just her presence, and soothed his weary soul.

Darium looked down to his pillow to see an arc of flowers placed around his head where he'd been sleeping. "Lippenbur lilies," he said, breathing in the comforting scent and slowly releasing his breath. This is what he had smelled on the other plane.

"Let me feel your forehead," she said, gently placing

her hand on him, making his body vibrate from her touch against his skin. "Your fever seems to have broken. I guess my healing herbs worked well after all. For a while, I wasn't sure they would help at all."

He noticed the bowl of water next to the bed with the piece of cloth in it. In the water floated many herbs and petals of flowers of all kinds.

"Y-you healed me," he said, surprised, yet grateful that she had been able to bring him back from that dark, wretched place.

"Well, I'm not sure about that, but I tried my best to bring down your fever and close the wounds." Her smile was intoxicating. "I'm still not even sure what it was that you were ailing from."

"What happened to me?" His head still felt thick with confusion.

"Don't you remember?"

"I remember a little. Mostly, that I was in a lot of pain."

"We're not really sure what happened to you, Darium. It was all so fast," she explained. "A battle broke out between the three kings at Macada Castle. It seemed as if some dark spirits from the Land of the Dead were there as well."

"Ah, now I remember." Darium's hand went to his chest as he thought of the stabbing, burning sensation he'd felt in his heart.

"You fought brilliantly, Darium, but the fight wasn't fair. You received a few wounds, but I've wrapped them with herbs and you should heal quickly."

"Aye," he said, looking down at the cloths wrapped around his arms and also one leg. He patted his chest again, looking for a wound or perhaps a burn mark, but thankfully, there wasn't one there. "My brothers were there," he remembered.

"Aye. Zann came in his wolf form to help, and Rhys lifted the gate to allow us to escape. If they hadn't been there to assist us, we might both be dead right now."

"Where are my brothers?" he asked anxiously, scanning the room but not seeing them. "Please, don't tell me something happen to them." He had one leg off the bed already when Talia stopped him.

"Nay, don't move. You need to rest. Your brothers are fine," she assured him. "Please, calm down. Rhys has gone back to Kasculbough and Zann went to tell my family where I am before heading out on his hunt. They are not harmed and will return at first light."

"Oh," he said, letting out a sigh of relief and laying back down. His head continued to throb. He reached up and placed his hand upon it.

"Does your head hurt?" she asked with extreme concern in her voice, rubbing her hand over the top of his. The only other person who ever cared for him in this manner was his mother. It felt good. He missed this type of comfort although he'd convinced himself over the years that he didn't need it any longer.

"It hurts, but it's naught compared to the ache in my heart."

"Oh, I'm sorry. Let me rub your temples." She sat close to him on the bed and used her fingertips to rub small circles against his temples. It felt so good that it instantly made him relax.

"Mmmm, that feels nice." His eyes closed and his breathing slowed. The dream that had haunted him faded in his mind. All he focused on now was his sweet Talia at his side.

"If that feels better, I can rub your chest next. Where exactly does it hurt?"

Her hand slid down to his chest, sending a flitting sensation of excitement through his body. He liked being touched by the fae. Because of who he was and what he did, Darium had lived most of his life as a loner. He'd learned to accept the way everyone shunned him, not wanting his presence near them. Since the death of his mother, Darium had closed off his heart. He didn't feel as if he deserved love. Especially not the love of a beautiful woman who thought naught of herself, but only of his own cares and comfort. His hand clasped over hers and he opened his eyes.

"Thank you, Talia," he said in a mere whisper. "No one has ever cared about me like this before. Not since my mother."

"Your brothers are to thank as well."

"Nay, that's not what I mean." He looked deeply into her eyes, getting lost in the bright green swirls that seemed so full of life and light. Her eyes drew him in, making him feel closer to her. Closer to nature. "What I mean is that no woman has ever been brave enough to care for me the way you do."

She giggled. "Darium, are you saying that you've never been with a woman before?"

Her innocence made him chuckle. "Nay. Of course not, sweetheart," he answered. "I'm a twenty-five-year old man, not a boy. I've had my share of lust and sating it with women, like any other man. I'm not talking about that. It's something more."

"Really?" Her smile faded and her hands covered his now. "Tell me, what do you mean?"

Something stirred in his memory, and in his head he heard a voice. It was her voice saying she loved him. He was sure now that he'd heard her say it right before the portal closed. This thought should have made him feel secure, but instead, it scared him. No one had ever said this to him before and he wasn't sure how he felt or how he should react. "I care for you, Talia." He tried to return her feelings, but couldn't say the same words she'd said to him.

"I care for you as well, Darium."

"No woman has ever been brave enough to say what you said to me."

"What did you hear me say?" She asked as if with caution. As if mayhap she hadn't really meant him to hear it after all. Or had she? Either way, he needed to know.

"Did you say–did you say you loved me?"

"Oh, that." She slowly slid her hands off of his. "I'm sorry. I didn't mean to make you feel uncomfortable. I don't know why I said it. I mean, we've only just met and I–"

Talia's words were cut off as Darium pulled her atop his prone body and covered her mouth with his. They shared a passionate kiss, that was slow and long. This surprised and at the same time pleased her. When their lips parted, she felt as if she needed to explain.

"Darium, I thought I had lost you forever when you went through that portal. I was afraid you were gone for good and would never return from the Land of the Dead."

"Is that the only reason you said it?" His silvery gray eyes drank her in, holding all the hope in the world.

Talia realized a man like Darium had probably never known true love with a woman before. His profession kept girls from ever wanting to be too close to him, she was sure.

Darium was a wonderful man and didn't deserve to be treated so harshly. She didn't feel it was fair. He deserved so much more. Sure, he was frightening at times, but it was only because of his profession. Everyone feared death, or at least everyone but Darium. Talia had been able to see into his heart and he was a good man underneath his rough outer exterior. He longed to be loved, even though she was sure he would never admit it. It was something he needed, probably more than anyone else. He also needed to drop those heavy walls he'd built around his heart, closing himself off from others. Talia decided that she would feel honored to be able to be the one to do it. Aye, it was time for Darium to feel love, and she was going to help him.

"It might have been the reason at first," she said, reaching out and tracing his lips with the tip of her finger. "However, since then, I have realized something."

"What is that?" He took her hand in his, gently kissing her finger.

"I realized what a wonderful, caring man you really are, Darium Blackseed. I think there is a side of you that no one but I have seen. I've been lucky enough to glimpse it, and I must say yes, I do love that part of you. I love not only that part, but all of you, Darium. I want you to know that."

"I have the feeling that this is where I'm supposed to say the same thing back to you."

"Only if you truly feel it in your heart." She wished more than anything that he would say he loved her, but she knew it would be hard for a man like him. Talia promised herself she would be patient, and not be upset if he didn't return the same feelings.

"I am not sure what I feel in my heart, other than the stabbing pain that happens every time someone or something appears through the portal from the Land of the Dead. However, I know how I feel when I'm around you, Talia. Although I can't be sure it's love because that is a new emotion for me, I think I love you, too."

She reached up and kissed him once more. "That is good enough for me. Now, I don't want to talk anymore right now."

"Nay. Neither do I," he told her, rubbing her back. His fingers made small circles, making her feel randy.

"Darium, make love to me," she blurted out, not able to hold back her emotions or thoughts any longer.

"What?" he asked, seeming surprised. His hand stilled and he barely breathed at all. "Is that what you really want, my little fae?"

She smiled, and nodded. "I am fae and cannot lie, and I believe you know that. So, yes, it is what I want, more than anything in life right now."

"Talia," he said softly, swallowing forcefully. He seemed suddenly sad and she didn't know why. "I can't make you any promises. You have to know that."

"I'm not asking for any. I just want this intimate time together with you, even if it is only done in lust."

He was silent for a minute, as if he were considering her suggestion. Then he let out a breath and shook his head. "Nay," he said, surprising her since she felt him growing hard beneath her and knew he really wanted her as much as she did him.

"Nay?" she asked, not understanding. The thought made her sad. She felt foolish now for ever asking him to make love to her in the first place. What had she done? She'd ruined everything between them. "All right," she whispered, starting to sit up. However, he did not let her go. Instead, he once again pulled her to him, wrapping his arms around her tightly.

"Let me explain," he said, his mouth right next to her ear. His cheek brushed against hers, and the scratchy stubble on his face felt invigorating, reminding her he was a mature man. "I meant nay, I won't do it just in lust. Talia, I have come to care about you and I have to admit, I do have strong feelings for you that I think must be love."

"You think?" Her heart lodged in her throat. Was this his way of only telling her what she wanted to hear? She was sure it wasn't easy for a man like him to be open with his feelings. Actually, she hadn't even been certain until now that he even had feelings at all.

"I do," he continued. "Although, I must admit I don't know how love is supposed to feel. It's been so long. I once knew it in a way as a child, but that was different. That was love for my mother."

She smiled, looking up at him. "Did you want to learn how to love? How to show those emotions with a woman, I mean?"

"I want to make love to you, if that's what you're asking. I also want you to know it is not being done in lust only. I feel different about you than any other woman I have ever been with in my life."

"Darium, are you going to keep talking, or can I remove my clothes now?" She giggled playfully.

"Sorry." He flashed her a quick smile. "I just wanted you to understand."

"I do understand. More than you know." She reached out boldly to touch him, wrapping her fingers around his hardened form. A playful giggle escaped her lips.

"Enough talking, you're right," he said, pushing up on the bed, reaching for the tie on his breeches.

"Nay. Let me," she told him, nimbly untying the string, slowly pulling his breeches down his legs. Her eyes drank in his beautiful manly form, and her jaw dropped when she saw his sheer size. Her core stirred within and warmth filled her being. All she could think about now was having him inside her, wondering how it would feel.

"Don't sit there with your mouth gaping open unless you intend to use it."

"What?" she asked, in confusion, her eyes darting back to his face. Then she saw his eyes drop below his waist, and she knew exactly what he meant. "Mayhap, I will," she said, getting on her knees with her rump in the air, lowering her mouth to him, keeping her eyes interlocked with his. She did not want to break the connection. Talia wasn't exactly sure how to do this, but with his guidance she was able to accomplish what he wanted. It made her feel pleased with herself when she heard his moans of pleasure.

"That's enough," he said, reaching out and pulling her gown over her head and throwing it to the floor. "It's time you felt some pleasure my playful little fae." He untied her undergarments, pulling them down slowly. It about drove her out of her mind.

"I can't wait," she said, helping him, then crawling atop him in a straddling position.

"You act as if you know what you're doing." He grinned. His eyes were hooded, his gaze so mesmerizing that it brought her to life even more.

"I don't know what I'm doing. Not really," she admitted. "It is just my nature to be aggressive and playful, I suppose. I'm sorry. Did you want to be on top?"

"Nay. I like this aggressive side of you, princess." He reached out and cupped her breasts, flicking his thumbs over her nipples, making them go instantly taut.

"Oooo," she cried, liking the excitement that now shot through her. She purposely drew closer to him so he could take her into his mouth. She might not have really known how to make love, but Darium seemed to be an expert at it.

He used his mouth, his lips, and even his tongue to suckle her, bringing her swells of great pleasure. All the while, his hands caressed her, slowly sliding down her sides, and over her buttocks, ending with a playful squeeze.

"Darium, you are exciting me so much," she told him through ragged breathing.

"Is that a bad thing?" he asked, chuckling under his breath.

"Oh, nay. It is a very good thing, indeed."

His hands slid around her hips next, and his fingers dipped beneath her as he readied her, making her feel even more excited than before. Then he gently spread her legs and he lowered her onto him a little at a time until she was able to take him in completely.

"Oh, my," she gasped, not knowing what to expect, but liking the feel of this joining together.

"Kiss me," he said. She followed his direction. When she did, he started the dance of love, moving his hips and helping her move hers to find the rhythm as he thrust in and out ever so slowly at first. It was wonderful, even if originally she felt a little scared. The more he kissed her and touched her, the more relaxed she became.

The dance of love continued and became even faster now, until she was so lightheaded and giddy that there was naught to do but to let herself go. She broke the kiss and cried out with elation, moving her hips faster and faster until she found her total release. Colors exploded behind her closed eyes, and she felt as if she were one with Darium, and one with all nature as well. He must have known it. In another minute, he'd reached his peak and found his release, too.

Their bodies joined together easily. It felt so perfect, so right, as if it was where they both belonged. She almost didn't want to break the connection. But then she heard the call of the plants and animals of the forest telling her it was daybreak. They warned her in her mind that someone approached the house.

"Darium," she said, through ragged breathing. "I think your brothers are here." She looked up at him now with wide eyes. When she listened again to nature in her head once more, she was sure now that it was Rhys and Zann who had come to see them.

Darium groaned. "Why can't my brothers ever have good timing?" He rolled out from under her, reaching to the floor for her garments and quickly handing them to her. "Cover up, sweetheart. I don't want to share you with anyone else. You may have seen one of my brothers naked, but damn if I'm going to let them see you the same way."

"Darium?" she asked, holding her gown to her chest, biting one lip as she looked over at him.

"Aye?" He stepped into his breeches.

"That was wonderful. I don't regret it at all."

"Neither do I. No regrets," he said with a smile, as if he were thinking of something.

She had wanted to approach the subject of love again, but didn't have time. She heard the footsteps outside the door, and quickly yanked her gown over her head, and pulled up her undergarments.

Darium stood there tying his breeches, looking up at her. He was barefooted and bare chested, with his long black hair with the white streak hanging down around his shoulders. He looked so handsome that she could almost cry. Then, he opened his mouth as if he were about to say something, but before he could, the door opened and his brothers burst into the room.

"Darium, you're awake. Great!" Rhys walked in followed by Zann right behind him.

"Damn it, brother, you had us worried," said Zann. They made their way over to the bed and stopped when they both realized just what had transpired between Darium and Talia.

"Oh. Mayhap we should return later?" asked Zann, flashing a smile.

"We didn't know that you . . . I mean that you were going to . . ." Rhys chuckled nervously, his eyes flashing over to Talia.

"Darium awoke a little while ago," she told the men, scooting off the bed and slipping into her shoes. "I've tended to his wounds the best I could."

"Aye," said Rhys, clearing his throat and looking back at his brother. "We see that."

"What did you two find out?" asked Darium, picking up his tunic and pulling it over his head, acting as if nothing had just transpired between them. With him, it seemed to always be business first.

"I told Talia's mother and sisters to beware, that Necos might not be the man they think he is," said Zann. "I also offered to take them back to the Whispering Dale so they'd be safe with the rest of the fae."

"What did they say?" asked Talia curiously.

"They refused to leave without you," Zann told her.

"Did Necos return to the fae's home last night?" Darium pulled back his hair, tying it with a leather strip.

"After my hunt, I kept watch over them until morning, but nay, he didn't show," said Zann.

"Good." Darium seemed pleased. "They are no longer safe around him, so it is good if he is not with them."

"That's my father you're speaking of," Talia reminded him, unwinding the faerie knots in her hair and smoothing it out with her fingers.

"Talia, it's not him," said Darium. "I saw the darkness in his eyes. His body has been taken over by an evil spirit. You're going to have to stay away from him."

"Darium's right," agreed Rhys. "It seems that those from all three kingdoms who have died recently are coming back to life."

"That's great," said Talia. "I mean, isn't it?"

"Nay," Darium answered. "What he means is that their bodies are being taken over by a dark force."

"That couldn't have happened to my father," said Talia, shaking her head and not wanting to believe it was true. "He was a good man, and still is, no matter what any of you think about him."

"Then how do you explain the fact that he died, went to the underworld, and is back again?" asked Zann.

"Without even a scratch to show for it?" added Rhys.

"Talia, no human can do that," said Darium in a low voice. "I know you don't want to believe your father is truly gone, but he is. You need to accept it and stop being in denial."

Talia looked at the three men, feeling fear fill her body. She was truly shaken to hear that they thought her father was somehow possessed and not himself. She had the feeling deep down that they were right, but it hurt too much to acknowledge it was true. Talia couldn't even imagine life without her father. Nay, they had to be wrong about this. She just couldn't accept it. The fear she felt was not for herself, but for her father this time. Because, if the men were right, then there was no hope for her father after all.

"You're going to kill my father, to try to expel the dark spirits that you think are in him, aren't you?" She felt angry, not wanting anyone to hurt those she loved. Even if the man truly wasn't her father anymore, it would be too hard to watch Darium and his brothers kill him.

"We're not sure yet how to do it, but yes, we'll have to send those dark entities back through the portal and then close it," said Darium, sitting down to don his boots.

"Do you think we can do it?" asked Zann.

"We have to," said Darium. "We don't have a choice. It's our destiny. Or at least, it is mine."

Talia no longer wanted to hear Darium speak of a destiny that was laden with doom. It was as if everything they'd shared between them had just diminished, and he was back to being the man he was on the first day that she'd met him. She didn't want that Darium. She wanted the one who was changing. She wanted the man who was slowly letting down the walls around his heart, realizing that he had choices and not just duties. Aye, she wanted the man who had been learning to love.

"I'm going back to my family," she announced, turning and running for the door.

"Talia, wait," Darium called out, jumping up to chase after her, but his brothers stopped him.

As Talia left the house, she heard what they were saying, or mayhap she just read their minds. She wasn't sure which, but then again it didn't really matter. Either way, she didn't like what they were saying.

"Let the fae go, brother," said Rhys. "We have more important things to deal with right now."

"I agree," said Zann.

"I can't let her go," protested Darium.

"Get your mind in the game," said Zann, snapping his fingers in Darium's face. "All the fae is going to do is distract you."

"That's right," said Rhys. "It could prove to be

deadly. You need to stay focused now. You've got to figure out how to fix this mess we're in. Only you can do it, brother. It's your destiny, and now it is time you fulfill it."

With that, Talia took off at a run through the woods, crying and needing to clear her head. This proved that Darium didn't want her as much as she wanted him after all. He was a Sin Eater first, and would never know love, even though she had hoped he was changing. He would always put his so-called destiny before anything else. Unfortunately for her, she wasn't part of this destiny at all.

Twelve

"Forget about the girl. Tell us what else happened when you went through the portal." Rhys closed the door to the cottage, not allowing Darium to watch Talia leave. It didn't feel right to just let her go. Especially since she helped to heal him and they had also made love. On the other hand, his brothers were right. He needed to focus on their problems and couldn't be distracted. He would go to Talia and talk to her later.

"It was awful," said Darium, pushing back a stray strand of hair that hung in his face. He sat down on a chair and pulled over a bowl of berries that Talia must have picked and left for him. He was too tired to care what he ate. "I not only saw Father in the Land of the Dead, but I also saw people that shouldn't be there. People who were dead and are now back here, alive again. I don't understand this at all."

"So, now that we have the dead walking the earth instead of staying put, what do we do about it?" asked Zann.

"The entities are using the bodies of the deceased," Darium told them. "I think because of this, even though

I sin ate, those souls aren't going to be leaving the underworld any time soon."

"Then we need to get those blasted spirits out of their bodies here, so they can go to The Haven where they belong," suggested Rhys.

"I guess so," agreed Darium, not really sure about a damned thing anymore.

"How are we going to do that? Did you ask Father about it?" Zann paced the floor like a hungry wolf even though he was in his human form.

"I did, but he won't say anything except that I know what to do. But I don't. Not really."

"Well, it is your destiny," said Rhys. "Mayhap the answer will just come to you."

"True," agreed Zann. "You are the one who is an emissary of the dead."

"I wouldn't use that word, since there is no peace from what I saw. Besides, I'm not so sure it really is my destiny after all," said Darium, thinking about what his father said. Perhaps he did have a choice, like Talia told him. Even so, wouldn't it be too late for him? He wondered about this, wishing he knew the answer. He'd been a Sin Eater for so long that nothing was going to save his darkened soul now.

"Well, if it's not your destiny, Darium, then whose is it?" asked Zann.

"That's right," said Rhys. "Someone has to close that portal and stop the dead from coming through. You don't really think that we can do it." Rhys motioned to himself as well as Zann.

"Nay. I suppose not," said Darium shaking his head. "Father also told me something that I never expected."

"What's that?" asked Zann.

"He told me he had regrets. Lots of them. Something to do with our family."

"I don't understand," said Rhys.

"He didn't explain." Darium started to pace. "He told me . . . he said he took his own life."

"What?" said his brothers at the same time.

"That's not how I remember it," said Rhys.

"Me either," agreed Zann. "We found him on the road, stabbed by bandits nearly ten years ago."

"It's only what he wanted us to think." Darium stopped pacing and faced his brothers. "Something he did–something to do with those regrets caused him to take his own life. He only wanted us to believe he was murdered, for some damned reason."

"What does this mean?" asked Zann.

"It means he had secrets." Rhys got up and started to pace now, something that he never did.

"It also means that there is no chance that Father will go anywhere but to The Dark Abyss now," said Darium softly. "Or, at least that is what I believe."

"He was headed there anyway, brother. Don't take it so hard." Zann could really be insensitive at times, but Darium supposed he couldn't blame him.

"I suppose it was Father's choice to end things that way," said Darium. "Choice," he repeated, Talia's words and also his father's coming back to him now.

"Darium? What are we going to do?" asked Rhys.

"We'll go back to Macada Castle," Darium told his brothers, pushing all thoughts of his father from his head. It was only going to be a distraction. Right now he needed to focus. "I'll sneak inside, and hope not to be discovered."

"You're going back to Macada Castle?" asked Zann. "Are you crazy?"

"Darium, you truly are daft to even consider it," agreed Rhys. "We were all almost killed there in case you're forgetting."

"Twice," mumbled Darium. "Believe me, I did not forget. However, I have to go back because there is someone I need to talk to. He might be the only one who can give me the answer I'm looking for."

"The king's son?" asked Rhys.

"Nay," Darium answered with a scowl.

"Then you must think King Sethor himself is going to help you," said Zann. "Forget it, he'll only order your head on a spike if he sees you again." Zann swiped his hand through the air to dismiss the thought.

"Nay, nay. Neither of them," said Darium. "I've got to try to find that stupid little elf mage." He strapped on his weapon belt as he spoke.

"Who?" asked Rhys.

"I think Talia said his name was Elden. Nay, Eldric. Mayhap. I can't remember." Darium shrugged. "Supposedly, he has some answer that will save the fae race as well."

"Wait, didn't you already talk to the elf?" asked Zann.

"I tried, but he wouldn't tell me a thing. He just played silly games."

"Why would he do that if he's truly a sage?" asked Rhys.

"Because," said Darium, chuckling and shaking his head. "He's also the court fool."

~

Talia didn't stop running through the forest until she made it back home. She barged into the house, slamming the door open against the wall, eager to see her family once again. But when she walked into the main room, she found all six of her sisters huddled together on the floor, crying. They looked up at her with fear in their eyes. She had never seen them like this before. They were usually so happy and always giggling.

"Talia!" cried Joy, the youngest of her sisters, running over and attaching herself to Talia's leg. She squeezed it so tightly that Talia wasn't even able to walk.

"Joy, what is the matter?" Talia gave her little sister a hug.

"Where have you been, sister?" asked Poppy. "We needed you and you weren't here."

"She's been warming the Sin Eater's bed," scoffed Shaylyn.

"That wolf man told us you were tending to the Sin Eater's wounds." Tia wiped a tear from her eye.

"I'm sorry," apologized Talia, not understanding what was the matter. "Yes, I was helping Darium. We were attacked at Macada Castle, and he was hurt and almost killed. I spent the night with him healing his wounds. Come. I've missed you all." She held out her arms, but none of the rest of her sisters approached her. Only little Joy still clung to her leg. Usually, the sisters always hugged. Why were they shunning her now? It made Talia sad. It wasn't a good feeling at all. She wondered if this is how Darium felt every day of his life.

"Joy, come back here, right now," scolded Shaylyn, holding out her arm.

Joy released Talia and ran back to the group of girls.

"What's going on here?" Talia closed the door and walked into the house, looking around the room. "Where is mother?"

"Mother is gone," cried Joy.

"Gone?" This truly surprised Talia to hear it. Her mother would never leave all the girls alone like this. "Where did she go and why did she leave you?"

"She didn't leave us, you did," said Aubrette,

making Talia realize what they were all so upset about now. "Mother was taken by force."

"What? Nay." Alarm filled Talia. How could this have happened? Her heart beat wildly in her chest. "Who took her? Where did they go?" She felt fear for her mother, and wished for her safety.

"It was Father," said Zia. "He was going to take Joy, but Mother wouldn't let him. She sacrificed herself instead."

"Take? Sacrifice? I don't understand any of this. It makes no sense. Why would Father take anyone anywhere? Tell me everything right now."

"Talia, he's not the father we remember. Not anymore." Aubrette ran to her, seeming to forgive her for not being there, but Shaylyn called her back.

"Aubrette, get away from her," said Shaylyn. "We don't know if she's really our sister anymore either."

"Oh, now I understand," said Talia, realizing that they saw the dark spirit controlling their father and wondered if Talia was possessed as well. "I am your sister and always will be. Stop this ridiculous talk right now." Talia walked over to the other girls, pushing her way into the center of the circle. "Now, tell me everything."

"Father's eyes turned black," said little Joy. "It scared me."

"What?" asked Talia, remembering what Darium had told her. It seemed as if she'd only been fooling herself about her father after all. Darium said she was in denial and now she realized he was right. "Are you sure?" she asked once more, just for confirmation.

"Talia, it wasn't Father. He was possessed or something," said Zia.

"Mother knew it. She didn't want him to harm us. That's why she convinced him to take her instead."

Poppy shook her head and looked at the ground. "I hope Mother is all right."

"Why didn't mother just call to nature to help her?" asked Talia. "I know the rest of you aren't strong enough yet to do it, but she could have."

"She didn't do it, because Father said he had you and would harm you if Mother even tried." Shaylyn relayed this information. Talia realized if she had been here, this deception never would have happened.

"That's a lie," yelled Talia. "No one was holding me captive. I was with Darium, I told you. I realize now I should have been here to help you and use my powers against the evil entity. Mother and I working together could have possibly stopped him. I'm so sorry. I thought Darium's brother Zann would watch over you."

"He was," said Tia. "This happened right after he left here at sunrise."

"Stay here and lock all the doors." Talia gave them all quick hugs and then headed for the exit.

"Wait. You can't go out there," protested Shaylyn.

"It's not safe, Sister," agreed Poppy.

Talia felt the weight of the world on her shoulders. "I feel as if this is all my fault. I should have been here to protect you. Plus, I should have believed Darium when he told me that I couldn't trust Father."

"Where are you going?" asked little Joy.

"I'm going to Macada Castle to find the sage. I'm sure he can help us."

"What about the Sin Eater?" asked Tia. "Can't he help?"

Talia stood in the doorway, holding on to it, feeling a knot forming deep in her belly. "Nay, I don't think Darium can help us," she answered.

"Why not?" asked Aubrette.

"Because, he has his destiny to fulfill," she told them. "And unfortunately, we are not a part of it."

~

"I can't do this," said Darium later that day as he and his brothers hid in the thicket outside of Macada Castle.

"Make up your mind," groaned Rhys. "You're the one who said you wanted to come here to talk to the elf."

"That's not what I mean." Darium found it hard to concentrate since all he could think about was Talia. "I never should have listened to you two. I should have gone after Talia right away before coming here. I'm going back to talk to her. I need to do it." He stood up and started to leave, when Zann pulled him back down to stay hidden.

"You fool! The guards on the battlement are patrolling. You were almost spotted. Just go see her later."

"Nay. I have feelings for the girl, and I want to make sure she knows it right away." Darium admitted to his brothers. "Plus, Talia said she loves me."

"Really?" asked Rhys.

"Loves you?" Zann looked at Rhys and they both started laughing.

"Oh, brother, you are being fooled by one of the tricks of the fae. Can't you see that?" asked Rhys.

It angered Darium that his brothers didn't think he could ever have a woman love him.

"Nay, I'm not being fooled. This is no trick, I tell you. Our feelings for each other are real," announced Darium. "I think, well I'm not sure but, mayhap I . . . love her too. Yes, I'm sure I do now. I should have told her I was positive about it before."

"Well, this is a fine time to go soft in the head. We've got a job to do, Darium," Rhys told him. "Focus. You have a destiny to fulfill."

"That's another thing I've been thinking about lately." Darium looked at the ground when he spoke. "Father said nothing is as it seems. He also told me that Sin Eating isn't my destiny. I don't believe I have to end up in the Land of the Dead or The Dark Abyss for eternity when I die after all."

"Now you're really spouting nonsense." Zann peeked out from around the bush and dove back down when another guard appeared on the battlements. "I don't know what you thought you heard, but I don't believe father would ever say that. You know as well as us that it is the way it's always been. You are the first born and so you just need to accept all that goes along with it."

"That's right, Darium. You know what to do," said Rhys.

Those were the same words his father had said to him when he asked about closing the portal. Perhaps Darium did know. Then doubt crept in and he didn't trust his thoughts anymore. The last thing he wanted was to make the wrong decision. He kept thinking of his father saying he had regrets. Darium didn't want a single regret when he died and left here forever.

"I do know what I have to do, you're right." Darium stood up to go once again, this time to follow his heart. If he died without ever telling Talia how he felt about her, he would take that regret to his grave with him. "I'm going back to find Talia. I need to talk to her and tell her exactly how I feel."

"Don't bother," said Zann, stretching his neck, looking at something.

"Don't try to stop me," said Darium. "I know what

to do now, and I'm leaving."

"Brother," said Zann. "You might want to go into the castle after all."

"Nay. Not now." Darium turned around in frustration. "I told you I—wait. Is that Talia?" He saw a woman sneaking into the castle through a postern door at the back of the keep. He wasn't exactly sure it was her at first, until the wind blew her hood off and he saw her faerie braid with all her flowers in her hair. "What does she think she's doing? I told her to go home and stay put. Can she never listen?"

"Mayhap you'd better go find out," suggested Rhys. "She is only going to alert them that we're here."

"Yes. Stop her before she gets herself killed," added Zann.

"Dammit, why does a fae act this way?" Darium changed his path, this time heading back to the castle.

"Will you be needing us to come to your rescue again?" Zann asked in a loud whisper as Darium walked by.

"If the fae is involved, then I'd have to say most likely so," Darium answered.

"If I'm still a knight for Kasculbough when this is all over, I'll be surprised," mumbled Rhys. "I cannot keep disappearing. I have duties, you know."

"Do what you want," said Darium. "I'm going in."

"It's your destiny," Zann reminded him. "Find a way to close the portal."

"I've got a new destiny now," he told his brothers. "This one includes protecting a troublesome fae with whom I think I am falling in love."

Thirteen

Talia had just managed to sneak inside Macada Castle by means of the postern gate when all of a sudden someone grabbed her from behind, clamping their hand over her mouth.

She squirmed and fought, trying to get away, and ended up biting the man.

"Ow, dammit, stop it, Talia," she heard from behind her, turning to see Darium, who still had his hand covering her mouth. Finally, he removed it.

"What are you doing here?" she asked. "I thought you had a destiny to fulfill."

"Aye," he told her. "That's what I'm trying to do. What are you doing here?"

"I'm here because my father has abducted my mother and I need the sage's help to try to set her free."

"Your mother is in danger? Egads, I knew I should have been watching over your family. I'm sorry, Talia."

"It's not your fault," she answered. "I never should have stayed away from my family for so long."

"You did it to help me. Now, I'm going to help you."

"Nay. I don't want your help." She frowned and

crossed her arms over her chest. "You have your work to do and I have mine, so leave me to it."

"Talia."

"I don't want to hear another word about it, Darium."

"Talia."

"I mean it. I know now what your priorities are and I'm sorry that I am getting in the way."

He grabbed her and kissed her hard, holding her tightly up against him. For a minute she almost forgot that she was angry with him. When their lips parted, her body vibrated. His essence clung to her, making her feel heady.

"Now, will you stop talking, and listen to me?" he asked.

She looked up at him and just nodded, not even able to even speak. He truly affected her in ways that she couldn't explain.

"I made a mistake."

"I know," she said, suddenly feeling sad again. "We never should have slept together."

"What?" That seemed to surprise him. "Is that what you really think?"

Her heart raced. She wanted to tell him it was, so they could both part and go their separate ways. However, her inability to lie had her shaking her head. "Nay, of course not," she said with a sigh, looking at the ground. "I loved every single minute of it."

"Well, so did I." He grinned, remembering their special time together. "I never should have let you walk out before I told you how I felt about you."

"Oh, I know how you feel, Darium. Don't bother to explain," she said. "You're a man who will never fall in love because you don't believe you deserve it. Also, because you don't have time for it. You've got a destiny to fulfill."

"I think since I met you, my destiny is changing."

"What?" she asked. It was her turn to be surprised now. "Do you really mean that?"

"I do," he answered. "I think I might be falling in love with you, Talia, but I'm not sure. You see, I don't know how it is supposed to feel."

"Darium."

"I understand, we just met and it's crazy to think this could really happen so fast, yet it seems that it has."

"Darium," she said once again, but he wasn't finished talking yet and kept on going.

"I thought it was my destiny to be a Sin Eater, but mayhap you were right. Mayhap it's something more than that and I really do have a choice after all."

She grabbed him by the tunic, pulling him hard against her body, kissing him just as passionately as he'd kissed her.

"What was that for?" he asked with a smile, touching his lips with his tongue.

"To shut you up."

"Huh?" His smile disappeared.

"I am delighted you finally want to talk to me about your feelings for me and your destiny and all, but I don't think this is really the time or place to do it." She nodded to a procession of soldiers who were lining up near the keep. King Sethor came down the stairs of the great hall, holding his hand high in the air to get everyone's attention.

"What's all this about?" asked Darium, craning his neck to see them.

"I'm not sure, but I don't believe we're going to like it."

"Soldiers, listen to me," called out the king. "I have

recently learned about the location of a portal that leads to the Land of the Dead."

The sky was black overhead now, the clouds looking fierce once again. The winds picked up, blowing things around the courtyard.

"We will have the strongest army when our fiercest warriors once again come back to life," explained King Sethor.

"Is this possible?" called out one of the men.

"How can that be?" asked another.

"Ask my son if you don't believe it." The king motioned to Muldor who walked out of the castle. "Ask my new advisor as well, who once used to work for my rival, King Grinwald of Evandorm. Now, he answers to me."

"Oh!" gasped Talia, quickly covering her mouth when she saw her father walk out with the king's son. "You were right, Darium. That really isn't my father," she said sadly, shaking her head. "He would never help King Sethor since he pledged his loyalty to Evandorm."

"Shhh," said Darium. "Let's listen and hear their plans."

"I'll also have the help of a fae to win this war against Evandorm and Kasculbough and to claim all of Mura as my own," continued the king.

"A fae?" gasped Talia. "Nay. No fae would ever help him do that!"

"Remove the covering of the iron-barred cage and show them the fae." The king waved his hand in the air. Then, to Talia's surprise, she saw the sage pull away a cloth to reveal her mother trapped inside the iron-barred box.

"Nay!" she cried, starting to lunge forward to help her mother.

"Talia, no," growled Darium, pulling her back to remain hidden.

"Let go of me, Darium," she said, trying to get out of his grip. "I've got to help her."

"Stop it," Darium commanded. "Your mother is a fae. She can call the elements of nature to her aid, so don't worry about her."

"Nay, she can't," said Talia, tears filling her eyes. "The power of the fae is void if we are surrounded by iron. I'm sure either the sage or my father must have told the king that."

"That damned elf should have helped her, but he seems to be answering to Sethor instead. He is getting on my nerves," spat Darium, watching the small man standing next to the cage.

"What are we going to do?" asked Talia.

"Can you pick a lock?" he asked, handing her his dagger.

"I don't know. I've never tried. What do you want me to do?"

"I'll cause a distraction while you free your mother. Then, take her and head back out the postern gate," Darium explained the plan to her.

"Nay, I won't," she answered, not liking this idea at all. "I'll cause the distraction instead. You pick the lock." She gently pushed his hand with the knife back to him.

"I won't let you put yourself in danger," he argued.

"I'm not going to. I will have some help." She closed her eyes and called to the animals and nature to come to her aid.

"What are you doing? Calling the birds again?" he asked.

"Aye, and a little extra help this time."

"What kind of help?" he asked.

"Seca should be here shortly."

"The stricat?" He made a face. "What is one wildcat going to do against an entire army of men?"

Darium didn't have to wait for his answer. He heard shouting from the guards, and looked up to see the stricat flying right over the wall and toward the courtyard. It hit the ground running. In leaps and bounds, the huge striped cat snarled and showed its long, sharp teeth. Darium was about to tell Talia that the cat would be killed, when all of a sudden a menagerie of animals started storming the castle. Birds swooped down from the sky, this time bringing with them raptors with sharp talons and beaks like razors. Behind the stricat was a procession of seyadillos with their chests puffed out, and their long tails dragging on the ground behind them. These animals had hides too tough to penetrate with an arrow. A group of large, slithering arcines followed, as well as a few skunets that lifted their tails high and blasted the soldiers with a foul spray.

Chaos broke out in the bailey with the men running in all directions, trying to fight off the animal attack.

"Good work," said Darium, looking over at the cage. "All right. I'll get your mother. You get the damned elf and tell him he's coming with us, like it or not."

Darium made his way over to the cage easily, no one stopping him since they were all busy fighting off the army of animals.

"Maeve, are you all right?" asked Darium, easily picking the lock with the tip of his dagger.

"I'm drained of energy because of these iron bars, but I'm not harmed," Maeve told him.

Darium opened the door and grabbed her hand, helping her out of the cage.

"She's not going anywhere," Darium heard, looking up to see Necos and Muldor coming at him with swords in their hands. Both of them had eyes that had turned totally black from being possessed.

"Necos, nay. Let us go," cried Maeve. "I am your wife. You sired my children."

"He's not your husband anymore, so pleading with him won't matter," said Darium. "These men have died and their bodies are only alive with the evil of the underworld." Darium drew his sword, although he knew it would be of little use against the dead.

"That can't stop us," said Necos, laughing heartily.

"You'll never win, Sin Eater," sneered the king's son. "As soon as we approach the portal, we'll kill all the soldiers and replace every one of them with spirits from the other side."

Their voices were deep and not their own anymore. Or at least Darium didn't think they'd sounded this way while they were alive.

"Maeve, get your daughter and go out the postern gate, quickly," Darium instructed the fae, speaking to her but keeping his eyes and sword pointed at the men. "My brothers are waiting out there and will help you."

Maeve ran off while Darium raised his blade higher. He had to give the women time to escape, even if he realized this was naught but a fool's errand. He couldn't kill these men with a blade since they were already dead. Still, he had to at least slow them down, so that's what he intended to do.

To his surprise, the clouds parted and a ray of sun poked through. Both Necos and Muldor hissed and raised their hands to cover their eyes. Then they turned and ran back into the castle.

"Interesting," said Darium to himself, looking up at the sky. "That was odd." It seemed the dark entities couldn't endure the bright light of the sun. He wondered how other light would affect them as well. Right now, this was the break he needed and he was thankful for it.

He turned and ran toward the postern gate. Once there, he found Maeve and Talia, trying to convince the elf to come with them. The stupid thing wouldn't go.

"I'm not leaving here. Sorry," said Elric stubbornly.

"Elric, we need your help," said Maeve.

"You're a sage and know the answers," added Talia.

"Mayhap yes, mayhap no." The elf bit at his fingernail, not in a rush to help at all.

"We don't have time for this," said Darium, using the hilt of his sword to hit the damned elf over the head. Elric's eyes rolled back in his head and he fell to the ground.

"Darium, how could you?" cried Talia. "He's a sage!"

"Well, now he's a sage who won't fight us." Darium reached down and picked up the small man, throwing him over his shoulder. "Let's go," he commanded. "Once we're safely away from here, call off your animals, Talia. They don't need to die for us."

"They won't," she said. "I only called the ones that could fend for themselves."

The group escaped through the postern gate and ran back to where Darium's brothers were waiting for them.

"What's this?" asked Rhys in surprise.

"We've got a little company," said Darium, throwing the elf over the top of Zann's horse.

"Wait. What are you doing?" asked Zann. "I don't want that thing on my horse. Take it off!"

"You're taking the elf with you, Zann, and I don't want to hear another word about it," Darium told his brother. "Rhys, you'll take Talia's mother with you. Talia will ride with me."

"Oh, that's a big horse. I don't think I can get up there," said Maeve, looking way up to the saddle of Rhys' warhorse. She was short, and the horse stood at least twice her height.

"No trouble." Rhys put his hands around the woman's waist and easily lifted her up and then climbed atop the horse with her.

"Come on, Talia," said Darium, mounting and holding out his hand for her.

"Wait," she said, looking back at the castle. She held her hand to her head. Darium realized she was silently calling off the army of animals who had come to their aid.

The birds flew up and away, and the stricat led the way out the gate with the rest of the animals following.

"Did any of them get hurt, Talia?" asked Maeve in concern.

"There are a few injuries, but no deaths," she reported, seeming as if she could tell just by talking to the animals in her mind. "It's nothing we won't be able to heal."

"How do you know that when you can't even see them?" asked Darium, helping her atop the horse.

"I suppose, you could say it's my destiny to know these things," she answered with a smile.

"We'll talk about destinies later, princess." Darium gave her a quick peck on the cheek. "Right now, we need to get to safety. Then, I'll tell all of you how we're going to rid ourselves of the dark spirits and close the portal to the Land of the Dead forever."

Fourteen

"We've got Sethor's soldiers on our ass," Rhys reported as the small group rode away from the castle in a hurry.

"Damn," spat Darium, looking over his shoulder to see a group of soldiers on horseback racing out the castle gate and heading in their direction. "I had hoped they wouldn't follow us."

"I shouldn't have called off the animals so soon," said Talia in an apologetic manner.

"Nay, it's fine." Darium didn't want to see the animals die if they did not have to.

"The soldiers will follow us to your house, for sure," said Zann, looking over his shoulder as they rode. "We won't be safe there. They want the fae and won't stop until they get what they're after."

"You're right. Change course," said Darium. "I just don't know where we can go to get away from them."

"I do. We can go to my home in the woods," suggested Talia.

"I don't think that's a good idea," Darium replied. "It's too dangerous for you and your family. We can't do that."

"Nay, she's right, we can go there," called out Maeve. "It won't be dangerous. Don't worry. We'll be inside a faerie ring. We'll stay invisible to others since it is magical and they won't be able to see us."

"A faerie ring?" asked Darium. "What's that?"

"It's a natural ring of growing mushrooms," explained Talia. "It is magic, and will hide us as well as our cottage since the house is inside the ring as well."

"So that's why no one could ever find your house," said Darium, starting to understand a little more about the fae. "All right. Let's do it, since we don't seem to have another choice." Darium, led the way.

Thankfully, it worked. They entered the faerie ring that encompassed a large circle in the forest. Once inside, they were invisible to the soldiers. Darium liked this little trick of how the fae were able to mask their home and even themselves from the eyes of humans.

"I know I saw them come this way," shouted one of the guards, stopping in a clearing and looking around.

"How could they all have disappeared so quickly?" asked another of King Sethor's men.

"Let's keep looking. They must be here somewhere."

"Let's try up on the hill," shouted another of the men, pointing the way. The small party of soldiers rode off, never seeing Darium and his friends although they were right in front of them.

"I like that trick," said Zann with a chuckle. The elf lying across his horse groaned and lifted his head.

"Where am I?" asked Elric.

"You're with us. You're safe now, sage," Talia informed him, sliding off Darium's horse.

"Oh, it's you, Sin Eater." Elric scrunched his nose and made a face at Darium. "Time for me to go."

"Grab him," Darium commanded as the elf moved quickly, slipping from Zann's hold.

"Don't let him leave," yelled Darium. "We need him."

"Elric, wait," called out Talia, but the elf zipped around so quickly that he was going to get away.

"Murk, stop him," Darium called to his raven. The bird flew after the sage, circling around the small man's head. Elric swatted at the bird, his arms waving wildly in the air like a madman.

"Shoo. Go away, you pesky bird," cried the elf. "Get away from me."

"Enough of this. We're just wasting time," Darium grunted.

"I'll get him." Rhys rode over to the elf, reaching down from his horse and snatching Elric up in one hand. He held him high above his head.

"Stop it! Let me go. Leave me alone." The elf kicked his feet and tried to hit Rhys with his fists, but couldn't reach him. Rhys used his strength to hold him up and away from his body.

"My brother is really strong," Darium told Elric. "Don't bother fighting him, you'll never be able to break free." Darium dismounted and so did the others. "Maeve, can we talk inside your home?"

"Of course," said Talia's mother, leading the way. Before they even got to the door, it burst open and Talia's six sisters ran out to greet them.

There was a lot of hugging and kissing and laughing going on. Darium had no use for anything like that. He looked over to Rhys and Zann and shook his head. "Let's get inside." The men entered the house and sat down at the table. Rhys still held the elf by the scruff of the neck of his colorful tunic. Elric struggled against his hold.

"Calm down, fool," Darium told Elric. "You're going to hurt yourself."

"Darium, his name is Elric!" Talia told him. "You need to respect him because he is a sage. You can't talk to him in that manner."

"He's dressed like a court fool, and I've yet to hear a single word of wisdom come out of his mouth yet," complained Darium. "He's more of a mage than a sage, I'd say."

"Mayhap if you gave him a chance to speak, he'd tell us what we want to know." Talia loyally stuck up for the elf.

"I doubt it." Darium looked at Talia and sighed. She had such pleading in her eyes that he couldn't deny her. "All right. Let the fool loose, Rhys," he told his brother. "I swear, if he tries to run, I'll skewer him to the wall with my blade."

"If you're sure." Rhys shrugged and released the elf. Darium half-expected the little man to run, but he didn't. Instead, he brushed of his clothes and straightened the tri-spiked multi-colored hat on his head. The little bells jangled as he pulled it tighter over his pointy ears.

"Girls, get our guests something to eat," Maeve instructed her daughters.

"Right away, Mother," they all said, hurrying around the home to prepare food.

"We're fine. We don't need anything," said Darium, remembering the last meal here that consisted of naught but berries, nuts, and roots vegetables from the earth. It wasn't an appetizing thought to him at all.

"Darium, you're being rude," whispered Talia. "It's not polite to turn down food offered by a fae."

"It's bad luck if you do," said the smallest girl, who Darium remembered as Joy.

"Well, we don't want any more bad luck, do we?" Darium answered. "Bring on the food."

"I really should be getting back to Kasculbough," said Rhys, getting up out of his chair.

"I've got to go, too. Sorry, we can't stay for the meal." Zann was up and right behind him as they headed for the door.

"Sit down. Both of you," Darium commanded, knowing they were trying to get out of eating the food of the fae. "We need to talk about closing that portal. This can't wait."

"He's right," Zann told Rhys, shrugging. They both came back to the table and sat down.

"Darium, how are we going to do that?" asked Talia.

"I have an idea, but before I tell you about it, I'd like to hear what the elf has to say." Darium stared at Elric, waiting for him to speak.

"Sage," Talia corrected Darium. "Elric, can you tell us how to close the portal? I'd also like to know how to save the fae race."

"I might be able to help, but what's in it for me?" asked Elric, stroking his pointy little chin.

Darium felt his blood starting to boil. He'd never really had dealings with elves before, but if they were all like this one, he could see why they were the favorite food of giants.

"I'll tell you what's in it for you," said Darium, gritting his teeth. "Your life. If you don't tell us what we need to know, I'll take you back to King Sethor, expose those pointy little ears of yours, and stand by watching as he kills you for the magical being you are. Or, perhaps he'll throw you to his giant, as a little snack."

"Oh!" cried Maeve, putting her hand to her mouth, looking horrified that he should speak in this manner. Darium didn't care. He needed answers, and would do whatever he had to in order to get them. They were quickly running out of time.

"Darium, mayhap you should let me talk to him," said Talia, resting her hand on his arm.

"Be my guest," he said, getting nowhere and hoping Talia could get results.

"Elric, why were you at Macada Castle in the first place?" she asked.

"That's what I'm wondering," mumbled Zann.

"That's my business, and I'm not saying," said the elf.

"Shouldn't you be back at Glint with the rest of your kind?" asked Zann.

Glint was the land of the elven kingdom. It was found on the other side of the Picajord Mountains.

"You won't be able to close the portal," said the sage. "Not without help, and I don't mean mine."

"Whose help, then?" asked Rhys as the fae girls laid down bowls of berries on the table. Shaylyn, the eldest of the sisters, carried over a large wooden bowl that took two hands to hold. The wooden vessel looked to be filled with naught but weeds of all shapes and colors.

"This looks . . . interesting," said Zann, picking up a purple leaf from the bowl and sniffing it. Even in his human form, he often had the characteristics of his shifting shape of a wolf. He made a face that said he didn't like it, throwing the leaf back with the others and handing the bowl to Darium without taking any. Darium shook his head, so Zann handed it to Rhys instead.

"You'll need magical help for sure," said the elf.

"I discovered that dark spirits don't like light," Darium informed everyone there.

"That's true," said Talia, bringing an earthen pitcher of liquid and several cups over to the table, setting them down in front of Darium. "I saw the king's son, and even Father's reaction to sunlight. They rushed inside when the clouds broke and the sun shone through."

"He's not your father, Talia. Not anymore," Maeve softly reminded her. "You can stop calling him that."

"I know." Talia looked so sad as she picked up a cup and poured liquid into it and handed it to Darium.

"What is this?" asked Darium, looking at the liquid inside the cup suspiciously, not sure he wanted to try it.

"It's dandelion wine," Talia informed him.

"No, thanks," he said, trying to hand the cup back to her.

"Try it. I'm sure you'll like it."

"Dandelion wine? That's my favorite." In the blink of an eye, the elf managed to steal the cup, drink down the liquid, and hand the cup back in just seconds. Darium would never get used to the magical creature's fast movements. All he saw was a blur.

"So, what are you thinking, brother?" Rhys was a big man - bigger than Zann or Darium, even though he was the youngest of the brothers. He pulled the entire large bowl of greens over to him and started picking at it, eating it with his fingers.

"Rhys, that is meant for everyone," Talia said sweetly, trying to hold back her giggle. Her sisters giggled behind their hands.

"Oh. Sorry," said Rhys, pushing the bowl to the center of the table. "Did anyone else want some? It actually doesn't taste as bad as it looks."

"Nay," said Zann, looking like he was salivating for some meat.

"We're good," said Darium, holding up his hand. "Now, can we get back to the conversation?"

Rhys smiled and pulled the bowl back in front of him. "Sure. Tell us your thoughts, brother."

Rhys was about to continue eating, but the little elf moved in a blur, zipping around the table. When he sat back down, to Darium's surprise, the bowl was empty.

"Hey! How did you do that?" Rhys picked up the bowl to inspect it, looking underneath it as well.

"For such a little thing, he sure can eat a lot," remarked Zann.

"I think it is light that kills off the spirits. I saw them flinch in the sun. I believe if we use torches, it could simulate enough light to do the same, if we get right up in their faces," said Darium, sticking to the matter at hand. "I think we can burn the spirits right out of the bodies they possess. Then, hopefully, they'll either disintegrate, or go back through the portal where they belong. Either way, we'll be rid of them."

"That's a great idea, but you still didn't tell us how to close the portal." Looking bored, and hungry, Zann picked up a bilberry and popped it into his mouth. He licked his lips, shrugged, and pulled the bowl over to him, helping himself to more.

"Hey, that's for all of us, Zann." Rhys reached out for a berry, but Zann slapped his hand away.

"I'm hungry, since the elf ate all the salad," whined Rhys.

"Stop it, you fools," commanded Darium. Next, he looked over at Elric. "Elf–I mean, Elric," he corrected himself, seeing the glare from Talia from the corners of his eyes. "Do you know how we can do it? Who can help us? I need to know."

"Aye, I'd like to know, too," said Talia. "Elric, you said they needed help. Whose help?"

The elf finally spoke. "Well, the torches might work on the dark spirits, or just slow them down. There's no way to know for sure. But the portal is different since it holds so much more evil. The light will have to be really strong. I think the only way to close the portal is to flood it with the bright light of the sun, the next time the portal opens."

"The sun?" asked Rhys. "How is that even possible?"

"I don't think it is," said Darium, getting up and pacing the floor. "Every time the portal opens, it does so only when the sky is black and the clouds are many. Then, when it closes again, the clouds leave."

"So, you're saying, we now have to somehow control the weather, too?" Zann popped a purple pazzleberry into his mouth and shook his head. "Impossible."

"I know. We're doomed." Darium ran a weary hand over his hair, not knowing how to accomplish this task.

"Nay, it's not impossible," said Maeve.

"That's right," said Talia's sister, Poppy. "An Elemental of the Air can control the weather easily."

"Really?" This got Darium's attention. "Can you do that?" he asked the girl.

His comment only seemed to make the Fae giggle even more.

"Did I say something funny?" he asked, looking over to Talia and then back to the girls.

"Nay, Darium," said Talia. "They aren't laughing at you. Not really. You see, you amuse them, and they like you."

"They do seem very happy," said Rhys. "I like that in a woman." He smiled at all the girls, once again, making them giggle.

"Well, if she can't do it, then I'm sure one of you can." Darium looked from one girl to the next.

"Darium, you don't understand," said Talia, sounding as if she were losing her patience. "My sisters are Fae, but not Elementals. Not yet, and possibly never. Since our father was human, it was only half a chance they'd be magical at all. You see, they didn't inherit the same abilities that I did from my mother."

"We're learning to do it, though," said Tia. "Slowly."

"The magic within us just needs to be awakened, so it'll take us a little longer to learn," added her twin, Zia.

"Besides, I told you that we are Fae of the earth, not the air," Talia continued.

"Then who is one of these air Elementals?" asked Darium, trying to understand how it all worked.

"Well, there are a few back in the Whispering Dale," said Talia. "Mayhap one of them can help us."

"Nay, this is too big a job for them. They aren't strong enough for a task like this," Maeve interrupted. "There is only one sylph that I know of, with powers that strong."

"Sylph?" Darium raised a brow in question.

"The Elemental of the Air," Talia explained. "Mother are you speaking of the sylph who resides on Lornoon?"

"Aye," her mother answered. "I've never met her but have heard her name is Portia-Maer. She also has the power to turn invisible, and holds the gift of the healing kiss. I'm sure she could close the portal easily."

"Then, let's call her," said Darium. "Can you do that?"

"She might hear our call on the air, but not from here, since the forest is so dense," said Maeve. "It'll have to be from the top of Mount Catskulp in the open air. That's our best chance for our request to travel to her on the wind."

"Mount Catskulp is the highest mountain of Mura," said Zann.

"And also the hardest to climb," added Rhys, taking a drink of dandelion wine, looking into the cup and smacking his lips afterwards. There wasn't much of anything that Rhys wouldn't eat or drink.

"Maeve is right," agreed Elric, leaning back on two legs of his chair as he rested his feet atop the table. His arms were crossed in front of him. "The mountain overlooks Portia's homeland of Lornoon. It's the only way she'll hear the call on the wind."

"All right. Do it, then," said Darium, looking back at Maeve.

"Nay. Mother, it's too much of a climb for you. You can't go," said Talia. "I'll do it instead."

"You?" Darium's head popped up in alarm. He didn't want Talia doing another thing that was dangerous or that might get her into trouble

"Nay, Daughter, it's too dangerous if you're caught," said her mother. "I should be the one to go."

"I won't let you do it, Mother," Talia continued to protest.

"We agree," said Shaylyn coming forward with her sisters right behind her. "Let Talia go, Mother. I will accompany her since I'm the next eldest."

"Thank you, sister, but your powers still need to be honed. I don't want to worry about you. I'll go alone." Talia's words sounded final. Darium didn't like this idea in the least.

"You'll not go alone," said Darium. "I'm going with you to protect you, Talia. Zann and Rhys, we'll get the slif and meet you back at the lake. You two watch over the portal whenever you can, and make sure King Sethor stays away from it."

The Fae all giggled again.

"What? What did I say to make them laugh, now?" asked Darium, raising up his palms in the air in surrender. Anything he seemed to say made these crazy girls laugh.

"It's pronounced sylph, not slif," Talia corrected him. "However, it does sound quite funny the way you said it."

"Whatever. Glad to have amused all of you. Now, let's go." Darium bounded from his chair, purposely hitting the feet of the elf as he passed by, heading to the door. The elf fell back and to the floor from losing his balance. Although Darium felt very little hope that this would really work, he had no other choice right now. One way or another, he was going to have to find a way to close that portal, if it's the last thing he ever did.

Fifteen

The ride up the mountain was treacherous, and Darium had to take it slow. Once it became too steep for his horse, he dismounted Lucifer, and helped Talia down as well. Looking out over the mountain range, it took his breath away. He had never been at this height before. Everything looked so beautiful from up here. In all his twenty-five years, he had never taken the time to climb up here, never feeling the need to do it.

From this high up, he could see each of the castles of the three kings of Mura. The Goeften Forest looked so green and lush. He couldn't see his little cottage because of all the trees. However, he could see the Lake of Souls and the water looked black even from this height. The thought of it being the place where the portal to the underworld had decided to materialize only made him wonder what other secrets the lake held. It sent a shiver up his spine.

"What's the matter?" asked Talia. "Why are we stopping? We still have a little ways to go to get to the top."

"I know." Darium looked over the edge as his raven flew in circles above his head. "It's too dangerous to continue to ride double on Lucifer, and I don't want to take him much further because I'm afraid he'll slip and break a leg on these loose stones. If we had stuck to the mountain range nearer to the coast, it wouldn't have been so dangerous."

"I understand," said Talia, looking around. "However, it is important we climb to the highest peak. There is cave up ahead and vegetation growing near it. There is even a small stream running through the area. It might be a good place to stop."

"Aye. We'll leave the horse there and continue to the top on foot."

"That sounds fine to me," she agreed.

"This little side trip is taking much longer than I'd anticipated. It'll be night soon," he told her.

"True." She perused him and nodded. "You look as if you're starting to tire, Darium."

"Are you?" he asked.

"Not really. I get energy from the earth."

"I'm fine, too," he said, wiping his brow and glancing up the mountain. It seemed to go on forever. He wondered if they would ever reach the top. "It's just that the air is thin up here and it is starting to be a chore just to breathe. It is even making me feel a little lightheaded."

"I'm sorry. I forgot that you don't have the endurance of a Fae. We are used to nature and it does not tire us, but makes us feel alive instead."

"I assure you, I have endurance," he said, his attention flicking from her face, down to her legs. Her body tempted him. Damn, why was he even thinking about something like this right now? He needed to remain focused on the task at hand. He reminded himself that the people of Mura were counting on him. The weight of the world felt heavy upon his shoulders now. It was up to him to close that portal, because no one else was going to be able to do it. He drank in the beauty of the Fae, her smile and the sound of her voice giving him hope and urging him to continue. There would be time to get to know her better, he told himself. Time later, to spend with Talia in his arms and with their lips caressing each other. He just needed to get through this first. Once he fulfilled this destiny, he would have time for all sorts of things.

"We can stop in the cave to rest," she told him. "My sisters sent food and dandelion wine along with us, so we can replenish ourselves."

"Great." He groaned as his empty stomach gurgled. How he wished that he had thought to bring along some food of his own. Or at least some real wine or ale. Weeds and berries weren't going to do much for him at all. The way he felt right now, he wondered if mayhap Talia was right. Did he have the endurance to carry on with this quest or not?

They made their way to the cave just as it started to rain and thunder. Lightning slashed across the vast sky. The pitter patter sound of the raindrops hitting the rocks and leaves on the trees around them almost sounded comforting although they were in the midst of a storm. He breathed in the fresh breeze, liking the feel of the cool wind against his face. He supposed he was getting delirious from hunger and exhaustion, because he swore he heard the whispers of voices in the air. As the wind picked up, he seemed to be brought back to life. Now, he felt as if he had the energy to continue after all. The only trouble was, the elements of nature were working against them.

"Damn," he scowled, realizing the storm was going to slow them down even more. He tied the horse to a tree, glad to see mountain foliage and a small stream for

Lucifer to drink from. Murk squawked in protest from a branch. "Come on, Murk." Darium held out his arm and the raven landed atop it. Then he followed Talia into the cave.

It was a large cave, and although he was tall, he didn't need to duck to enter. The ceiling of the enclosure was well over his head. He blinked, trying to get used to the darkness inside. It smelled musty. Moisture covered parts of the interior, making it damp. The strong feeling of life he'd experienced just minutes ago, suddenly vanished. He felt a chill run through his body. Then the light-headed feeling was back again. He didn't understand this at all. Darium wondered if he were getting sick. Nay, he decided. His kind never seemed to fall ill, so it couldn't be that.

Talia looked back over her shoulder, realizing that Darium wasn't at all happy. She couldn't blame him. Because of the storm, their little trip to the top of the mountain would be delayed. At times like this, she wished she was an Elemental of the Air instead of the earth. Then, she would be able to control the weather. Or, if she was an Elemental of Fire, she'd be able to light a flame instantly right now to warm their bones.

"Well, I suppose I'll try to find some dry wood to make a fire." He looked around and was getting ready to go back into the storm, when she stopped him.

"Darium, there is some dry wood in here from the last time I climbed the mountain," she told him. "I'm sure I'll be able to start a fire using the wood and stones. Just give me a few minutes." By asking for help from nature, she should have flames to warm their bones soon. However, inside a cave wasn't the strongest place for her Elemental magic to work. Still, she had to try.

"I had hoped this storm wouldn't last long, but by the looks of it, I don't think it'll let up anytime soon." Darium stood at the entrance to the cave, staring hopelessly out at the rain. His horse neighed, seeming spooked by the lightning and thunder. Talia didn't like to have to leave the animal outside. She felt its fear, and knew Lucifer wanted to be near them.

"Lucifer is frightened of the storm," she told Darium, hitting stones and sticks together trying to get a spark.

"Nay, he's fine. He's a horse. He's used to the elements of nature," Darium answered, dismissing her own concerns.

"Nay, he's not fine. Lucifer wants to be near us," she told him. "You're forgetting, I can read minds and also communicate with all nature. He is asking to come into the cave."

"You're right. I'm sorry. But inside the cave?" Darium asked in surprise.

"He doesn't mind being inside the cave, I assure you." She stopped what she was doing and closed her eyes. She entered Lucifer's mind to calm him. *It's all right*, she told him with her thoughts. *We'll bring you inside the cave with us so you'll be safe.*

"What are you doing?" Darium asked, causing her eyes to pop open.

"I was speaking to Lucifer," she told him. "Darium, the entrance of the cave is high and we can all fit in here easily. Bring him inside."

"If you insist." Darium shook his head and left the cave, going out into the pouring rain. Murk stayed inside the entrance squawking his disapproval, not wanting to go into the storm and get wet.

"I don't care what you think," she told the bird.

"Lucifer would like to be dry and warm, just the same as you, so stop complaining."

She was having a hard time making fire. Then, she realized that if she actually asked nature for help, which she hadn't done yet, it would do her bidding for her. "Please, we need fire to keep warm from the rain," she said, gently running her fingers along the length of the twigs in her hand. "I could use your help too," she said to the stones, even though getting rocks to listen to her wasn't always easy.

Murk squawked and hopped around the floor pecking at invisible bugs.

Thankfully, she managed to light a spark. Feeding some dried moss and kindling to it and blowing at the spark gently, she was then able to get a flame. "Thank you," she said with a smile, letting out a deep breath. By the time Darium returned with Lucifer, she had a blazing fire going.

"What? You did it?" he asked in surprise, never imagining that she could.

"I have more talents than you think." She stood up and brushed off her hands. When she looked up at him, his eyes were hooded and he had a sultry expression on his face. It caused a wave of excitement to rush through her.

"I'd like to see some more of those talents." He smiled at her and then turned to unsaddle the horse and wipe it down.

"Mayhap that can be arranged." She grinned, tending to the fire.

"That storm seemed to come out of nowhere," he commented, echoing her own thoughts. "One minute it was sunny with a clear sky, and the next, the storm rolled in and the sky was clouded over."

"It was odd, since the plants and animals didn't even

know it was coming," she admitted. "They can usually feel it long before it arrives, and they warn me. I can usually feel it too, but not this time."

"I hope it has nothing to do with the portal," he mumbled.

"Nay, I don't think so," she answered. "I've seen this before, and it is usually when an Elemental of the Air makes it happen."

"Really?" he asked, looking back over his shoulder at her. "So, mayhap this Portia-Maer did it? Do you think she is trying to stop us for some reason from even contacting her at all?"

"Nay, I don't believe it was her. I'm sure she doesn't even know yet that we are going to ask for her help."

"Then who did it?" he asked, sounding confused.

"I'm not sure. But since there is naught we can do about it, I suggest we just enjoy it. Storms clean the air and water the plants. It is a good thing even though it slowed us down."

"I never thought about it in that way before."

"Besides, it'll give us a little time together to get to know each other better." She shyly peeked up at him, feeing a blush rise to her cheeks.

"I suppose so."

"Darium, I really don't know much about you at all. Can you tell me something more?"

"Like what?" he asked, still tending to the horse.

"I don't know. Anything at all will be fine."

"Lucifer looks hungry. What did your sisters pack in the travel bag?" He rustled through it, groaning and pulling out a leather bag filled with greens. "Well, this won't go to waste at least. I know someone who likes weeds." He opened the bag and placed it down in front of Lucifer. "Here you go, boy." The horse eagerly stuck its nose into the bag as Darium rubbed its neck.

"For your information, I happen to like those weeds, as you call them. They are a delicacy to the Fae of the earth."

"Oh." He looked back at the bag, reaching down for it. "Sorry. I should have offered some to you first."

"Nay," she answered with a giggle. "Leave it for Lucifer. He's hungrier than I am. Just come over here and sit down so we can talk."

"All right." He headed over to her. Murk squawked and then flew to the entrance of the cave, landing on a rock for a perch as the bird stared out into the storm.

"I'm afraid I just used the only blanket I had, to wipe down the horse," he apologized. "I don't have anything else that is dry for us to sit on."

"Don't worry about it," she said, not caring at all. "Our clothes will dry quickly if we stay close to the fire."

"At least we have my cloak, I suppose. It's a little wet, but it'll do." He sprawled out the cloak and then removed his boots and weapon belt before sitting down and getting settled. Then, he held out his arms for her.

She went willingly, snuggling up against him, loving the feel of their bodies touching, even though they were both wet from the rain. Darium used a branch to poke at the fire.

"You already know my brothers," said Darium. "And I told you about my father."

"Yes, but I still don't understand."

"Understand what?" he asked.

"Your family has magic."

"Only on my father's side."

"I know you explained that the first born son inherits the role of Sin Eater. So . . . your grandfather and great-grandfather had this trait as well? I know you already tried to explain, but I am still confused."

"It's all right. I'd be happy to explain things until

you understand them. Answering your question, nay. Not at all. My grandfather and great-grandfather were not first sons like my father and me. Let me explain this to you, trying to make it easier to understand. In the Blackseed family, the first born boy is always a Sin Eater. The second, a shifter. The third has great strength. Rhys actually has the power to heal himself, too, for some reason."

"Oh, that must come in handy."

"He rarely has to use it. No one has ever managed to injure him, or win in a fight."

"So your grandfather and great-grandfather were second and third born then?"

"That's right. They had older brothers, but unfortunately, those brothers have died and so have their children."

"I'm sorry," she answered. "What happens to the fourth or fifth born sons?"

"I'm not sure. For the last several generations, only three boys have been born. Mayhap it's some kind of curse." He picked up a twig, broke it with one hand and tossed it into the fire.

"It sounds like your bloodline is strong with magic. Especially since Zann has the power to shapeshift at will."

"I suppose so."

"Tell me more about that."

"Nay. Someday, you'll just have to ask Zann about it."

"All right, then," she answered with a shrug. "Tell me what kind of magic you have, Darium. I know you are a Sin Eater, but you must have other skills as well. Magical ones."

"I can read minds on occasion. Besides that, I'm just a Sin Eater, doomed to spend eternity in The Dark

Abyss. I don't really have any magic. I have the worst of the family curse, and hate being the first born. My brothers got off easy."

"I agree that it doesn't seem fair. I mean, the first born sons of knights are always their father's heirs."

"I'm the heir of death and doom," he said, trying to make light of the situation.

"I still can't believe that."

"Well, I'm living proof, sweetheart. I don't have any special abilities that are really desirable, I assure you."

"What about your mother?" she asked. "You don't ever speak of her."

"That's because I don't remember much of her," he said. "She died when I was just a boy. My brothers were too young to really remember much of her at all. We grew up with just my father, until he died when we were in our teens." Talia could feel his emotions. They were feelings of loneliness and somehow of being abandoned.

"Tell me what you do remember about your mother, Darium. I would like to know."

"I was six when she died."

"What is it that took her life?"

"I'm not sure. I used to ask my father about it, but he'd never answer me. Eventually, I stopped asking. My parents used to fight a lot, I remember that. It seemed they could never agree on anything. Then one day my father took me to the Land of the Dead, although my mother didn't want him to do it. The next day when I woke up, I couldn't find my mother anywhere. That's when my father told me she died in the night very suddenly. He said he buried her before my brothers and I awoke."

"He did what?" she asked in astonishment. "Why would he do such a thing without letting you say your goodbyes?"

"Ambrose Blackseed was not a sentimental man. He cared for no one really except for himself. He said he hadn't wanted me or my brothers to see her dead, and that is why he didn't wake us. He wouldn't even show us where he'd buried her body so we could pay our respects."

"That seems odd and makes no sense, Darium. If he wasn't sentimental or caring, why did he suddenly worry about how you or your brothers would react to seeing her dead? I don't understand."

"Neither do I. It no longer matters. Neither of my parents are here anymore, and I need to move on with my life and not let my memories of them hold me back."

"Darium, if your father was training you to be a Sin Eater, then it seems to me, being around the dead is something he'd want you to be comfortable with. Yet, he did just the opposite by not letting you say goodbye to your dead mother."

"Aye. I suppose so. I never thought of it that way."

"What else do you remember?"

"I remember my mother was a beautiful woman. She had long, blonde hair and clear blue eyes. She also loved storms. I never knew anyone who actually liked the wind and rain." He chuckled lowly and smiled, seeming to remember.

"She did?" Talia giggled. "I've never heard of anyone besides the plants or perhaps an Elemental of the Air that really liked the rain. Your mother sounds like she was a very special person."

"She was." Darium's face softened and almost seemed to glow as he reminisced about his late mother. "Mother loved the outdoors as well. In a way, she was a lot like you. She always brought fresh flowers into the house and told me to sniff them to calm myself."

"Did it work?"

"Aye. Every time. I suppose that is why I like sniffing those lippenbur lilies of yours so much."

"I'm sorry I'm not wearing any in my hair today, but they only grow in the Whispering Dale. I'll have to go back there to collect more soon."

"Mother used to hum a tune to me that also calmed me," he continued. "It was the same tune you were humming, Talia, when I was wounded."

"Really? That is a song of the Fae. I wonder how she knew it?"

"Perhaps, she was lucky enough to have a Fae friend, just like I have you." He pulled her closer and kissed her gently. "I often used to wonder how she and my father ever fell in love in the first place since they were so different from each other."

"What do you mean?"

"Well, remember my father was always surrounded by death, ever since he was born. Darkness was his world, not light. His was the opposite of my mother's world, it seemed. Or as far as I can remember. It's been so long, that I might not be getting this right."

"Didn't you wonder more about it, and ask your father questions?"

"My father refused to talk about Mother after she died. It made him upset. So, my brothers and I just kept quiet rather than to anger him." A shadow crossed his face and Talia could feel his pain.

"I can tell this is making you very sad, Darium. Mayhap we should speak of something else."

"I agree." He released a deep breath and looked over at her. "What about your family, Talia? How did your mother, being an Elemental, end up marrying a mortal man?"

"Love does strange things, I guess," she told him with a smile. "My father ran across my mother one day when he was out exploring and wound up at the Whispering Dale. Once he knew her secret, he fell in love and married her. But humans are not accepted in the Whispering Dale, so he couldn't stay."

"Your father was married but left his wife?" asked Darium.

"Yes, he had to. Besides, he was a guard at the castle and lived there and worked there every day. He couldn't stay in the Whispering Dale even if he had wanted to."

"Then why didn't your mother move to the castle with him?"

"Darium, she has magic. My father knew she wasn't safe and told her to stay in the Dale. He traveled back and forth to see us as children, but was never able to stay with us for long."

"That's sad," he said.

"It is, but was necessary. Especially after I and my sisters were born. My father cared enough about us to want to keep us safe. That is why he told us to live in the Whispering Dale with the others of our kind."

"I see."

"Darium, there is something else I want to speak of."

"What is it?"

"There are not many male Fae, as I've already told you. I haven't had the chance to talk to the sage about it yet, but I think he might know a way to help us save the true Fae line from dying off."

"Don't count on the elf for anything. Tell me about your sisters, Talia. Will they ever be like you? An Elemental, I mean?"

"I'm not sure. I was the lucky one. I only hope they are able to find their powers within them. The older they get, the more and more human they become. I really need to speak with the sage about it."

"Talia, I doubt that mage knows anything other than trickery and deceit. Even if you do speak to him about it, you cannot believe a word he says. You can't trust him."

"Now, that's not nice, Darium," she said, not liking anyone speaking bad about magical beings. "Also, he is a sage, not a mage. Don't call him that or it'll anger him."

"All right, I won't do it to his face, since it upsets you. Don't tell the elf my true feelings about him." He chuckled, his low voice rumbling, sounding so masculine and sexy. She ran her hand up his arm, feeling the need to touch him.

"You are a handsome and remarkable man, Darium." She looked up into his silver-toned eyes, watching the light of the fire dance within them. She didn't see death when she looked into his eyes. Nay, what she saw was light and life.

"No one has ever told me that before, Talia. I admit, it is a nice thing to hear." He picked up her hand and gently kissed it.

"Well, mayhap it's about time someone did." She reached out and touched his face, seeing him looking at her lips. He wanted her to kiss him, and so she did. It was a tender kiss, but oh, so sweet. She loved the taste of his lips. They were soft and yet tantalizing at the same time. This man was so compelling.

"I have never met anyone like you." He cupped her cheek in his large palm. His other arm drew her closer to him. "I don't know what I did to deserve someone like you in my life."

"Stop saying that, Darium. I'm the lucky one to have you. You deserve so much more than me."

"Do I?" he asked, gently running his fingers up and down her back now. "I never thought I could feel this way about any girl. Woman," he corrected himself, his eyes partially closing.

"Darium, you are a man with needs and wants, just like any other. I am not speaking about coupling. I mean, life in general"

"I grew up hearing that I had a destiny to fulfill," he told her. "I wanted to be a good son, and do the right thing. My father always told me not to complain about the hand fate dealt me. He said it was an honor to be a Sin Eater, but I never saw it that way. So many times I wished I was Rhys or even Zann. Then, my life would be different."

"Your life can be different. You have to want it and believe it first, or nothing is going to change."

His head lowered and he seemed to think for a while as he continued to rub her hand with his. "Talia," he said, his head slowly raising. "I saw my father in the Land of the Dead when I entered the portal. It almost seemed like he was telling me that everything I believed about being a Sin Eater is not true."

"Like what?" she asked, laying her head against his broad, warm chest.

"Like the fact my destiny was decided for me the day I was born. Before I was born, actually."

"You mean because you are the first born and had to follow in your father's footsteps?"

"Yes. I remember my mother always fighting him about this. She would tell my father that I should be able to choose what I want to do, not be told."

"That's the same thing I said." Talia looked up into his eyes. "I still mean it. Make your own choices and decisions, Darium. Don't do something just because you feel you have to. Life is too short for that. You're here to live just like everyone else, so start living. Do things because you want to, not because you feel obligated."

"I like that advice," he said, the corners of his mouth pursing upward. "I like it a lot. I think I'll exercise that suggestion right now." His fingers trailed down her bodice and he started to unlace it.

"That's not exactly what I meant," she said, looking down at his hand.

"Did you want me to stop?"

"You didn't hear me say that, did you?"

"Well, no."

"It is a choice you're making, Darium. No matter who you are. It is always a choice. I'm making one right now too. So, there is nothing wrong with what we're about to do."

"I'm confused. So, you answer is . . ."

She grabbed him and kissed him deeply, showing him the passion she had in her heart, bringing it out through her kisses. "Does that answer your silly question?" She reached out and tapped him on the nose.

"I think so." He took her hand, sucking her finger into his mouth. His eyes stared into hers all the while. A heat engulfed her, and it wasn't from the flames of the fire. Nay, this was because Darium brought her to life in ways that she never thought were possible.

His head dipped down and he kissed her neck, running his tongue down to her cleavage. She knew where this was leading and it excited her to think of making love to Darium once again. His hot tongue lapped at the top of her breasts as he pushed them both together and buried his face between them, making her giggle. Then he pulled down her bodice, cupping both her bare breasts in his hands.

Talia's breath hitched when his mouth covered one nipple and he suckled her, causing a vibrating sensation to start up between her thighs. Then he playfully, but gently, pulled at the taut nub with his teeth. This action was so sensual to her that it nearly drove her out of her mind.

"Oooh, do it again," she cried, arching her back, pushing herself deeper into his mouth. He removed her gown and shift, and laid her back atop his cloak.

"Remove your clothes, Darium. Quickly," she begged him, feeling herself starting to climb.

"Not quite yet. Not all of my clothes, anyway," he told her, taking off his tunic only.

She loved the look of his masculine chest and taut stomach. His tanned skin was smattered with curly dark hairs that ran a path all the way down, disappearing under the band of his breeches. The biceps in his arms as he held himself up over her were so delicious-looking that she couldn't help but reach out to squeeze them. They were huge and rock hard. She heard a moan lodge at the back of her throat, not even aware she had made it.

"You like that?" he asked in a low voice, winking at her now.

"I do." She winked back. "I like this as well." She let her hands trail down his chest, as she felt each muscle under his skin, loving the heat emanating between them when they touched.

"There is a lot I like about you, too, princess."

"Like what?" she asked. "Even though I told you, I am not a princess."

"To me, you are. I like everything about you, Talia. Like this, for instance," he said, kissing her nose. "And this." He kissed her mouth next. "And even this." He ran his tongue down her chest. Then he let his tongue swirl around her navel as he untied her undergarments, sliding them down and off her legs. "I have something I would like to try with you," he told her in a breathy whisper.

"Will I like it?" she asked. "Tell me what it is." Her curious Fae nature made her want to know more.

"You'll love it," he promised, lowering his head between her thighs, continuing to use his lips and tongue to pleasure her in her most private spot.

"Oh!" she gasped, not realizing at first what he was about to do. Then he raised up her legs and put them over his shoulders, giving him more access to bring her to satisfied heights of pleasure without even entering her with his manhood at all. He was right. She did like it, very much.

She squealed with delight, running her hands through his hair as she gripped his head. She was climbing a height of ecstasy that was as high as this mountain, and she was about to reach the top. With her eyes closed, her breathing labored. Then she heard herself moaning out loud in delight, and even squealing with excitement as she reached her peak.

Her body vibrated for Darium. Tears streamed down her cheeks.

He looked up in surprise. "Are you crying?" he asked, removing her legs from his shoulders and gently placing them down atop the cloak. "I'm sorry, sweetheart. I didn't mean to scare you." His tongue shot out to lick his lips.

"These are not sad tears but tears of happiness," she explained. "I never thought I could feel this way. I found my release, and it was wonderful. I loved it, just as you said I would."

"Oh. I see," he said, almost seeming confused as if he should continue or not. "Well, mayhap we should stop then, since you have been sated?"

"You stop right now, and I swear I'll make you cry," she told him playfully, giggling when she said it. "And it won't be happy tears this time."

"I'm not sure what that means, but I think I'd better continue."

"I think so, too," she answered, not able to wait for more.

It only took a moment for Darium to remove his breeches and settle himself gently atop Talia, holding up his weight with his arms so he wouldn't crush her. He entered her then, slipping in and out, guided by her own wetness. As the dance of love continued, it became faster and faster, both of them heating up and climbing that peak as well. He thrust in and out, making her feel so excited, that she could no longer hold back any sounds of passion.

They made love right there in the cave atop his cloak, and it was exhilarating. It wasn't something most girls would like, she supposed, but she was Fae and an Elemental of Nature. To her, the only thing better would be making love in the forest, right down on the earth and in the grass. Spending intimate time with Darium was not only something she liked and enjoyed, but something she would remember forever.

Sixteen

Darium awoke the next morning, surprised to find that Talia was no longer in his arms. They had made love and fallen asleep in front of the fire last night, holding each other while they slept in the cave.

"Talia?" He raised his head and looked around. The first rays of sun were shining. It had stopped raining and he could hear the birds singing outside the cave. He could see Lucifer saddled and ready to go, tied to a tree. The horse was munching on some foliage. "Where are you, sweetheart?" He got up and dressed quickly, hearing the sound of his raven outside the cave, shrieking about something. "What is going on?"

The fire was somehow still burning, although he knew they hadn't had enough wood to last the night. He walked over and donned his weapon belt, walking out of the cave to find Talia sitting on the ground with her legs crossed. Her hands were on her knees with her palms facing upwards. Her face was toward the sun. A smile and peaceful look engulfed her. She was fully dressed.

"Sorry to interrupt you," he said, clearing his throat.

Her eyes popped open and she jumped to her feet. "Oh, you're up. Good."

"Why didn't you wake me?"

"You were sleeping so soundly, and the rain only stopped a few hours ago."

"How did that fire last throughout the night?"

"I called to the animals in nature to bring more sticks to me. I also had some of the birds collect berries so we could break our fast." She opened a cloth to show him a handful of berries inside. "I took care of Lucifer for you, as well."

"I see. You are very efficient." Darium was hungry, so he shared the berries with her that she held out to him. "What's Murk making such a fuss about?" He looked over to his raven sitting atop a rock above the cave.

"He's just upset that I asked him to go back to my mother and give her the message that we were fine and would return soon."

"My raven did that?" Darium glanced at the raven and then back at her, astonished and slightly amused to hear this. "I didn't know he could do such a thing."

"Of course he can," Talia answered with a giggle. "The only reason Murk has never done something like this before, is because I am the first one to ever ask him. Remember, my mother and I can talk to the animals."

"Aye, I guess so," he said with a nod, being very impressed with her skills. It made him want to know how to do it, too.

"By the way, Murk is just as stubborn as you are. Even though he did deliver my message to my mother, it wasn't without complaining about it."

"Murk did that," he said again, smiling and looking back at his bird. "Don't ever pretend you don't hear me again," he warned the bird. "Because if you do, I'll know you're faking it."

"He also told me that you tend to forget about him unless you need his help. He doesn't like that at all."

"He said that, did he?" Now, Darium glared at the bird. The raven stopped squawking and looked the other way.

"Since it is no longer raining, I think we should continue on to the top of the mountain so I can call for Portia-Maer." Talia stood up and stretched with her hands above her head. "The faster we do it, the faster she will be here."

"How long will it take for her to get here?" he asked.

"Not long. That is, if she's not too busy."

They quickly extinguished the fire and prepared to leave.

"The Fae sure have some odd names," he told her as they climbed the mountain with Murk leading the way.

"Well, you and your brothers have names that are a little unusual too. I don't see what you mean by that."

"I suppose you're right. Of course, I've always heard that it was my mother who named us. If my father had had any say about it, we would probably be named William, Frank, and Robert."

She giggled at that. "I think I like the name Darium much better. It fits you." As always, her sweet little giggle sounded magical to him, much like a chime. He still wasn't sure if Talia was doing it just because she was happy, nervous, or if he'd once again said something that was funny.

"I'm not sure about my name, but I've grown used to it."

"Well, I think your mother did a fine job naming you and your brothers. They are all wonderful names and not really odd at all."

"I suppose. Of course, her name was a little unusual as well."

"What was her name?" asked Talia.

"Her name was Alaina."

"Alaina? You think that is an unusual or odd name? I find it rather common."

"Well, that's what everyone called her, but her real name was Alai Na-Dae."

"It was?" Talia asked in surprise, stopping and turning to face him. "Really?"

"Really," he told her, knowing how stupid the name sounded once he said it aloud.

"What do you know about your mother's parents?" asked Talia.

"Nothing at all," he replied. "My grandparents on both sides died before I was born. My parents never spoke of them to us at all."

"Do you know where your mother's family came from? I mean, are they from Mura or perhaps somewhere else like Lornoon?"

"I don't know," he said, wondering why she was asking all these questions. He supposed it was just the nature of the Fae to be so curious. "Like I told you, I don't know anything about them at all. Why are you asking me this, Talia?"

"I'm just curious," she told him, but he didn't believe that was her only reason at all. He tried to read her mind the way he'd been able to do the day he first met her, but it wasn't working for some reason. She turned and continued to hike up the mountain.

"Darium, stop it," she warned him, over her shoulder, startling him and making him feel embarrassed that he'd been caught.

"Stop what?" he asked, trying to sound innocent even though he was not.

"You can't pretend you weren't trying to read my mind just now. I felt it. Besides, since I'm able to read your mind, I know what you were doing."

"Sorry," he apologized as they neared the top of the mountain. "It's just that sometimes I am able to read minds and other times I can't. I don't understand why. I was just wondering if I could still do it."

She stopped and turned around and put her hands on her hips. "Mmm-hmm," she said with a knowing smile.

"Oh, all right. I suppose you know that's not what I was really doing."

"You're not very good at lying," she told him.

They continued on for a little longer and then they stopped when they approached the summit. Even though the wind was blowing, the sun shone down brightly on them, warming Darium completely. He felt so alive up here. Being closer to the sky and clouds made him so happy. He supposed it was only because now he was closer to The Haven as well, and further from The Dark Abyss, which was a place he never wanted to see.

"We're at the top of the mountain, Darium. Isn't it a beautiful view from up here?" asked Talia, looking down at the land and sea below them.

"It is the most beautiful thing I've ever seen." Darium reached out and put his arm around Talia. "Well, almost the most beautiful," he told her, kissing her atop her head.

"Look! I think that is Lornoon." Talia pointed to the outline of an island in the distance. It was a clear day and not hard to see. It looked to have a lot of mountains, just like Mura.

"Lornoon," he repeated, feeling such a strong curiosity to learn more about it.

"It's where the four strongest Elementals live," said Talia, knowing what he was thinking.

"You mean, Elementals like this Portia Miner?"

That made her giggle again. "Portia-Maer," she corrected him. "And to answer your question, yes and no."

"What?" he asked, looking down at her in confusion.

"I mean, Portia is an Elemental of the Air, and I've heard the most powerful of that element. It is said she has three good friends who are also the best at what they do. "I believe their names are Brynn-Riletta, Elemental of Fire; Ebba-Tyne, Elemental of Water; and Rae-Nyst, who is an Elemental of the Earth, like me."

"Don't ask me to remember those names, because I won't," he told her. "Why is it that all those Elementals have two names, but you just have one?"

"I have two as well," she told him. "Talia-Glenn. Although, I choose to just go by Talia. My whole family does the same."

"Oh. I thought Glenn was a surname."

"Nay, silly," she answered. "Fae don't have surnames."

"Well, thanks for explaining that one." He looked further in the distance, shading his eyes. "I wonder what that land is?" he said, pointing to another island further away.

"I'm not sure, but I think it might be Tamiras, the land of sand and sheiks."

"Really," he said. "So Elementals like sand?"

"Not Elementals of the water," she explained. "That dry type of environment could kill them. Each Elemental has an element that gives them power, but there is also one that can take it away as well."

"There is so much I need to learn."

"There will be time later to talk more about this,"

said Talia. "Right now, we need to call out to the wind, asking it to take our request for help to Portia-Maer."

"All right," he said, noticing his raven landing on a rock not far from him. "What do we do?"

"*We* don't do anything," she told him. "I'm the only one who can do this, so you just sit back and watch."

"Fine," he said with a shrug and a sigh, sitting down on a rock feeling worthless since he didn't have magic like her or his brothers. His raven flew over and landed on his shoulder. "I just wanted to help," he told Murk, running a finger over the raven's head. "I guess the only thing I'm good at is dealing with the dead." He ended with a sigh.

"Powers of the wind, the air, and the sky that be; a request for assistance is sent to thee." Talia chanted, holding her hands above her head and turning her face up to the sun. "Go quickly with my message, please; and bring the Elemental, Portia-Maer to me."

She sat down and turned her face to the sun again, closing her eyes and smiling. Darium waited, looking around, but didn't see anyone. Nothing happened. He looked back at Talia, but she almost seemed as if she were asleep. If she hadn't had that big smile plastered across her face, he would have thought she was taking a nap. She didn't speak a word to Darium. Finally, he could stay silent no longer.

"Well? Talia?" he asked, clearing his throat, not wanting to startle her in case she was really still working on getting the sylph here. "Talia? Where is she?" he asked, softly.

"Give it time," said Talia, talking to him without turning her head. Her eyes were still closed. "The wind will carry the message to her in Lornoon. It takes time to get there. Besides, she might be too busy to help us."

"She might be too busy to help us?" He got up so abruptly, that he scared his raven. Murk jerked and squawked and flew away. "What does that mean?" His patience was wearing thin. He walked over to her.

"It just means we have to wait." She peeked out at him, opening one eye.

"I can't wait, Talia. *We* can't wait. We're on a tight schedule." He paced back and forth atop the mountain. "We've already wasted too much time spending the night in the cave. We have to move this along quickly."

"What did you say?" Her eyes opened and she turned her head to face him now. "You think the time we spent together last night in the cave was just a waste?"

Darium stopped pacing, feeling like hitting himself over the head, now that he realized how that sounded. "Nay, that's not what I meant at all." He continued to pace back and forth on the edge of the mountain as he spoke. "I just meant that we don't know what is going on back at the portal. I don't think our time together was a waste at all. I mean . . . " He slipped when his foot encountered a loose rock. His arms flayed around wildly as he tried to regain his balance, but he teetered on the edge of the mountain. "Nay!" he cried out, not being able to right himself. He went over the edge.

Darium found himself plummeting to the ground, since he'd been so careless as to fall in the first place. If he hadn't been so lost in his thoughts, he would have realized the stones under his feet were loose. Something wound around his ankle and he jolted to a stop. He swung back and forth, finding himself hanging by a vine wrapped around his foot.

"Darium? Are you all right?" shouted Talia from the top of the mountain. She was on her hands and knees and looking over the edge. "I called out for the vines to help you."

"Do I look like I'm all right?" he ground out, hanging upside down as Murk flew past him, circling around and doing it a second time. "Have the vine pull me up before I fall to my death."

"I'm afraid I can't," was her answer.

"What! Why not?" He tried to grab for the vine to pull himself up, but couldn't reach it from his position.

"The vine isn't strong enough to hold your weight for very long."

"It's not? Oh, crap. Dammit, we've got to do something, quickly."

A strong wind picked up, and he swung back and forth, almost hitting his head on the cliffs. He continued to try to reach for the vine, but just couldn't. Then, to his surprise, he felt himself being lifted up by the air, and dropped gently back atop the mountain.

"Talia, thank you! How did you do that? It was amazing." He untangled the vine from his leg and ran to her and hugged her. "You saved my life."

"I sent the vine only, Darium," she told him. "I had nothing to do with bringing you back up here, I'm sorry to say. I don't have that type of power."

"Then, how did it happen?" he asked, feeling very confused.

"I think I know." Talia's eyes lit up and she pointed behind him. When he turned to look, he never expected to see a woman standing there. He stumbled backward in surprise and almost fell off the mountain again. Talia reached out and grabbed him, pulling him to safety.

"You'd better be careful," said the woman. "Next time, I might not be here to save you."

"Are you Portia-Maer?" asked Talia excitedly. "I called for you. I sent the message on the wind."

"Yes, I know. I am Portia-Maer, and I received your message," said the blonde-haired woman. She was beautiful, and wore a crown of flowers in her hair and a white, flowing dress. "You're Talia-Glenn, the Earth Elemental and daughter of Maeve, aren't you?"

"I am," she confirmed. "How did you know this?"

"My friend, Rae-Nyst, is an Elemental of the Earth as well. She has met your mother long ago and told me about you."

"Thank you for coming," said Talia with a nod. "This is my–my friend, Darium. He . . . I mean we . . . need your help. Everyone on Mura does."

Talia could tell that by calling Darium her friend, it had upset him. She had only said it because she wasn't sure what to call him or how he would react. They were lovers now, but she didn't think that was a proper way to introduce him. It wouldn't put either of them in a good light.

"What is this all about?" asked Portia with concern in her voice.

"There is a tear in the veil between the two worlds," Darium told her. "I need to close the portal to the Land of the Dead, because dark spirits are starting to come through."

"That's not good," said Portia.

"Can you help me do it?" he asked, anxiously. "I need intense sunlight. Since you are an Elemental of the Air, I thought mayhap you could control the weather for me and blow the clouds away the next time the portal opens."

"Why do you have such an interest in this, Darium?" she asked, curious as all Fae are.

"I'm a Sin Eater," he told her. "It's my duty."

"He thinks it's his destiny," Talia, remarked. "His late father was a Sin Eater, too."

"I see," said Portia, seeming to be in deep thought. "Was your mother a Sin Eater as well?"

"Nay, of course not," said Darium, losing his patience once again. "She was human. Now, can you help us or not?"

"We're going to use torches to burn out the dark spirits that have entered the dead bodies of humans who are once again walking the earth," explained Talia. "But the sage told us that we need intense sunlight to close the portal and keep the rest of the entities inside."

"My, this is a critical situation," said Portia. "However, I'm not sure your plans will work."

"Nothing will work if we don't hurry. That is, if we're not already too late," said Darium.

"Can you help us, Portia-Maer? Please?" asked Talia. "You're the only one who has enough power to do it."

"Are you sure about that?" she asked.

"My mother said she didn't know of any other Elementals of the Air who would be able to handle this task," said Talia.

"I'll do it, but I must tell you that I'm not sure I'll be able to close the portal alone."

"What? Why not?" spat Darium. "You are an Elemental. You're supposed to be able to do those types of things."

"Darium, please don't be disrespectful," said Talia in a soft voice.

"Sorry," he told Portia. "It's just that if you can't do it, then no one can. And if that happens, I'm afraid that all of Mura is doomed."

"Let's go," said Portia. "We have no time to lose.

The most powerful time to do this is when the sun is at the highest peak."

"Let's start down the mountain," said Darium. "It'll take a while and I'm not sure we'll even make it back before nightfall. It's more treacherous to climb down than it was to get up here."

"Then allow me to help you," said Portia with a flick of her hand over her head. A whirlwind of air formed a cyclone, blowing so hard that Darium was sure they'd all be thrown from the cliffs.

"Talia, hold on to me," he called out into the whirling wind, grabbing her and holding her close to his body.

"It's all right, Darium. Portia is helping us. Relax," came Talia's reply.

"Relax? Relax, you say! Are you crazy?" He shouted into wind, doing all he could to stay upright. The wind started to move his body. Holding on tightly to Talia, they skidded across the ground. "Aaaaaah," he cried out, trying to dig his heels into the dirt to stop him, but with no results. Then, to his horror, his feet actually left the ground. He and Talia were lifted up into the air, and moved over the side of the mountain. It was evident that they were about to die.

"She's bringing us down the mountain by using her powers of the air," Talia explained calmly. "Don't forget Lucifer, Darium's horse," she called out to Portia.

Darium's head spun and his stomach lurched as he and Talia, his horse, and Portia, rode the wind in circles, spinning round and round until they went lower and lower and finally reached the ground. Then, the wind stopped, and their feet were stable upon the land once again. Darium stood there breathing hard and feeling dizzy, still gripping on to Talia, not wanting to let her go. He looked over to see Lucifer nearby munching on grass, as if nothing had happened. Murk cried out from overhead, flying in circles above them.

"Portia-Maer, that was wonderful," said Talia, slipping out of Darium's hold, looking like she had actually enjoyed that terrorizing trip.

"Aye. Thank you," said Darium, trying to be polite and grateful to the Fae, then remembering Fae didn't like to be thanked. "Thank you, I think," said Darium, patting his body, making sure he was still in one piece, not really knowing what to say.

"Darium, over here," called out a voice.

Darium turned to see Zann and Rhys waving their arms above their heads from over by the Lake of Souls.

He ran to join them.

"It seems there is a storm brewing," said Rhys.

"Aye, I'll say." Darium was still thinking about his whirlwind ride down the mountain. He looked up at the darkening sky, searching once again for the cyclone that brought him down here, but it was nowhere to be seen.

"That means the portal is about to open," said Zann. "And as if that's not bad enough, we have another little problem now, too, brother."

"What's that?" asked Darium, right before he heard the sound of thundering hoofbeats. King Sethor and his army of men appeared atop the hill, heading right toward him. Sethor's son, Muldor, and Talia's father, Necos, were leading the way. "Oh, crap. This is bad. This cannot be happening right now. Not with the portal about to open."

"It's even worse than you think," said Rhys. "The kings of Kasculbough and Evandorm are also headed this way with their men."

"There's going to be a war, Talia," shouted Darium, feeling anxiety coursing through him. Quickly, get back to the woods with your mother and sisters where you'll be safe. Now go. Hurry."

"Too late for that. We're here to help you." Maeve appeared with Talia's six sisters in tow.

"Damn," Darium ground out. Why were they here and what else could possibly happen? Things were going from bad to worse.

"Mother, the girls can't help," protested Talia. "They have only a small amount of power and they have not yet learned how to control it. They'll be hurt or even killed. They shouldn't be here at all."

"I agree," mumbled Darium.

"Nay. You're wrong," said Maeve. "They have their full powers now, Talia. Elric told us what to do to tap into them, and it worked. They might not be as skilled as you or me, but they can still be of some help."

"The elf did that?" asked Darium in surprise, not believing Elric would ever help anyone besides himself. "So, it seems the fool really knew something after all." He nodded, being impressed.

"You call me a fool once more and I'll show you what else I can do," said the elf, peeking out from behind Maeve. Elric looked up to see King Sethor. Worry creased his forehead. "It's time for me to go. Goodbye."

"Wait!" cried out Talia. "You still have to tell us how to help the Fae race."

"Later," said the elf, zipping away in a blur.

"It figures," grunted Darium. "When there is trouble brewing, that elf is the first one to disappear."

"Darium, take a torch," said Rhys, handing a lit one to him and another to Zann. "I see the portal starting to open." The air became colder. The clouds totally covered the sky now, blocking out any ray of light. Wailing was heard from the Land of the Dead. Darium's joints ached and started to stiffen. He felt a slight pain in his heart.

The kings all arrived and rode down to the lake at the same time with their armies of soldiers following.

"What's this?" asked King Sethor. "Why are you two here?" He raked his eyes over the other two kings.

"We're here for the same reason as you," growled King Grinwald of Evandorm.

"That's right," agreed King Osric of Kasculbough. "You're not the only one who wants warriors who are invincible. Now get out of my way, Sethor."

"Wait, King Osric," said Rhys, stepping up to him. "You don't understand what's all involved. You don't want dark spirits as warriors, I assure you. It's not a good thing."

"They're evil, and will destroy us all," added Zann. "Besides, all three of you have banned magic."

"I've changed my mind about magic," said Sethor. "And I also don't believe a word you say."

"It's true," cried out Talia.

"Well, we'll just see about that, won't we? Now get out of my way, everyone. I am about to go through that damned portal." King Sethor was determined, and Darium had no doubts the foolish man would try to do it.

"Nay. I can't let anyone enter the portal, I'm sorry," said Darium, stepping in front of the portal as it started to open. He held his torch high. "The spirits will invade your dead. They already have started to do so."

"What kind of nonsense is this?" asked Sethor.

"That's not your son," said Talia. "My King, a dark entity has taken over Muldor's body."

"Nay, this is my son," yelled Sethor. "Don't you think I would know the one I sired?"

"That's also not my father next to you," continued Talia, nodding at Necos with tears in her eyes.

"Necos, you traitor," yelled the king of Evandorm. "You are my enemy now that you joined up with Sethor."

"He's loyal to neither of you, I assure you," said Talia. "He is not the man you think he is."

"Talia, Daughter, how can you say that? Of course, I am." Necos tried to convince the kings.

"Nay, you're not!" Maeve ripped the torch out of Zann's hand and stomped over to Necos who had already dismounted his horse. "My husband is dead, and you'll not use his body. I won't let you. He doesn't deserve this. Now out with you!" she screamed, shoving the flame near the man's face. She waved the fire back and forth in front of his eyes, so close it almost touched him.

"Naaaay," shrieked Necos, stepping backward, raising up his arms and covering his eyes.

"Look at the flame!" Darium yelled, but the man blocked his face and looked at the dark sky instead. Darium rushed over and grabbed the man, struggling with him as Necos kept turning his face away from the flame, with his eyes closed.

"I'll get him," said Zann, handing Talia his torch and walking over and pulling the man's hands away as Darium held him still. The next time Maeve used the torch, Necos' gaze met the fire. His eyes turned black and his body stiffened as he shrieked. It sounded frightening, just like the cries coming from the Land of the Dead. A black wisp of an evil spirit rose from his body. It wailed even louder before burning up in the fire of the torch. The ashes of the evil spirit fell to the ground at Maeve's feet. The physical body of Necos, now void of the entity, fell dead to the ground.

"Necos!" cried Maeve, looking downward, holding one hand over her mouth. "What have I done?" She gave the torch back to Darium and dropped to her knees at the body of her husband, cradling his head in her arms. Talia handed her torch back to Zann and ran to join her mother.

Darium took the torch and held it up to King Sethor's son next, and they went through the same thing with him.

Talia watched in horror as Zann and Rhys helped Darium, and one by one, the dark spirits that had invaded the dead humans were all extinguished. But just as things seemed to be improving, the portal opened up wider, and a swirling force from within it started to pull men toward it. The men shouted, pawing at the ground as their bodies were pulled closer and closer to the portal. The portal was trying to take the living into the Land of the Dead, and away from Mura forever.

"Nay!" cried Talia, using her powers to ask the vines and shrubs to hold back the men. All three of the kings were now in attack mode.

"Draw your weapons!" cried King Grinwald.

"Fight!" yelled King Kasculbough.

"My son," shouted King Sethor, dismounting his horse and falling to his knees when he realized his son, Muldor was truly dead.

"We could use a little help here, Portia-Maer," yelled Darium, trying to keep from being pulled inside the portal, and at the same time trying to help the others as well. The torches had blown out, so Darium and his brothers threw them to the ground. Men flew through the air toward the portal, being slowed down by limbs of trees, bending down at Talia's request to grab them.

Others were dragged over the ground, gripping on to vines, trying not to be pulled in. Darium held on to a tree with one hand, and on to a soldier with the other, trying to avoid the pull of the portal. Wind, dust and dirt swirled around them, making it hard to see. The noise became unbearable as the sounds from the portal grew louder and louder. Wailing and hissing sounds filled the air. "Make a human chain," Darium shouted into the wind, instructing everyone to hold on to each other.

"I'll hold everyone back," Rhys shouted, using his strength to pull at the head of the human chain, dragging the people away from the portal. One man broke off, screaming, getting sucked in.

"I've got him," called out Zann, springing at him, and dragging him back out at the last second.

"Girls, use your powers to help the soldiers from being pulled into the portal," commanded Maeve. Talia's sisters did all they could, but it was getting hard to hold back the men. The Land of the Dead was a powerful place, and its forces inside the portal were getting stronger and stronger.

"I'll try to close it," said Portia, holding her hands over her head. She started to part the clouds in the sky so the sun would shine through, but then she hit the ground, being pulled toward the portal as well.

"Nay!" shouted Darium, pushing a soldier over to his brothers as he went diving for the Fae. He was able to grab her by the leg, but it took all his strength to hold her there, so she wouldn't be pulled into the Land of the Dead. He realized that any living being besides a Sin Eater would never be able to survive a trip through the portal and back again. It was important that the Elemental didn't enter the portal, or they would have no hope of ever closing it.

"It is too strong," yelled Portia. "It keeps blocking the sun when I move the clouds away."

"Don't worry. I'm here to help." Darium heard the voice of another woman from behind him, but couldn't turn to look. He used all his strength trying to help the Fae.

He heard Portia and another woman chanting together. Then, he was thankful to see the black clouds part and the sun shine through brightly.

"It's working," yelled Darium, looking up at the sky and then back to the portal, all the while still holding on to Portia's leg. He was able to pull her further away from the portal as it started to lose power and the opening became smaller.

"Keep going," Talia called out to the Elementals. "We need to close the portal completely. We're almost there."

The chanting of Portia and the other woman seemed to do the trick. The force from inside the portal released, and Darium was able to let go of Portia and help her to her feet. The rest of the soldiers scrambled to their feet as well and ran back to their kings.

Darium heard the screaming of the spirits from inside the portal as the opening became smaller and smaller. It was just about closed now.

"You did it!" he shouted to Portia. "Thank you, so much."

"I didn't do it by myself," said Portia. "I don't think I could have done it without a little help from my good friend, Alai Na-Dae."

"What did you say?" Darium was surprised to hear his late mother's name springing from the lips of the Fae.

"Hello, Darium. Hello, all my boys," said a sweet voice. He turned to see both Rhys and Zann standing there with their jaws dropped open. Then, he laid his eyes on someone he thought long gone since he was a child, someone that he never thought he'd ever see again.

"Mother?" he asked, barely able to speak because of the lump in his throat. His eyes settled on the beautiful face of his mother standing behind Portia. She looked a little older, and her hair was peppered with gray, but she was still just as beautiful as he remembered her. She wore a wispy pink and white gown with a crown of colorful flowers in her hair. If he wasn't mistaken, they looked like lippenbur lilies. "Mother, how can this be?" he asked in total astonishment to see her smiling face. "I thought . . . we thought . . . you were dead," he said, looking over at his brothers and then back to his mother again. His brothers were too much in shock to move or even speak.

"Nay, I'm alive as you can very well see," said Alaina.

"Is she . . . possessed by the dark spirits of the portal?" Zann was finally able to mumble.

The Fae all giggled, and that told Darium that it wasn't so.

"Nay, I'm alive. I never died, boys," said their mother. "It was only what your father wanted you to believe."

"Mother! You're a–a Fae?" asked Darium, astonished and unable to believe this.

"You helped to close the portal?" asked Rhys. "I don't understand."

"I am and I did," she answered, making Darium's head spin. For some reason that awful stab to his heart was back and his stomach clenched again. Mayhap this was just all too overwhelming, because he also felt as if it was getting hard to breathe.

"Darium," said Talia.

"Not now," he told her, lifting his hand. "Mother,

are you saying you're an Elemental of the Air like Portia-Maer?"

"Exactly," she told him, still smiling. At one time his mother's smile comforted him, but now all it did was confuse him. Why was she even here at all? How could this be real?

"Darium, listen to me," said Talia once again.

"Wait, sweetheart. I need to know more."

Darium looked out at the sea of faces, realizing that everyone's eyes suddenly opened wide and they all started to shout at once. He couldn't understand a word anyone said since there was so much noise and they were all speaking at the same time.

The stab to his heart became even worse, and he doubled over, clutching his chest. That is when he felt someone grab him from behind and pull him hard. His body flew backwards and he felt the sensation of being sucked into the portal.

"What in damnation is going on?" he shouted.

"Come, Darium," came an eerie, sickening answer from inside the portal.

"Nay!" he cried out, realizing what was happening now. He'd been too fast to think the portal was totally closed, and also too distracted by the appearance of his mother to be paying any attention to it. He'd been careless and now would pay for his mistake.

Darium grabbed for Talia, who had her arms outstretched, trying to help him, but they did not touch. As if everything turned to slow motion, his body propelled backwards while his mother, Portia, and his brothers, ran toward the portal trying to help him as well.

He tried to shake off the force that was pulling him backwards, but he felt so sick that he didn't have the strength to do it. Darkness loomed all around him and black entities swirled in a circle above his head. The opening to the portal got smaller and smaller, as he looked out now from inside the Land of the Dead.

"Nay, this can't be happening again," he cried, trying to crawl for the portal. The pain in his chest and stomach was so bad that it made it hard for him to move. His head swarmed and he became so dizzy that he could no longer see straight.

He somehow managed to approach the opening of the portal, reaching for Talia as she reached toward him, but it was too late. The portal snapped closed. The last thing Darium saw was Talia's face and the look of complete horror upon it.

He was able to read her mind easily this time, although it wasn't a thought he wanted to hear or know right now. As the last bit of sunlight disappeared and the portal claimed him, he heard the thoughts in Talia's head. She was afraid that she had lost Darium forever and that she would never see him again.

He supposed it wasn't just Talia's thoughts, because he had the same thought lodged in his own mind as well.

Then he heard a hissing voice in his head, the words burning into his mind just like a branding iron against his skin.

We are what we are.

We do what we do.

Fate brings us here and our destinies are decided before we are even born. We must travel the road that the hand of fate has dealt us.

No one can alter their destiny even if it is naught but a burden to behold.

We can do nothing to change it.

He realized now that he couldn't escape his fate. Darium was a Sin Eater, like it or not. He was doomed to end up here sooner or later, just like his father before him. Only now, he had a feeling that leaving the Land of the Dead was no longer a choice that he could control. Nay, he was here to stay. That thought didn't bother him as much as the thought that he would never hold Talia in his arms again or feel her sweet lips pressed up against his.

"This was always my destiny," he said to himself, laying in a fetal position on the ground, trying to ignore the darkness all around him. He hoped he would die quickly now, so he never had to feel this horrendous pain again. Then again, the physical pain was nothing compared to the mental anguish and emotional pain he was going through at the moment. Once he left here and entered The Dark Abyss, he wondered if he'd even remember Talia at all.

He didn't want to leave Talia. He also didn't want to leave his mother after he just discovered that she had never really died. What was going on here?

His last thoughts before he lost consciousness were that he almost believed what Talia had tried to convince him of. For a short time only he felt hope in his life for the first time ever. Aye, he had truly believed that perhaps his destiny wasn't to be a Sin Eater and end up in The Dark Abyss for all eternity. Then again, he was here feeling like this, and the portal was closed, leaving those he cared about behind.

There was no choice.

It didn't matter.

There were no decisions to be made, because they'd already been made for him, the day he was born the eldest son of a Sin Eater.

Fate had dealt him a hand that he had no choice but to accept.

He couldn't change it.

He had found love for the first time in his life with

Talia. A woman loved him and cared for him, and he felt the same way about her. Hope had budded like a seedling sprouting after a hard winter's frost. However, that seedling never made it far. All hope was lost now, and his fate was sealed.

His destiny, like it or not, had just been fulfilled.

Seventeen

"Darium!" screamed Talia, holding out her hands, reaching for him as the portal closed completely and he disappeared from sight. "Nay! This can't be happening. Not again." She spun around and looked at her mother and the other Fae. "Someone, do something! We need to save him."

"Those women have magic," said King Sethor. "Seize them and kill them!"

"I thought you didn't care about banning magic anymore," snapped Talia. "Now that it isn't to your advantage, you've changed your mind, I see."

"I'll have no part of this." The King of Kasculbough was the first to protest. "Sir Rhys, I'll expect you back at the castle soon now that the portal is closed."

"Aye, my king," said Rhys with a respectful bow.

"One of us has to carry out our orders of allowing no magic," bellowed King Sethor, still on the ground cradling his dead son. "Look what it's done."

"I'm not getting involved with dark magic or anyone who has anything to do with it," called out the king of Evandorm.

"But what about our laws?" asked Sethor.

"You can carry them out if you want, since you're the one who lost your son. I won't do it." The king of Evandorm and his men turned and rode away without looking back.

"This is the fault of the Fae," screamed Sethor, getting to his feet.

"Nay," said Talia bravely, walking over to confront the man. "This is your fault. Your greediness and quarreling was what caused the portal of the Land of the Dead to open and the dark spirits to be released in the first place. The Fae are to be thanked since they are the ones who closed it."

"I lost my son!" yelled the king.

"And I lost my father because of you. Plus, I just lost the man I love," she shouted back, pointing at where the portal had been. She started crying now.

"You mean the Sin Eater?" asked the king, seeming bewildered. "No one could love him. What does it even matter that he's gone? He's only a Sin Eater and he can easily be replaced."

"King Sethor, I think it's time you take your men and leave," said Talia's mother.

"Aye," agreed Talia. "After all, you've seen the power of the Fae folk and you must know that you, too, King Sethor can easily be replaced. I warn you, do not anger us again or you will be sorry."

"Talia, nay," warned her mother, shaking her head, trying to keep her quiet and not goad a king. Talia's words were only meant to frighten the man, since the Fae would never truly use their powers to hurt anyone if it wasn't in self-defense.

Two of Sethor's men lifted up his dead son and threw him over a horse. The body of Talia's father still laid there but Sethor's men didn't want it, and didn't care.

"We're not going anywhere," growled the king. "Not before I have my revenge."

"Your vengeful ways have already cost you your son," Talia pointed out to him. "How much more are you willing to lose?"

"Are you threatening a king?" Sethor drew his blade.

"You're not the only one who lost a son today," said the woman called Alai Na-Dae. "I think they need a little help leaving, Portia-Maer."

"I agree," Portia answered. Together, the two Elementals of the Air held out their hands. The winds picked up, creating swirling air in the form of a funnel.

"What's happening?" screamed Sethor, holding up his hand to hide his eyes from the dirt and dust circling around him and hitting him in the face.

"My King, we must leave," yelled one of the soldiers. His men turned and rode away without waiting for their leader.

"I'll not leave until I am finished here." Sethor tried to walk forward with his sword pointing the way, but the wind held him back. Then, to Talia's amazement, he and his horse were lifted off the ground and rose higher and higher into the air inside the funnel.

"Nay, let me down!" screamed Sethor, with fear in his voice, kicking and screaming in fear.

"You'll not bother the Fae ever again," said Portia. Then, with a flick of her wrist, the funnel lifted even higher into the sky and disappeared.

"That was amazing!" yelled Talia's sister, Poppy.

"I want to be a sylph and do that," said little Joy.

"Me too," agreed Zia.

"Girls, we're Fae of the earth, not the air," their mother reminded them. "We can't do that."

"Did you . . . did you kill him?" Talia asked, turning to speak to the Elementals of the Air.

"Nay, Talia, we just sent King Sethor and his horse back to his castle where they belong," Portia explained. "It is not in our nature to hurt or kill anyone purposely."

"I don't think any of the kings will be bothering us again," said Maeve dropping back down to her knees at the side of her dead husband.

"That's all fine, but what about Darium?" Talia wiped a tear from her cheek.

"I know you're upset. So am I," said Alai Na-Dae, putting her arm around Talia's shoulders.

"Thank you, Alai Na-Dae," said Talia.

"Just call me Alaina. All my friends do," said the woman with a smile. She had blonde hair like Darium's brother, Zann, but Talia could see the resemblance of Darium in her face too.

"Alaina, are you really Darium's mother?" Talia asked.

"I am," answered the woman. "As well as the mother of these boys." She held out her arm to Rhys and Zann, but they just stood there, not sure what to do.

"I don't really remember you . . . much," said Zann. "Rhys and I were too young."

"You died," said Rhys, acting as if he were suspicious of her.

"There is so much to tell you, boys, but first we have to figure out a way to save your brother," said their mother.

"He's gone," cried Talia. "Darium's been sucked into the Land of the Dead and he will never return now that the portal is closed forever."

"Never say never." Alaina smiled kindly, keeping a positive attitude, but Talia read her mind and knew that she, too, worried about her son and wondered if Darium would ever return.

Darium's pain subsided slightly, and he was finally able to stand up again. He looked around in the fog, wondering how he was going to get out of here. Sure, he'd been here as a child with his father, and also recently, but he honestly didn't know how to make the portal open again to let him back out. He tried thinking back to his childhood, remembering how they made the portal open back then. It had been such a horrifying experience at six years old, that Darium tried to block the memories from his mind, never wanting to relive them. Ironic, since here he was, needing to know. He kept coming back and wasn't sure why.

"Darium," came a voice that Darium knew well. He turned to see his father standing before him. This time, his father didn't look frightening and as if death had consumed him. He looked like he had in Darium's recent dream. His body was not covered with oozing sores and his flesh was not rotten. This time, he looked just like the man Darium had known his entire life.

"Father? Why do you look normal when I've seen you decaying and with oozing sores?" he asked him.

"I chose this image for you. So you wouldn't be frightened or repulsed by me," his father answered. "But realize, it won't last long."

"I don't understand what's going on."

"I don't have long, Darium, before I am taken to The Dark Abyss. It is time for me to leave permanently now. I wanted to tell you first, that it is your choice if you stay here in the Land of the Dead, or go back to the land of the living."

"I don't have choices left, now that I'm dead. It was my destiny to follow in your footsteps, and that is exactly what I did."

"Nay. You're not dead, Darium. Not yet, anyway. However, if you don't leave here soon, you will be."

"Then tell me how to open the portal. I know you did it when you brought me here as a child, and recently helped to close it when I left the last time."

"Son, I foolishly brought you here as a child because I wanted to prove something to your mother. She was always against you being a Sin Eater, but I was determined that it was your calling. We got trapped here, Darium, I'm sorry to say. We would have died that day if your mother hadn't been the one to open the portal and release us from the other side."

"Mother just helped to close the portal, Father. She is alive, and she's a–a Fae."

Ambrose smiled slightly and nodded. "That's right, Darium. She's not just a Fae, she's a powerful Elemental of the Air. I felt her presence from in here, and it makes me happy."

This all seemed like naught but another dream. Darium was no longer sure what to believe was real.

"Why did you never tell us this? My brothers and I thought she was just human. You told us she died! We believed you. Why would you do such a horrible thing? What kind of a man are you?"

"I was wrong, Darium. I made wrong choices and for that I deserve to rot in The Dark Abyss for all eternity, but you don't."

"Tell me what happened."

His father winced, and his hands balled up tightly into fists. His eyes closed and then reopened. "I did it because I thought I was helping you boys, but I discovered I was only hurting you instead. I don't have time to explain more, I'm sorry." The sores started to appear on his body again and his eyes became sunken on his face. The image he had held for Darium's sake had started to crumble quickly. "It is almost time for me to go to The Dark Abyss now. Once I go there, you will never see me again."

"Never mind that," Darium spat, not feeling remorse for his father at all anymore after hearing what he did. "Just tell me this: Do I really have a choice about my destiny, or will the sins I ate condemn me to The Dark Abyss for all eternity as well?"

"You have the love of a wonderful woman." His father seemed to become very sad. "I had that too, but I sent her away. I believed I couldn't change my destiny, but I was wrong, son. It is too late for me, but you still have a chance. Change your destiny now . . . before it's . . . too late."

Darium's father reached out for him, but Darium stepped back, seeing the darkness overtaking the man once again. Then the dark souls started to surround him. Darium felt the sharp pain back in his chest. It also felt as if there were a million hands tugging him in all directions, but only to hold him here.

"Use your . . . powers, son. You can . . . open the portal." It was a struggle to speak, but his father tried to help him. Darium couldn't help his father. He knew it was his father's time to move on and that he would never see him again.

"Powers?" asked Darium, clutching his chest and trying to swipe at the entities by swinging his sword out of habit, not because it would do a thing to stop them. "I don't have any powers, Father. I'm the son who got nothing but the skill of sin eating in case you've forgotten."

"I taught you what I know. But your mother . . . taught you her skills . . . as well. You just don't . . . remember." His father screeched in horror, then dissipated into a swirl of black fog and disappeared into the ground. When Darium looked down, he saw the faces of many men staring back at him from a deep hole in the ground. They were warriors who were trapped in The Dark Abyss and would be there forever. They were men who had earned their places by the horrible deeds they did when they were alive. They would be there for eternity, and so would his father. It was the last place Darium ever wanted to be.

"Think, think," he spoke to himself, digging deep down into his mind for anything that he could remember about his mother or anything she could have possibly taught him as a child that he had forgotten. He needed to do something to leave here, but he no longer knew what. As hard as he tried to remember, he couldn't think of a single thing.

It was an absurd thought that he had the power of an Elemental of the Air. Still, he didn't feel as if his father had been lying. His head felt as if it were about to split open now, and thoughts like this only made it hurt worse. The powers his father spoke of were only something special given to a Fae. Females. Or so he thought. Could he possibly be one of those male Fae that Talia told him were few and far in between? He didn't know what to believe anymore, and neither did he care at the moment. All he wanted was for the pain to stop and to get out of place forever.

Suddenly, he heard the soft sound of his mother humming in his head. It was the tune that had always calmed him as a child. It was the same tune that Talia had hummed to him when she watched over him and healed his wounds. Music of the Fae, he realized. The tune must be magical. It made him feel safe and free from worry.

Even with all the loud wailing and screaming around him, he was still able to hear the song of the Fae in his head. He tried his hardest to focus on it, and it started to get louder and louder, eventually drowning out the sounds of the Land of the Dead.

Darium hummed the tune as well now, since it was the only thing about his mother that he could remember. It truly did seem to calm him, and also to chase away the pain in his body.

The evil spirits continued to swirl around him, hissing in his ear, trying to bring him to the dark side, but Darium would not go. He decided that if the light was what repelled these dark spirits and also what closed the portal in the first place, then possibly it was what could reopen the portal as well. The only trouble was, there was no light in this dark and haunting place.

Still your mind, Darium, came his mother's voice in his head. Darium could read minds at certain times, and he wondered if that was from his sin eating or from being part Fae instead. It didn't matter. He was reading his mother's mind right now. *Use the power of the air, my son. You have the power within you. Feel it. Call to it. You can do it. Return to the land of the living. We are all awaiting you here.*

Darium tried to ignore the dark spirits lurking around him as he hummed to himself, and tried to remember how he saw Portia use the power of the air to close the portal. He couldn't remember the words she used, but mayhap his intent would be strong enough to do it, he hoped. After sheathing his sword, Darium held out his hands, looking at them as if he'd never seen them before. His damned hands were starting to glow! Something made him hold out his palms in front of him, and he tried to mimic what he saw the Elemental do. Then he closed his eyes the way he'd seen Talia do when she spoke to the earth, and raised her face to the sun. He tried to envision sun on his face, and to feel its warmth.

To his amazement, with his eyes closed, he could almost feel it. The sounds of the shrieking from the underworld started to fade. Instead, he swore he could hear Talia's voice coming from somewhere nearby.

Darium, please come back to me. I can't lose you. You are a good man and I love you. Please, return, she said, jolting him enough that he opened his eyes, seeing air moving and swirling in front of him. It was happening. The portal was starting to open again! There was light and energy coming from his hands.

That's right, Son. Open the portal with your powers, came his mother's words in his mind once again.

Darium didn't know if any of this was really happening or if he was only dreaming. Either way, he wanted the nightmare to end so he could be with Talia and his brothers . . . and even his mother once again.

With that thought, the swirling air and light emanating from his hands lit up the portal completely. The more Darium's desire to leave here grew, so did the opening before him. Then, he saw Talia on the other side, looking in at him. She watched him with wide eyes and called out to him.

"Darium, you've returned!" A smile lit up her face, making her look even more beautiful than he'd remembered. He wanted to go to her now more than anything. He would not stay here in the Land of the Dead for a minute longer. Out there, with the living is where he needed to be.

"He's not through the portal yet," his mother told Talia.

When the portal opened wide enough for him to fit through, he stepped forward, but felt the tugging of the doomed souls behind him, forcing him to stay. He was about to try to fight them off, but had another idea instead. He hummed the tune his mother used to sing to him, getting louder and louder, focusing only on the tune. He used the magic of sound. When he felt the hold on him start to slacken, he forcefully pushed out of their grasps and dove through the portal, landing in the grass by the lake.

"You did it, Darium!" cried Talia, bending down to be with him. But by the look of horror on her face he realized that in opening the portal again, he'd also given the dark spirits another chance to escape. He jumped to his feet and spun around, holding out his palms.

"Nay!" he shouted. "Go back," he commanded, watching in amazement as some kind of light barrier shot out of his palms, keeping the entities from coming through. Air swirled all around him, and he wondered if he was the one doing it now.

"We'll help you," called out Portia as she and Darium's mother ran over and used their powers as well to push aside the clouds and bring forth the sun. Instantly, the portal snapped closed and all was sunny and quiet and peaceful once again. Darium was back in the land of the living, leaving the land of the damned behind. He let out a deep breath, never feeling as relieved and as thankful as he did at this very minute.

"Darium? Did you just . . . do that?" asked Rhys, hurrying over to his side, looking at him oddly.

"Damn, I can't believe it, brother. You're a faerie," said Zann, shaking his head and laughing.

"An Elemental," Darium corrected his brothers, pulling Talia into his arms and kissing her. "I have powers to control an element, and that is even more than any ordinary Fae can do. Or at least, I think that's what I am. Right now, I'm not sure of anything. All I know is that it feels damned good to be back where I belong, with all of you, again."

Eighteen

Talia had never been happier than she was right now. Darium, who she thought she'd lost forever, was now back in the land of the living. Not only that, but it seemed that they had more in common than they had originally thought.

The sound of her mother crying, caused Talia to realize that her mother was mourning the death of her husband.

"Mother," said Talia, not knowing what to do.

"Does anyone have food and drink?" asked Darium.

"Not now, Darium," said Talia.

"Nay, not for me," he said, walking over to Maeve and the dead body of Necos. "I'm going to sin eat so he has a chance to get to The Haven."

"You would do this for him? After everything that happened?" asked Maeve, looking up to Darium with tears in her eyes.

"I'm doing it for you, Maeve. And for Talia and her sisters," said Darium.

"We have some bread and a little wine with us." Shaylyn took the items from her bag and brought them over to Darium.

"Good. This will be fine," Darium told her. He put the items atop Talia's dead father's chest, and then did his sin eating, the way Talia had seen him do before.

"There," said Darium, standing up and helping Maeve to her feet. "He'll have the chance to go to The Haven now," he told them all.

"Thank you, Darium." Talia's mother reached out and hugged him. "I am sorry I was so fast to judge you before. You are a good man, and I am sorry not to have seen it."

"What will we do with father's body?" asked Tia.

"Shall we bury it?" asked Zia.

"We don't have a shovel," said little Joy.

"Talia and I are Elementals of the Earth. We don't need shovels," said Maeve. The two of them used their powers, asking the dirt to move, making a hole that could be used for Necos' grave.

"I'll move him," said Rhys, picking up the body and placing it in the hole. Then, Portia used her powers to blow the dirt and fill the hole back in again.

The Fae surrounded the gravesite and did a quick ceremony, and then Talia, turned back to Darium once again.

"Darium, thank you so much for what you just did for my father."

"It's my job," he answered.

"It is such good news that you're an Elemental." Talia held his hand as they all headed back to his small house.

"I still can't believe it. It's so weird," mumbled Zann, eyeing up his brother like he was some sort of oddity. Talia chuckled inwardly, since Zann being a shapeshifter, was more of an oddity than all of them put together. She found the situation amusing. "So, brother, you're not just a Sin Eater after all," Zann continued. "How does it feel to know that?"

"Just a Sin Eater, Zann?" Darium looked over to his brother and scowled.

"He only means that you have powers now, like us," explained Rhys from atop his horse. "That's great. We're happy for you."

"Even if we still don't understand any of this," Zann mumbled under his breath.

The entourage stopped in front of Darium's cottage.

"You are all welcome to come in, although I don't have a lot to offer." Darium seemed uneasy, and Talia knew why. She'd seen the inside of his house. It was messy and disorderly and she doubted anyone would want to visit in there. She decided she needed to save him from embarrassment.

"Perhaps we can all go back to our house. Is that all right, Mother?" asked Talia.

"Of course, my dear," answered Maeve. "But since we are here I would think Alaina would like to see the place. After all, she has told me this was once her home as well."

"Mayhap that's not such a good idea," said Darium. "I'm not really prepared for entertaining guests." Talia read his mind. He was horrified to have anyone other than his brothers over. Especially with all Talia's family, and now his mother too. He'd been a loner so long, that he didn't know how to socialize. He certainly didn't know how to clean or entertain anyone other than Rhys or Zann.

"Darium, you're not going to embarrass yourself by having us in," said his mother. "Remember, I used to live here too."

"I know. However, it might not be exactly the way

you remember it, Mother." He kept trying, but the women wouldn't take no for an answer.

"Portia, follow me inside where we can all visit and talk." Alaina pushed past Darium who was trying to block the door.

"Mother!" he called out to stop her as she opened the door and stepped inside.

"Damn," he mumbled under his breath, a look of doom washing over his face.

"She's your mother, Darium." Talia squeezed his hand and smiled. "She won't care how messy it is. Trust me."

"I want her to remember the house as it was when she lived here and made it look and feel so cozy. She'll be so disappointed in me, Talia."

"Nay. No mother is ever disappointed in her child. Just give her a chance and you'll see."

"I hope you're right. This is not the homecoming I wanted for a mother that I didn't even know was still alive."

"Oh, well, this is a surprise," commented his mother from inside the house.

"I can explain!" Darium ran after the women, rushing through the door. He came to an abrupt stop and his mouth fell open. The house was tidy! Not only that, but the windows sparkled because they were so clean. There were colorful curtains with a design of little flowers hanging on the windows which were not there before. The table was set with clean dishes and bowls of food. Real food. There was even meat! He looked across the living area to see the doors to the two bedrooms open. Those rooms were clean as well. Darium had moved his bed out to the main part of the house years ago, preferring it there. However, when he grew up, there was one bedroom for his parents and the other for him and his brothers. "What the . . . " Darium had no idea where this all came from or how it even happened.

"You look like you're more than ready for visitors, Darium," remarked his mother. "I don't know what you were so worried about. The house looks great. Just as good as when I left it so many years ago."

"Yes, it does. I–I don't understand how," said Darium, turning a slow circle, taking in the changes made everywhere in the house. The floors had been swept and washed. There were no piles of dirty clothes, and everything was in its place. He had a hard time believing this is truly where he lived. It didn't look like his house at all. It was so much better.

"You have me to thank, you big oaf!"

Darium spun around to see the damned elf lying on his bed picking his teeth with a small stick of wood.

"Elric?" asked Talia. "You did all this?"

"Well, if I'm being honest, when I saw the Sin Eater go through the portal to the land of the damned, I didn't think he'd ever be coming back."

"So, you took over my house as your own." Darium was ready to strangle the irritating elf.

"Uh . . . I suppose I was being a little too proactive. Gotta go." Elric zipped away in a blur and disappeared out the door. Darium would never get used to anyone moving that fast.

"Sit down everyone, please," said Darium's mother.

The men sat at the table while Talia's sisters hopped atop the bed. Maeve was on a chair, and Talia sat on Darium's lap. Alaina stayed standing while Portia stood at the back of the room.

"I hope someone is going to explain to me what is going on," said Darium, still feeling a little queasy, and very much confused. Thankfully, the pain had all left him, but he felt so tired that he could probably sleep for a sennight without waking and still need more rest.

"Darium, Zann, and Rhys, I want to apologize for leaving you when you were just boys." Alaina's eyes filled with tears.

"Why did you do it?" asked Rhys.

"Why did father lie to us and say you were dead?" Zann got up and started pacing the floor, too upset to even eat the food in front of him.

"I am an Elemental, as you all know," explained Alaina. "I fell in love with Ambrose, even though I knew he was a Sin Eater and that our union wouldn't work. Still, we got married."

"Why not? Why couldn't it work?" asked Talia, glancing up at Darium. He could tell she was worried about their relationship since they seemed to be following in the same direction as his parents.

"If we would have had daughters, we would have raised them as Fae," explained Alaina. "But when all boys were born, we realized quickly that our sons were only inheriting the traits of Ambrose's side of the family."

"You mean the super strength of Rhys and Zann's shapeshifting?" asked Talia.

"Aye," said Alaina. "You see, we weren't sure what would happen when we wed and had children since we are both different . . . kinds."

"I don't understand," said Darium. "So, am I not supposed to have the powers of an Elemental? And why do I? Where were they all these years and how did I not know about them?"

"Slow down, Son," said his mother. "I will tell you everything, but you need to remain patient."

"I'm not patient, Mother. I can't help it, I have never been," said Darium.

"True, but Fae have lots of patience as well as curiosity," his mother told him. "That means you do, too."

"All right. I'll try," said Darium. "Go ahead."

"I realized you did inherit the magic of the Fae, Darium," explained his mother. "I fought with your father because I wanted you to be able to use this power. He refused, saying it was the destiny of his eldest son to be a Sin Eater, just like him."

"So that's why you left? Because you couldn't agree?" Rhys didn't look like he liked his mother's explanation in the least. Neither did Darium.

"Nay, but that is why Ambrose took you to the Land of the Dead with him, Darium. He wanted you to be what he thought you should be. He did it to take you away from me."

"I've been there now more times than I care for, and never want to go back again," Darium told her.

"Exactly," said his mother. "Your father knew it was a dangerous journey and wasn't even sure what would happen if you went there. Still, he took you there to spite me. You both almost died because of it."

"Aye. Father told me that it was you who saved us."

"I used all my powers to open the portal and bring you out again. Then, I almost died because it took so much energy to do it. I knew we couldn't go on this way so we made an agreement. Ambrose would raise you boys, and I left for Lornoon to live with the Elementals there."

"So, you gave us up that easy? How could you?" Zann's eyes were in slits and his jaw clenched in anger.

"You think it was easy?" She started to cry again. "It was the hardest thing I ever had to do. I didn't want to leave my children behind."

"Then why did you?" asked Darium. "I don't understand."

"I did it for you boys. I knew it wouldn't be a loving home since Ambrose and I ended up despising each other. He threatened me many times, telling me he was going to take you boys away from me. I didn't want that, of course, but I also didn't want to have to live every day in fear. He never hurt me, but then again, I never gave him the chance. I also didn't want any of you to discover the awful truth that we were not a loving family. I thought it would be better if you remembered me in a good way instead. It was your father's idea to send me away and to tell you three that I was dead. He said it was for your own safety, and also your own well-being, and I believed him. I soon discovered what a mistake I made, but realized I could never come back. The damage had already been done."

"We could have helped, Mother," said Darium. "You didn't even give us that chance."

"You might be right," said Alaina. "However, your father started to change. I was frightened that he might become violent. I saw a dark side of him that I didn't like in the least. This side of him was only directed toward me. As bad as it became, I knew he still loved the three of you and that he would never purposely hurt you. Still, I didn't want any of you to get caught in the midst of it."

"How did you know he wouldn't hurt us?" asked Zann.

"I read his mind," she answered. "It was the only comforting thing about it all. I couldn't change him. The more I tried, the worse it became. After a while, the only thing left to do was to leave him. Sadly, that meant leaving the three of you as well. I had convinced myself it was for the best."

"Why couldn't you have taken us with you instead of leaving us with father?" asked Zann. "You left us with a man that you knew was turning evil!"

"Nay, that's not true," said their mother. "Not really. I told you, Ambrose would never hurt you. He was only mean to me. I wanted to take you with me, but the only place I could go nearby was the Whispering Dale with the other Fae. The other Fae didn't want me to bring you boys because they thought Ambrose would come there after you and cause trouble. I didn't want anyone getting caught up in the middle of my problems. It wasn't right."

"Then why didn't you take us to Lornoon instead?" asked Darium. "I hear humans and Fae are allowed to live together there."

"I should have. I know that now. I was confused about what to do. Now I'm sorry that I didn't."

"Did you know when father died?" asked Rhys.

"Yes. I knew of his demise. I heard it on the wind. I also heard that he had regrets and took his own life because of his choices."

"I still don't understand why you didn't return to us," said Zann. "At least with father gone, you didn't have to worry about him anymore."

"I am a Fae, son," said Alaina, softly. "I wouldn't have been able to lie about what really happened in the past. Or about how your father died. I didn't think it would do any good for any of you to know it."

"We deserved to know the truth," said Darium.

"Of course, you are right. I know that now." Their mother looked down to her hands, wringing them together. "We all have choices, and I, as well as your father, made some wrong ones, I admit. I wanted you boys to remember us in a different light. Since I couldn't lie, I stayed away. I know now what a horrible mistake I've made."

"I still don't understand how you could do this to us." Zann's anger was growing.

"It was wrong," said Darium. "You were our mother and we were lied to."

"Your father lied to you, not me," said Alaina once again. "That is why your father banned me from ever coming back to see any of you. He didn't want me to tell you. He is the one who concocted the lie, but knew if I ever returned I would tell you three the truth. He wouldn't allow it."

"I still say you abandoned us," snapped Zann.

"Mayhap you're right, Zann," she said softly, wiping tears from her eyes. "We all make mistakes, and no one is perfect. If I could do it all over again, I would fight harder to keep you boys with me instead of letting Ambrose raise you."

"Did you ever fall in love again and marry another man?" asked Darium. "Do we have half brothers or sisters?"

"Nay, I didn't," she said, looking sad and lonely. "As horrible as a man that Ambrose was at times, I still had love in my heart for him. That part never changed."

"Didn't he love you, too?" asked Talia.

"At one time, yes. But he put his so-called destiny of sin eating first, and that, I believe, is what doomed our marriage."

Darium looked at Talia, and they exchanged glances. He didn't need to read her mind to know what she was thinking, because he was thinking it too. She'd been trying to tell him all along that he could choose his destiny, but he had been stubborn. He had been acting no different than his late father.

"I'm not sure what to think of all this." Rhys didn't seem any warmer toward Alaina than Zann did.

"I didn't want to leave any of you," their mother confessed. "Ambrose never knew it, but I often watched the three of you growing up, staying hidden and crying in the shadows. My husband was a dangerous man. He changed from the man I once loved," she said, crying harder now, softening Darium's heart toward her. He didn't like to see anyone cry, especially not Fae who lived to giggle. "If I would have stayed, you boys would have suffered for it. No child should be pulled in two directions by their parents."

"Mayhap not, but it was our choice to make," said Darium. "A choice we were never allowed."

"Aye, and I am sorry," said his mother, once again.

"You left us!" snapped Zann, shaking his head now, not being able to accept it.

"She did it to help us, Brother," Darium explained, understanding what one would do for love. Just since he met Talia, his life had changed. He would give up his own life over and over again just to save hers if he had to. That was no different from what his mother did with them in a way. He saw now that her intent was good. She may have made a choice she now regretted but still, it was done in love.

"You have powers, Darium. You could have fought Father," said Rhys.

"I didn't know about the powers," Darium reminded him.

"Nay," answered their mother. "The Fae only uses their powers for good. Never to purposely hurt someone. There is nothing Darium could have done, even if he was aware of his Fae powers at the time."

"She's right," Darium told his brothers. "We all make mistakes, and whether or not we agree with our parents' decisions, it no longer matters. All that matters is that we have our mother back again. So even if it took many years, we still have a chance to get to know her."

"I'd like to get to know all of my sons," said Alaina with a sniffle. "That said, if you boys don't want me here, I'll understand. I'll leave for Lornoon right now if it'll make you happy."

"Nay!" Darium put Talia on her feet and stood up. He walked over and took his mother's hands in his. "You are our mother, and we will take care of you for the rest of your life, no matter where you live. However, I hope you will decide to stay right here with us."

"What?" Zann's head snapped around. "You're only taking her side because you got something out of this and we didn't, Darium."

"What did I get?" asked Darium, turning to look at his brother. "A little power, mayhap? So what?"

"It's not fair." Zann continued to pace, looking more and more upset.

"So, was it fair when the two of you had powers and all I had was a mark on my soul and a promise of spending eternity in The Dark Abyss?" asked Darium. "Stop being so selfish, Zann."

"I'm finished here." Zann shot out the door, not waiting to hear another word.

"Wait, Zann!" Rhys jumped up to follow, stopping and turning back before he walked out of the house. "It will take some time, but he'll come around. Welcome home, Mother. I never knew you really, but hope there is still time to fix that."

"There is, as long as the three of you still want me," Alaina said crying.

"Two out of three isn't all that bad." Rhys turned and left, going after his brother, leaving the door wide open.

"Darium, do you think you should go after Zann too?" asked Talia.

"Nay," Darium answered. "By now, he's shifted into his wolf form and I'd never catch him anyway."

"Darium, I hope you and your brothers can forgive me," said his mother. "I am so, so sorry."

"There is nothing to forgive," he told her. "You did what you thought was best for your children, just like any good parent would do."

"Does this mean Darium won't have to be a Sin Eater anymore?" asked little Joy from the bed.

"Does it?" asked Talia anxiously, running over to Darium.

"Do you want to continue being a Sin Eater?" asked his mother.

"That depends," Darium answered.

"Depends?" Talia was shocked to hear him say this. "On what?"

"Talia, I give people hope," he said, taking her hands in his, looking deeply into her eyes, wishing that she could understand.

"You take on the sins of others and in the end will pay for it," she replied.

"Well, mayhap yes, and mayhap no."

"I don't understand," said Talia.

Darium explained what he meant. "When I was in the underworld, I saw people there that by all right shouldn't have been there since I sin ate for them."

"Like the king's son," said Talia.

Darium slowly nodded. "This made me think. What if sin eating isn't at all about freeing a deceased one's soul, but rather it is done for those that are left behind? To give them hope," he added.

"I'm confused," said Talia. "So, are you going to be

doomed to the underworld forever because of who you are, or not?"

"I can't answer that, Talia. However, I see things from a different angle now. Instead of feeling like I'm doomed by saving the dead, I see it as doing something good by giving the living hope."

"I don't understand," said Tia. "So do you take on the sins of others or not?"

"I'm not sure I can answer that," Darium told her. "All I can say is that we all will end up where we belong in the end, judged on the things we do while we are alive. Not because we took on someone else's sins. I don't believe it works that way at all, anymore."

"Oh," said Talia with a sniffle, wiping a tear from her eye. "I thought that is what happened to all Sin Eaters."

"I don't believe anyone really knows for sure," said Darium. "Father didn't seem to."

"Are you willing to risk your soul by continuing to do it?" asked Talia.

Darium flashed her an assuring smile. "Like I said, isn't it better to give hope to the living than to think I am freeing the dead? Whatever I do, I'll make my own choices now and not believe it is my destiny to do something beyond my control. No one, nothing will decide for me, but myself. And when I do die, I will have no regrets."

"I like that," said Talia, flashing him a smile. Darium had a positive outlook now, and his near-death experience seemed to have changed him.

"However," Darium added. "Now that I have a new skill, I will say that I'll be spending less time sin eating and more time learning how to flip the weather."

The Fae all giggled from the bed.

"I've never heard it put quite that way before." It

was Portia-Maer who spoke now. She'd been so quiet that Darium had almost forgotten she was even there, standing at the back of the room.

"Thank you, Portia, for your help," said Darium. "I hope someday to come to Lornoon and meet the other Elementals as well as your family."

"You're always welcome, Darium. You all are." She headed to the door. "Alaina, I don't think I have to ask if you'll be returning with me, because I already know the answer."

"I'm staying here where I belong." Alaina put her arm around Darium in a half-hug.

"I'll be going then. But before I do . . ." She walked over and kissed Darium on the cheek.

"Thank you. I mean, I think." Darium was certainly confused now, having no idea why she kissed him, or if he should thank another Fae, or how he should even act at all.

"I have the healing power of the kiss," Portia explained. "Now, your soul is healed from anything in the past that might tie you to the underworld, and you have a fresh start. Even if you do continue to sin eat, it'll be for a different purpose now. Therefore, you won't bear anyone's darkness other than your own upon your soul."

"Talia, did you hear that?" Darium looked down to Talia with excitement. When he looked back up, Portia-Maer was gone. In the air hung the strong scent of lilacs. "Where did she go and why do I smell lilacs?" Darium looked around the room while the Fae continued to giggle from the bed.

"Portia also has the power of invisibility," explained his mother. "When you smell lilacs you know she is near, because that is her scent."

"Really?" Darium found this all so intriguing. He

had a new mission now, to find out more about the Fae folk, and also what he was capable of doing. "So, if I'm an Elemental now, will I be able to turn invisible too? Or what about that healing kiss thing? It could come in handy."

"Son, you are only half-Fae," his mother reminded him. "Be happy for what you have."

"I am very happy." He kissed Talia atop the head. "As a matter of fact, I'm happy that you're all here to hear what I'm about to say."

"What is that?" asked Talia, staring up at him with bright green eyes filled with happiness and hope.

Darium got down on one knee, cradling Talia's hands in his. He looked straight into her beautiful eyes and poured out his heart to her. "I want to marry you, Talia-Glenn. Will you be my wife?"

He heard Talia's mother gasp from behind him. Talia's sisters all giggled from the bed.

"I will," she cried, throwing herself at him so hard that she landed atop him on the ground. They both laughed. Darium stood up and picked her up in his arms.

There came a slow clapping from behind the open door. Then, the door moved and the elf walked out. "Congratulations," he said in his wiry little voice. "You just figured out how to save the Fae race, and I didn't even have to tell you."

"What do you mean?" asked Darium. "I don't understand."

"Of course not, because you're an oaf," said the elf.

"Well, if you were a sage instead of just a mage, mayhap I'd understand your nonsense," retorted Darium.

"I think I understand," said Alaina. "Now that there

is a male Fae, even if he is only half-Fae, any children you two have will start to strengthen the race."

"Rhys and Zann are half-Fae as well," stated Darium. "So, does this go for them, too?"

"They are," said his mother. "Only time will tell if they inherited any of the qualities of the Fae, but it is also in their blood, yes."

"Oh, have all boys then. Please," said Maeve jumping out of her chair.

"Now, wait a minute," said Darium, putting Talia back on her feet. "Even if we do have boys, how do we know they won't be shapeshifters or Sin Eaters or just super strong?"

"You don't," said Alaina. "Just like I didn't know either. In time, I think the mixed marriages will be strengthened and perhaps children from the union will have a choice."

"Yes," agreed Elric. "They will be able to use any or all of their powers. The choice will be up to them."

"So . . . our children will be able to choose their own destinies?" asked Darium, thinking of the conversation he had in the underworld with his father. He understood now that this is what he was trying to tell him. "Even though it might be too late for my father, it isn't too late for us or any children we may bring into this world?"

"I believe that is right," said Talia, beaming with happiness.

"So do I." This time, Darium truly did believe that he, or anyone, could choose their own destiny and that it wouldn't be chosen for them. "Belief is a powerful tool. Almost as powerful as love." He looked over at Talia and winked.

"So, when's the wedding?" asked Shaylyn from the bed. "Can I be your bridesmaid, Sister?"

"I'd like to get married right away," said Talia. "I want all of my sisters as bridesmaids."

"I want to be a flower girl," said Joy, jumping up and down on the bed.

"I wish your father could be here," said Maeve, looking and sounding very sad. "He was a good man, and left this earth too soon. He is probably in that horrible Land of the Dead right now." She started to cry again.

"Stop with the tears, Fae," said the elf, snapping his fingers. "What the big oaf didn't tell you is that the Land of the Dead is only a holding place."

"What do you mean?" asked Talia.

"Look, I don't make the rules, all right?" The elf rolled his eyes and shook his head. "It's like when you get on a horse to go somewhere. You don't stay on the damned horse the rest of your life. You get off when you get to your destination."

"That makes sense," said Darium, feeling better about everything now. "Maeve, I may have seen your husband in the Land of the Dead, but remember, I also sin ate for him. I'm sure he won't be staying there long. Just like the mage said."

"I'm a sage, you simpkin. I've got the knowledge of an elder, but you . . . you've got the brain of a pea. Everyone's stay in the Land of the Dead is different. While your father was there for many years, some only stay a day. Gotta go." With that, the elf spun around and shot out the door in a blur.

Everyone laughed, and this time Darium laughed along with them. Mayhap part of him was getting used to the pesky little elf. Then again, mayhap not.

"We've got to make plans for the wedding," said Maeve, rushing over to talk to Alaina. All the girls started chatting at once, so excited that they couldn't shut up. It was honestly giving Darium a headache. He strolled over to the door, seeing his raven outside in a tree. His horse was there too. It would be so easy to slip away from all this noise.

"Darium? Where are you going?" Talia called out, seeing him sneaking out the door. "We have to plan the menu for the wedding."

"Just have whatever you want, sweetheart."

"Darium. You know you don't want to eat berries and roots."

"If I'm a Fae now, princess, so I guess I need to start getting used to that kind of food. However, be sure to have a big juicy steak for Zann. I promised him one, and I won't go back on my word. I'll be back soon. I want to go find and talk to my brothers. I have the feeling they might not be as happy for me as the rest of your family about our upcoming marriage."

Nineteen

"Rhys, Zann, wait up." Darium rode down to the Lake of Souls, surprised to see Zann still in his human form. Rhys had dismounted his horse and the two of them were sitting on a rock talking.

"What do you want?" Zann sounded grouchy. Darium realized it probably wasn't a good idea to approach them now, with Zann being so angry, but he really needed to talk with his brothers.

He dismounted, sending his raven off to scout the area. "You two left before I had a chance to tell you my good news."

"We know your good news," said Zann, still sulking. "You're more powerful now than both of us put together. Too bad Father isn't here to hear it."

"Is that what's bothering you?" asked Darium. He sat down next to him. Zann begrudgingly moved over. "Father knows all about my new powers," he assured his brothers. "I saw him in the Land of the Dead. He was the one to tell me to use them to leave the portal. Also, that I need to choose my own destiny."

"What do you want, Darium?" asked Zann.

"I want to tell you that Talia and I are going to be married."

Both his brothers looked over at him in surprise.

"Well . . . that's great, Darium," said Rhys. "Congratulations."

"So, the Fae now have their claws in you and they'll never let you go," complained Zann. "I suppose next you'll be moving in with the Fae folk in the Whispering Dale, forgetting all about your own brothers."

"Now, wait a minute. That's not fair," said Darium. "You're making this all about you, when it is my life, and my choice, Zann."

"No, I'm not. I'm only speaking the truth. Right, Rhys?" Zann asked his brother.

Rhys looked at Darium, then back at Zann, seeming like he didn't know how to respond. Then he looked back at Darium again, without saying a word.

"Rhys, tell him that we won't put up with him abandoning us the way Mother did. And Father, too." Zann continued to try to get Rhys on his side.

"Zann, Father's dead," said Rhys. "And Mother told us her reasons. Get over it. And get over the fact that for once in his life, Darium actually has something to look forward to."

"Huh?" Zann seemed shaken that Rhys wasn't supporting him at this crucial time.

"I'm not going to abandon either of you. We're family," said Darium. "I do, however want to ask both of you to stand up for me at my wedding."

"I'll do it," said Rhys eagerly.

"How about you, Zann? I really want you there on my special day." Darium thought he saw his brother softening, but wasn't sure yet which way he'd go.

"I don't know," said Zann, still pouting. "Where are you and Talia going to live?"

"We haven't talked about it yet, but I'd like to stay right where I am for now. I want Mother to live with us. That is, as long as Talia doesn't mind."

"What about me?" asked Zann. "I live there too."

"You do?" Darium chuckled. "Zann, you only stay there when you have no bed to warm for a wench, and that is usually not more than once a month. If you want to stay there with us, I don't mind, but of course I'm going to have to see how Talia feels about it as well."

"Forget it. I don't want to live in a house full of Fae."

"I think I need to remind you two that you are both half-Fae as well."

"We are?" Zann's head snapped up and he made a face.

"I guess we are," said Rhys, also making a face and shaking his head in disbelief. "The thought never entered my mind until now."

"Will we have . . . Fae powers too?" asked Zann, suddenly becoming interested.

"I don't know," said Darium. "I'm not sure anyone knows. I suppose we'll all find out in time."

"Hmmm," said Zann, seeming to think about this more. "I hope we're not all going to start that damned giggling that the faeries do constantly."

That broke the tension and all three of them laughed.

"So . . . does that mean you're standing up to my wedding or not?" Darium asked Zann.

"Only if you promise to serve something other than weeds and berries." Zann glanced over and grinned.

"How does a big fat juicy steak sound?" asked Darium. "I already told Talia to be sure to have it ready for you, as I've promised."

"Sounds like just the right bait to trap a wolf." Zann

burst out laughing, and so did Rhys and Darium. They made up with half-hugs and slaps on the back, just like brothers do.

"When is the wedding?" asked Rhys.

"Tomorrow," said Darium. "I don't think I want to go home until five minutes before the ceremony, though."

"Why not?" asked Zann.

"Too many Fae giggling like that is going to drive me mad."

"A few of them look to be about Talia's age, no?" asked Zann. Darium could see right where this was leading.

"Oh, no. I don't want either of you to lay a hand on Talia's sisters. Other than mayhap to dance with them. Do you understand?" Darium looked from one brother to the next.

"No wench, no bed for me for the night," Zann reminded him. "So, unless you want me hanging around on your wedding night, you might want to double think that, brother."

"Nay, you can't be there on our wedding night! I won't even let Mother be there," said Darium. "If you have to, find yourself a nice wolf to curl up with, but my wedding night is not going to be shared with anyone but my wife."

"He's only jesting, Darium. Right, Zann?" Rhys elbowed his brother.

"Yeah. Sure," said Zann, not at all sounding convincing.

"Well, I guess I should get back, then." Darium turned to go, swearing he saw the flash of something out of the corner of his eye. "Did you two see that?"

"What?" asked Rhys.

"I didn't see anything," Zann answered. "What was it?"

"I'm not sure. If I didn't think it sounded crazy, I'd say I swore I saw the flash of a portal opening up at the edge of the water."

"Nay. The portal of the Land of the Dead is opening again?" asked Rhys. "I thought we solved that problem."

"Please say it isn't so." Zann let out a long sigh.

"Nay, I don't think that's what it was," said Darium, thinking about it. "It wasn't dark or foreboding this time. Plus, I didn't feel any pain. This time, it was actually light and colorful."

"Brother, I think you must have hit your head too hard getting pulled into that portal." Rhys stood up and stretched and yawned.

"Mayhap it's just your super Fae powers acting up," said Zann with an edge to his voice.

"Elemental. Call it Elemental powers, not Fae," Darium corrected his brother. "And nay, I don't think that's what it was. I swear it was the flash of some kind of other portal. It happened so quickly and then disappeared, so I'm not sure."

"Well, let's just hope you're wrong, Darium, because I think the land of Mura has seen its share of portals, and I don't care to see another one for a long time." Rhys headed over to his horse.

"Aye, and neither do I ever want to see another portal either." Zann left his spot at the lake and followed Rhys. Darium was right behind him, but heard the cry of his raven. When he turned around, he saw it again. It was the flash of another portal in a different spot, he was sure of it. It was so fast, that it almost seemed like he'd imagined it. Or had he?

"I didn't see that," Darium mumbled to himself,

hurrying after his brothers. He tried to convince himself he just saw colors from hitting his head, like Zann said. He mounted his horse and rode back home without even turning around to look. He didn't want another damned portal to appear. He didn't need any more trouble. He swore nothing was going to ruin his wedding, because it was the most important day of his life.

Twenty

Talia waited nervously for the wedding to begin the next day, standing under an archway of flowers that her sisters had constructed for her special day. The ceremony would be held in a circle of standing stones that was used for such occasions. It wasn't the usual faerie ring, but it was a powerful spot in the forest and would be perfect for such a celebration.

She was dressed in her favorite gown of green. On her head she wore a crown of twisted vines with flowers woven into it. Most of the flowers, of course, were lippenbur lilies. Colored ribbons hung from the crown, marking the tradition of a typical Fae wedding.

Talia's mother had wanted to have the wedding in the Whispering Dale, or at least to invite the rest of their Fae friends to join them. Talia knew how hard this all was for Darium, so she said no. Darium was still getting used to being part Fae, and she didn't want to overwhelm him. Therefore, Talia insisted that the only ones present for their wedding would be their families. The wedding was to be held just outside their home in the forest. Of course, the sage would be there too because he was coming to perform the ceremony. Talia hadn't had the courage to tell Darium about that yet.

"All right, Talia, it's time," said her sister, Shaylyn. "The men are waiting at the rock altar in the stone circle. Mother and Alaina are already there, and our sisters are waiting outside the circle for us to walk in."

"I'm nervous, Shaylyn," Talia admitted to her sister.

"Why?"

"Because, I'm marrying such a handsome, wonderful man, and I'm afraid something bad might happen to stop it."

"*You* stop it, Sister. Your worry is only going to attract trouble. Now, let's go before Darium finds out about Elric and strangles him before he gets the chance to officiate the wedding."

"I'm ready," said Talia, taking in a deep breath of the forest air and slowly releasing it. In her mind, she called to the animals and plants and trees, letting them know she was about to marry the man she loved.

"I've got the basket of flower petals," called out Joy, running to meet them, holding the handle of a woven basket filled with petals of flowers of all types."

"We're ready, too," said Tia, holding the hand of her twin, Zia.

"When do we walk in?" asked Poppy excitedly.

"Did you see how handsome the men look?" Aubrette's cheeks blushed.

"Go on, Joy, you go first and the rest of you girls follow. Shaylyn will walk out right before me," Talia told her sisters.

Joy skipped down the aisle, tossing petals in the air. Tia and Zia went next, walking slowly bringing one foot to the other with each step, stopping in between, not wanting to do it wrong. Poppy couldn't wait, and actually passed up the twins. Then, Aubrette almost tripped, because her eyes were on the men instead of where she was going.

"Are you ready, sister?" Shaylyn gave Talia a hug and handed her a bouquet of lippenbur lilies. "Now, be sure to toss the bouquet right to me. I'm the next eldest so I need to catch it and get married after you."

"I understand," said Talia with a giggle, following her sister to the stone altar in the middle of the standing stone ring. Large stones three times the height of a person made up a sacred circle in the center of the woods. Talia's heartbeat picked up with excitement. She had looked forward to being married for a long time now and this is the day when it would finally happen. Darium looked so handsome that Talia almost cried out when she laid her eyes upon him. Next to him stood Rhys and Zann, who had finally seemed to accept the fact that they, as well as their brother, were half-Fae.

"Talia, you look beautiful." Darium took her hand and they turned back to the stone altar. "Now what?" he whispered. "Is that it? Are we married?"

All of her sisters heard him, and giggled yet again. Talia tried her hardest not to laugh as well. Darium had so much to learn.

"Almost," she told him. "First, the officiator needs to give us a blessing and we'll repeat our vows."

"Oh, all right. So where is he? Did he forget to show up?"

"Calm down you big oaf, and learn some patience."

Darium groaned inwardly and closed his eyes. He figured things were going too smoothly. When he heard the voice of the elf from behind him it was all he could do not to turn around and slug the little man.

"Talia, please tell me that when I open my eyes I won't see that damned elf standing here."

"Darium, please. It is required of all Fae weddings to have a sage present."

"Of course, it is." Darium opened his eyes and there was the little guy, this time in green, looking smug. At least he wasn't wearing his foolish jester clothes. The sound of those little bells would have pushed Darium over the edge. If this wasn't required for a Fae wedding, Darium swore he would have turned and walked away. "Well, let's get this over with."

"Darium!" gasped Talia.

"I'm sorry, princess, I didn't mean it like that." He took her hand and kissed her fingers.

"I know what you meant." She smiled and giggled in that cute little way that wasn't at all irritating like when all her sisters did it.

The elf scowled at them. "Talia, do you really want to marry Darium Blackseed, the big–"

"I do," said Talia before Elric could finish.

"Sin Eater, do you want to marry Talia-Glenn?" asked the elf next.

"Don't call him that," Talia whispered to Elric.

"Fine." Elric rolled his eyes again and started over. "Fae man, do you–"

"Use his real name," Talia warned the sage.

In Darium's opinion, for being a sage, the man did and said the stupidest things. It was getting hard to believe he wasn't just purposely doing things that he knew would aggravate Darium.

Darium looked over to both of his brothers who just shook their heads and shrugged.

"Okay, okay. Darium Blackseed do you want to marry Talia-Glenn?" came the wiry little voice of the pesky elf once more. It wasn't much of a ceremony, but then again, Darium didn't care since he just wanted the elf gone.

"Yes, I do want to marry her," Darium answered. "With all my heart and soul. I love Talia, and want to spend the rest of my life with her, raising a family and starting a new life together." He looked deeply into Talia's eyes when he said it, meaning every word of it.

"A simple yes would have been sufficient," complained Elric.

"I love Darium, too," said Talia.

"Darium, the rings. You forgot to get rings," whispered Rhys.

"Oh, nay. Talia, I am so sorry." Darium shook his head.

"Nay, I have them." Talia, took two rings from her sister, Shaylyn that were naught but circles woven from green vines from the earth.

"Those are our wedding rings?" Darium was about to laugh until he realized she was serious.

"They are magical and will never wilt or fade," said Maeve.

"It is special to the Fae," Darium's mother told him.

"All right," he said, wanting to learn the way of the Fae. He put one ring on Talia's finger, and she put the other on his.

"Darium, I am so happy," said Talia.

"You could never be as happy as I feel right now," Darium told her.

"Enough! You're married. Now pay me my fee and I'll be on my way." The elf stood there with his hand outstretched, tapping his toe impatiently.

"Fee?" asked Darium. "I didn't know there was a fee."

Talia leaned over and whispered to him. "Sorry, I

forgot to tell you about that part."

"No problem. I've got it." Darium pulled a coin out of his pouch and handed it Elric. "Here you are."

"Don't insult me with your petty little sin eating money." Elric crossed his arms and stuck his pointy chin in the air.

"Oh, you want more. Is this enough?" Darium held out two coins this time, but the sage wasn't interested in them either.

"Darium, it isn't coins that we pay him with," explained Talia.

"It's not? Then what does he want?"

"He wants something personal from us. It's the way of the elves."

"Personal?" Darium didn't like the sound of this at all. The last thing he wanted was to have to give up any of his belongings to the elf. "Like what?" Darium glared at the elf from the corners of his eyes. "Our first-born child?"

That made everyone in the stone circle laugh, including his brothers.

"Well, I wouldn't doubt it," Darium told Rhys and Zann.

"Hold still," said Talia, taking a pair of scissors from her sister and looking over to Darium. "He wants locks of our hair."

"Make sure to get both colors from the skunet. I want both the black and white," said the elf anxiously, rubbing his hands together.

"Is it all right?" Talia asked Darium his permission before clipping his hair.

"Uh . . . sure. Snip away," he said, thinking this was an odd thing to want from anyone. "I needed a haircut anyway."

Talia snipped Darium's hair and then snipped off a

long lock of her own hair and handed the scissors back to her sister. Then she wove her hair together with Darium's two-toned hair into a small braid of faerie knots. "There," she said, handing the beautiful braid to the elf.

"Aaaaaah, yes," said Elric, snatching the braid from her, quickly inspecting it by sniffing it and even licking the end. The damned elf was even crazier than Darium had originally thought. "I never had a Sin Eater's hair before." Elric chuckled and zipped away in a blur.

"He's not going to hold power over us now, or be able to make us do things he wants us to, is he?" asked Darium, still feeling a little uneasy about giving his hair to the elf. By the sound of all the giggles from behind him, he realized he was worrying too much. "Never mind. Just kiss me, Wife."

"Gladly," said Talia, looking over to Shaylyn and throwing her the bouquet of flowers. Then she wrapped her arms around Darium's neck and kissed him long and passionately in front of everyone. The women clapped and his brothers whistled. Darium picked up Talia in his arms, turning around, once again seeing a colorful flash that looked to him like a portal. This time, it was just outside the stone circle. What was happening here?

"Did you see that?" he asked Talia.

"Oh, you mean all the animals?" she answered. "I invited them here to join us. I hope you don't mind."

It was then that Darium first noticed the stricat sitting nearby, as well as every animal in the forest, including the skunets which he hoped were not going to spray anyone during his wedding.

"Nay, that's not what I mean. I do love having the animals present, but I was speaking of something else."

"What in the world are you talking about,

Darium?"

"I–I swear I keep seeing flashes of another portal opening."

"Mayhap it has something to do with your newfound powers?" asked Talia with a shrug.

"Nay. It was a portal, I'm sure of it."

"Nay, it wasn't. The portal to the Land of the Dead is closed and will not open again. We've seen to it. It's over, Darium. Stop worrying," she told him.

"But I–"

"Husband, this is our wedding day and I don't want you speaking about portals again."

"You're right," he said, once again looking out to where he saw the flash. "I suppose I'm just still a little jumpy about everything that happened lately."

"I agree." Talia reached up and kissed him on the mouth, making him forget about anything else. "Darium, you no longer have to worry about such things. And remember, you don't have to be a Sin Eater if you don't want to, anymore. Even if you do, since Portia used her healing kiss on you, the dead ones' sins won't darken your soul. You're part Fae now, and the Fae folk like to have fun, so lighten up and start living."

"You're right," he told her, putting her down on her feet and hugging her, feeling the love emanating between them. "I have a new destiny now, and it has nothing to do with sin eating or the Land of the Dead, I promise you."

"I'm so glad to hear that, Husband. Now, you can start living your new life with me, and get used to embracing your Fae side. We'll live in light and love and happiness as we were meant to, never again having to feel **_Bedeviled_**."

From the Author

While researching the medieval times, I came across information that startled me and fascinated me all at the same time. I had never heard of a Sin Eater, but it was a real thing!

Sin Eaters were called in when a person died suddenly and didn't have the chance for a last confession. The idea behind this was that someone else, who was alive, would take on all the deceased one's sins, therefore freeing up the soul of the dead loved one so they could make it to Heaven.

Food and drink were placed upon the dead body and a prayer was said. Then, the Sin Eater ate the food and drank the liquid, and supposedly took on the deceased one's sins. Nice for the soul of the dead party. I'm sure it was a relief for those they left behind as well. However, it was not so good for the Sin Eater, since it only damned him or her to hell for all eternity.

Who would even consider taking on such a horrible job, I wondered? Well, back then there were many people who were dirt poor and who would do whatever they had to do just to earn some money for food for their family.

This sparked the idea of putting a Sin Eater in my

FROM THE AUTHOR

book. A Sin Eater who wasn't doing it just for the money, but who was born into the profession. I wanted someone who thought his destiny was to carry on the work of his sin eating father. Hence, my hero has a job that no one, not even himself, wants. Of course, I put a twist on it, as you saw. This might have started as something to do with Christianity, but in my story they have their own religion. I have wanted for a long time now to invent my own world. So, this is a fantasy setting, tying back to some of my other paranormal books.

Remember, we all have choices, and you are the only one who can create your own destiny. Sometimes, we just need to be reminded, that's all.

If you enjoyed this story, I would love for you to leave a review for me. The next book in the series is ***Bewitched***. As you continue on the journey, you will find out more about Darium's brothers, Rhys and Zann and their powers as well.

Portia-Maer, the Elemental of the Air made an appearance in *Bedeviled*, but she has a book and a story all of her own. You can find it in ***The Sword and the Sylph*** – Book 3 of my ***Elemental Magick Series.*** Be sure to check out the books about her Fae friends as well in ***The Dragon and the Dreamwalker, The Duke and the Dryad,*** and ***The Sheik and the Siren.***

Another paranormal series I have that I think you'd enjoy is based on fairy tales. It is called the ***Tangled Tales Series***. Each book is a twisted, tangled, romantic retelling of a favorite fairy tale. Watch for some of these characters making appearances coming up in the rest of the ***Portals of Destiny Series.***

FROM THE AUTHOR

If you'd like to find out more about me or all the books I have, please visit my website at **http://elizabethrosenovels.com** or stop by my **Amazon page**. I have about 100 books and counting, and write medieval, contemporary, paranormal, fantasy, and western romance.

Elizabeth Rose

About the Author

Elizabeth Rose is an Amazon All-Star, and bestselling, award-winning author of nearly 100 books and counting! Her first book was published back in 2000, but she has been writing stories ever since high school. She is the author of fantasy/paranormal, medieval, small town contemporary, and western romance. You'll find sexy, alpha heroes and strong, independent heroines in her books. Sometimes her heroines can even swing a sword.

Her earlier fantasy romance novels started out with her **Greek Myth Series**, inspired by the TV shows *Legendary Journeys of Hercules* and *Xena: Warrior Princess*. One of the books, **The Oracle of Delphi** was featured on the History Channel during a documentary of the Oracle. Elizabeth joins Oliver Heber Books with her **Portals of Destiny Series** which brings back characters from some of her other fantasy series, making guest appearances.

She loves adding humor to her work, because everyone needs to laugh more in life. Her **Bad Boys of Sweetwater: Tarnished Saints Series,** focuses on 12 brothers, a bunch of kids, and lots of humor. This small-town romance series was inspired by people, places, and things in her own life. The location is the lake and small town of Michigan where she grew up visiting her grandparents.

Living in the suburbs of Chicago with her husband, Elizabeth has two grown sons and one granddog – so far. A lover of nature, she can be found in the summer swinging in her 'writing hammock' in her secret garden, creating her next novel. Her secret garden is what inspired her medieval series, **Secrets of the Heart**, which of course centers around a secret garden too!

Visit elizabethrosenovels.com where you will find book trailers, sneak peeks at upcoming covers, excerpts from her books, as well as original recipes of food that her characters eat in her stories. If you'd like to sign up for her newsletter, join her private readers' group, or follow her on social media, just copy and paste the following links.

Join Elizabeth's Newsletter
Join Elizabeth's Facebook Group

Also by Elizabeth Rose

Tangled Tales Series
Lady and the Wolf (Red Riding Hood)
Just a Kiss (Frog Prince)
Beast Lord (Beauty and the Beast)
Touch of Gold (Rumpelstiltskin)
Lady in the Tower (Rapunzel)
A Perfect Fit (Cinderella)
Heart of Ice (Snow Queen)

Elemental Magick Series
The Dragon and the Dreamwalker
The Duke and the Dryad: Earth
The Sword and the Sylph: Air
The Sheik and the Siren: Water

Greek Myth Fantasy Series
Kyros' Secret
The Oracle of Delphi
The Thief of Olympus
The Pandora Curse

Once Upon a Rhyme
Mary, Mary (Mary, Mary Quite Contrary)
Muffet (Little Miss Muffet)
Blue (Little Boy Blue)

Dark Encounters
Familiar
The Caretaker of Showman's Hill
The Curse of the Condor

CPSIA information can be obtained
at www.ICGtesting.com
Printed in the USA
LVHW110750030522
717814LV00006B/747